When the Tide Ebbs

Book One
GRAVE ENCOUNTERS

A 1930's Epic Love Story

KAY CHANDLER
A multi-award-winning author

This is a work of fiction. Characters, places and incidents are the products of the author's imagination or are used factiously.

Scripture taken from the King James Version of the Holy Bible

Cover Design by Chase Chandler

FOR

Camille, Keith
Chad, Stephanie
Chase and Jenn

PROLOGUE

I was only eight years old the day the church ladies came calling—but the bitter memory left a lingering, raunchy taste in my mouth as sour as a green persimmon.

Mama's hazel eyes lit up like a neon Packard sign when she peered out the window and saw them coming down the road, all dressed up in their go-to-meeting clothes. She spat on her fingers and dabbed at a smudge on my face before jerking her long auburn hair up into a twist, securing it with a comb. We were about to have company and it was important to Mama that we make a good impression. She yanked off her apron and took a quick glance in the cracked mirror, which hung on a nail above the oak washstand.

"Kiah," she said, parting my hair with her hand, "when our guests knock on the door, use your manners. Be a gentleman. Invite them in and offer the older lady the rocking chair." There were only two chairs in our quarters on the Poor Farm—a ladder back and a rickety old rocker Mama salvaged from the dump.

"Well, I reckon they'll just have to take turns sitting, Mama, since there are three of 'em." But it wasn't hard to tell which one was the oldest. Or the meanest. Mrs. Ola Mae Dobbins. She was my Sunday School teacher and I wasn't fond of the old goat.

I didn't tell Mama, but the woman didn't like me from the first day I walked in her class. In fact, I heard her tell her prune-faced husband I was a little buzzard. Or at least, that's what it sounded like to me at the time, and I was old enough to know a buzzard wasn't something people admired. I was eleven before I learned from a bully in the schoolyard what she really called me. I found out later being called a buzzard wasn't the worse thing in the world.

Even now, an indigestible rage regurgitates within my gut as I recall the wounded look on Mama's face when the ladies said the church elected them to inform us we weren't welcome in their fellowship. Funny word, "fellowship." In my young mind, I pictured a big white boat reserved for a few hen-pecked men wearing top hats and morning coats and a bunch of nosey old biddies, all appointed by God to check off the passenger list, before setting sail.

I peeked out from behind Mama's skirt as Mrs. Ola Mae explained the church's position. Said the Bible warned against mixing with our kind, being as how I didn't have a daddy. Tears welled in my eyes as I imagined Mrs. Ola Mae sailing toward heaven's pearly gates on the big fine Fellow Ship—smirking, as she waved goodbye to those of us who missed the boat.

Mama nodded and said she understood. But I knew she didn't. And neither did I.

Chapter 1

Pivan Falls, Mississippi, 1929

The bitterness inside me festered like a painful boil. Looking back, I reckon it was about two months shy of my seventeenth birthday when I decided to make a dual vow to never show myself inside a church building again, nor allow myself to fall for a dame.

I'll admit such a vow was akin to making a solemn oath never to eat maggot stew. Wouldn't happen and I knew it. Still, I didn't believe in taking chances. To be safe, I stayed far removed from anything with a steeple or anyone wearing a skirt. I make no apologies for being cynical. I had my reasons. I'd learned more about love than I cared to know by witnessing its devastation upon Mama. Though she'd never admit it, I was living proof that reckless love had led her to no good end. I would not be so foolhardy.

Let me be clear. I'm a normal, healthy, red-blooded American male, who isn't immune to having my head turned by the sight of a good-looking chickadee. But I figured if I was stupid enough to put myself in harm's way, then I deserved any pain inflicted upon me by hoity-toity church folks or silly, conniving females. How was I to know the prettiest girl in the land of cotton—a parson's daughter, no less—would move to Mississippi and set her sights on the likes of me? I'd never seen a real live angel until the day Zann Pruitt stood at the front of the class beside our teacher, Mr. Thatcher.

He rapped a gavel on his desk. "Class, I'd like to introduce a new pupil."

Sweat popped out on my brow. She was prettier than a newborn calf. Little in stature, but not frail looking. Her fine features and bones were sculpted to perfection. Her cheeks had a healthy, rosy glow like a ripened peach and thick, fluttering lashes framed big, ebony orbs. Long raven locks fell in folds on her shoulders like shiny black silk, and the form-fitting calico dresses, which she wore so well, were decked out with rows and rows of colorful rick-rack. No doubt about it, the girl was a cool drink of water to thirsty eyes; yet, I figured if I should suffer such an ailment, boric acid was a much safer remedy.

Arnold Evers stood with his hand raised. "Excuse me, Mr. Thatcher, but if the little lady needs help catching up, I'll be more than happy to assist. I'm available every Saturday night." Giggles erupted. I grimaced, knowing the kind of assistance he had in mind, and I could look at her and tell she was *not* that kind of girl. Arnold prided himself on being a ladies man and for reasons I couldn't understand, the girls did seem to go for him. But why should I care? So what if he was three inches taller than me, had hair the color of autumn wheat, wore dungarees that fit and owned store-bought shirts? It didn't change the fact he was a low-down rascal.

"Thank you, Arnold," Mr. Thatcher said, "but looking over her records, I don't think she'll need your assistance. Miss Pruitt has excellent marks."

"Then maybe she can help me. I could sure learn a lot from someone like her."

The class broke out in thunderous laughter, though I failed to grasp the humor.

She looked at Arnold and smiled. Her voice was soft and melodic. "I thank you for your kindness—"

I bristled. Kindness? Was that what she thought? I likened her naïve remark to that of a biddy telling a chicken hawk, "Thanks for offering me a lift." If only she knew Arnold Evers the way I knew him.

He ran his fingers through his sleek hair. "Just want to make you feel welcome, ma'am."

Mr. Thatcher's brow furrowed. "Have a seat, please, Arnold."

My heart pounded when Mr. Thatcher led her down the aisle and sat her within arm's reach of my desk. Out of the corner of my eye, I saw the smile fade from her lips as she thumbed through her math book. She raised her hand. "Pardon me, Mr. Thatcher, but it seems your class is ahead of me in mathematics. I fear I may need tutoring to catch up."

Arnold let out a "hot-diggedy-dog," and winked. "Don't forget, I chose first, sugar."

Mr. Thatcher shot a menacing look his way, but didn't respond. Seemed to me he should've made Arnold stay after school for a month or so, for being such an ignoramus. Instead, Mr. Thatcher made his way back down the aisle and gently laid his hand on my shoulder.

"Miss Pruitt, if you need help, this is your man. Kiah Grave is a math genius."

I made a futile attempt to focus my gaze on the knothole in the pine flooring. My mouth felt as if it had been swabbed with a cotton boll as I slid down in my desk and snuck a peek.

Zann batted long lashes, glanced at me and smiled. "I'll keep that in mind."

My head swelled. Not because Mr. Thatcher called me a genius, but he called me a man. Zann's man. It wasn't that I had a hankering to belong to any cockeyed female, because I didn't, but I can't deny it was a boost to my ego. She was a pretty thing for sure, but so is a young colt or a freshly furrowed field and as many times as I've looked at both, I've never been tempted to fall in love with either. Yet, even when I tried to keep my eyes glued on the blackboard, it was impossible not to glimpse the poised frame on the other side of the aisle, since her desk was diagonally across from mine. For fear of being misunderstood, love had nothing to do with it. I still had control over my emotions, even though I seemed to have lost control of my eyes, which kept shifting in her direction against my will. Regardless of how many times I reminded myself not to look her way, it was as futile as reminding a yard dog not to suck eggs.

A real dish—the way she sat with her head held high, her shapely legs crossed at the ankles—but she had a strange habit, which I found most annoying. She'd glide her pencil slowly across her mouth, yet she never gripped it between her teeth. Never. She sort of slid it, playful like, over perfect-shaped pink lips, then she'd tap it lightly against the wooden desk. Why it bothered me, I can't explain, but I wanted to reach across the aisle, grab that stupid pencil and yell, "What's wrong with you? Go ahead and sink your teeth into it, or let it be. Stop teasing it."

I swallowed hard. There was nothing wrong with her, but there was definitely something wrong with a fellow who'd fixate on a wooden pencil until he was ready to turn loose of his senses and make a blubbering idiot of himself. Suppose I really did scream out in class?

I'd remember to ask Mama if insanity ran in the family. I shrugged. What would Mama know about my paternal bloodline, the aristocratic Lancasters, who checked out before I was born?

My lip curled at the amusing notion that I could've possibly inherited something from my highfalutin ancestors, if nothing but lunacy.

I did my dead-level best to discourage any romantic notions Zann might have, but from the first day she walked into our little two-room school building, she stuck to me like a tick on a hound's ear. When she slipped me a note in class, I raised my upper lip and snarled. I wanted her to notice I didn't read it, so I made a show of wadding it up and cramming the paper into the top pocket of my overalls. I glanced over to make sure she saw me. I expected her to be furious. Instead, she flashed those pearly white teeth and her wide eyes transformed into tiny slits, as if she knew I couldn't wait to get home and smooth out the crumpled note. I'd never met anyone so exasperating.

To complicate matters, her daddy was the Baptist preacher in Pivan Falls. He was also the Methodist preacher. I reckon you might say he was also the Presbyterian preacher, since he was the only preacher for miles around. When anyone in the community married, died, or had need for a man of the cloth, they called on Zann's father, Parson Pruitt.

Of all the boys in school, I had the least going for me. I was shy, slow to make friends, and I had curls. Yeah, curls. Tight, kinky ringlets that looked like thick wool on an unsheared sheep. What was the girl thinking? Me, a penniless, gangly, curly-haired loser. Not that being poor in 1929 put me in a unique category.

There was poor--and *dirt* poor. We were at the bottom of the second category.

I owned two pair of overalls. One, so short the legs barely touched the top of my brogans. The other, Mama bought at a rummage sale for a quarter. The day I tried them on, her jaw dropped. But being the optimist she was, she lifted her brow and said, "Maybe they're a little large, son, but look on the bright side. There's growing room in them."

"You're right about that, Mama," I smarted back. "I could grow a nice-sized family in size 38 overalls. The little wife and I could occupy one leg, and there's ample room in the other leg for half-dozen kiddies."

Mama paid me no mind. She yanked the straps up until the bib reached my chin. I reckon she figured a fellow with no plans to choose a bride would have no cause to worry about where he'd raise a family. I pulled them off and slung them on the floor.

"Mama," I growled, "I can't wear these to school."

But I did. I didn't have to be a Harvard scholar to understand I had a serious problem when I showed up wearing my big-man britches and Zann Pruitt continued to follow me around.

She was like fly paper. I couldn't seem to free myself from her. When she entered the room, my hands got all sweaty and I hassled like an ol' coon dog who's trailed his prey 'til his tongue hangs out. However, it didn't mean I was ready to change my mind about love. I wasn't. To look was one thing, but falling in love or getting religion was entirely different.

I had plenty of reasons for feeling as I did and it was all Mama's fault. Not that she meant to turn me against love, but she did, just the same. She'd lean back in her chair and with a starry-eyed expression, repeat the familiar, grating words.

"My, my, Kiah, I do declare, son, if you ain't the spittin' image of Will Lancaster."

I knew what came next and jerked back to keep her from running her fingers through my hair.

"You have his dark curls, blue eyes and deep dimples. Built like him, too. Long arms, trim waist and broad shoulders. Ah, what a handsome man. Your daddy was such a—"

Hearing her call the man my daddy made me want to puke. Any man who'd skedaddle after bringing a child into the world, leaving it nameless to be ridiculed and labeled by pious snobs wasn't worth the Mississippi mud caked on the bottom of his shoe. Nevertheless, I supposed with his money and fancy duds, he could cruise into heaven on the big fine Fellow Ship with Mrs. Ola Mae and all her cronies.

Well, I'd prove to all the religious do-gooders that buzzards have wings and can fly same as an eagle. I was bright and I knew it. I had dreams of becoming a Harvard Professor, though I shared my ambitions with no one. After all, who'd believe a poor Mississippi buzzard could soar to such heights?

Although Zann never asked about the man who sired me, I

was sure she'd heard the gossip about Mama and me. Yet strangely enough, she treated me like I was good as the next fellow. Maybe, even better. She waited for me before school, after school and at lunch. When I saw she wasn't going to leave me alone, I quit trying so hard to get rid of her.

Before I knew what was happening, she began to grow on me. Sort of like a seed wart I once had. I tried every remedy in the book to rid myself of the unwanted growth on my hand. Nothing worked. Then one day, I realized I still had the wart, but it didn't bother me anymore. I'd gotten accustomed to seeing it there. It became as much a part of me as the five fingers on that hand. And that's how it was with Zann. Without my approval she attached herself to me, but I eventually became accustomed to having her around.

Zann wasn't only beautiful, she was smart. She never missed a single question on history exams, and there wasn't a word in the dictionary she couldn't spell. That's why I was surprised when she approached me one morning before school with a proposition. It was almost time for the bell, and I'd just walked up to the pump for a drink of water. I was in serious pain. I must have grown three inches overnight. I had on my short overalls and they were so tight they were cutting me in two. If I bent down to drink, I was likely to come up twins. Nevertheless, I was thirsty enough to try it. Should my body divide, I'd let my brother have the girl *and* the overalls, then maybe Mama would see the need to buy me a new pair.

"Hi Kiah," Zann said in a near whisper, swaying from side to side. Her porcelain-like hands clasped together tightly near her tiny waist.

Relieved that neither I nor my britches had split on the way down, I straightened, and with the back of my hand, wiped water from my lips.

"Whatcha want, Zann?" My left eye twitched when she smiled. My knees knocked. The girl was a picture of everything lovely, balled up and neatly packaged in flesh and blood. I ran my hands through my tousled hair, as she stood batting those thick lashes. My face heated up. I could only imagine how I must look to her, wearing patched overalls, three sizes too small, and a tacky, hand-made shirt with a frayed collar.

Mama did the best she could when she stitched up the unbleached muslin shirt, but a seamstress she was not. I could hardly wait for cooler weather when I could pack away the horrid shirt that made me look like a throwed-away scalawag, and pull out my red flannel store-bought shirt, which made me feel like a man. I swallowed. If only I could be wearing the red flannel at this very moment. I shrugged. Why should I care? I wanted to deny it had anything to do with Zann Pruitt.

"Kiah?" She repeated, her smile fading.

I could see she was fretting over something, the way her brows shot up between her eyes, drooping slightly on either end. When her lower lip quivered, I tried to appear unmoved.

14

"Yeah?"

"Kiah—" Her voice cracked.

After her third attempt, my heart softened, yet I had an image to uphold. Didn't want the fellows to think I was getting sweet on her, in case anyone happened to be looking.

"Go ahead. Spit it out, Zann, the bell's gonna ring," I grumbled.

Her eyes glassed over and she whimpered, "I make A's in everything but math. I don't know what's wrong with me. I can't seem to catch on. I was wondering . . . Kiah, would you mind coming to my house after school to tutor me?"

From where I stood, I could see nothing at all wrong with her. But go to her house? Uh-uh. No way. Not me. I suggested studying down at the old covered bridge, about a mile from the school house. It was my special place. A place of solitude. Except for an occasional kid walking through the woods with a slingshot, I never saw anyone, and I went there often. Problems dwindled and sometimes disappeared whenever I'd sit under the old bridge, listening to the sounds of the forest. Seemed the perfect spot. Besides, no one was likely to see us there.

She didn't cotton to the idea. So be it. If she really needed help, there were nine other fellows in the classroom salivating for such an opportunity.

In spite of my resolve, it was hard saying 'no' to Zann. She was nice. I reckon she was about the nicest girl I'd ever met. I wanted to help her, but I had a dilemma. A real problem. In case I've given the impression I was afraid of breaking my vow and falling in love, allow me to be frank. That was *not* the dilemma. As beautiful as she was, I didn't consider her a threat, because I figured if I ever did have a notion to fall for a dame, it wouldn't be with someone like her. She was . . . well, she was sweet. Not the kind of girl you'd think of in a romantic sort of way. After all, she was the preacher's kid. And that, in a peapod, became the crux of the problem.

Her daddy being a man of God was the precise reason I couldn't study at her house. I figured if he did his job, he'd try to convince me to attend his church and then I'd say something we'd both regret. On the other hand, if he *didn't* try to talk me into going to church, then I'd have no respect for the man, since he'd be neglecting his duty. To eliminate the problem, I'd keep my distance, which meant staying clear of the parsonage *and* the parson.

However, studying at my house wasn't an option, either. No way would I escort a girl inside the iron fence at Rooster Run, and especially not a nice, refined girl like Zann Pruitt.

I expected her to eventually tire of asking for my help, but for days she pecked away at me like a woodpecker pecking on a chimney, wasting energy and getting nowhere.

"Please, Kiah, won't you reconsider? I'm going to fail the college entrance exam next fall if I don't get help, and math comes easy for you. Sometimes I get so frustrated, I just start bawling."

That's all it took. The notion of something making her cry made me want to come up with a solution. Yet as much as I wanted to oblige, I remained firm."We study at the bridge or you can find someone else to tutor you."

She nodded. "Okay, you win. This afternoon at the bridge. But I'm warning you, Kiah—"

My teeth made a grinding noise. *Warn me*? Did she honestly think I had an ulterior motive for wanting to lure her off to a secluded spot? Whose idea was it to study together? Not mine. Who sat in class every day, batting long lashes and flashing teeth at whom? Not this cat, and not at her. My jaw tightened. She could find another tutor, if she was afraid of me.

When she finished the sentence, I let out a deep breath and almost laughed aloud

"Yes, I must warn you. Your job won't be an easy one. I hate math."

Was that all? That was the warning? When the bell rang that afternoon, she shoved her books into my hands.

"Kiah, I need to run home and tell Mama where I'll be, so she won't worry. I'll meet you under the bridge in about thirty minutes."

"I won't hold my breath."

"What's that supposed to mean?"

"Nothing. Forget it."

I didn't doubt she was telling the truth, yet I didn't expect her to meet me there. Her mother would put a stop to our little get-together as soon as she heard of her daughter's intent to meet with Fendora Grave's son, on a seldom traveled road under an old bridge. I couldn't blame Mrs. Pruitt. If I had a daughter, I'd be slow in letting her meet with the likes of me in a secluded area, also. Still, it hurt. Would my father's curse be branded on me forever?

I trudged down the winding, dusty road, kicking sand as I walked. The fluffy white clouds above my head reminded me of the bubbling foam on top of a pot of Lima beans just before they boil over. I sucked in a deep breath. The scent of freshly dug peanuts from a nearby farm hung heavily in the humid air. The kudzu vines, recently brought in by the Soil Conservationists to ward off erosion, had begun to wither and turn yellow, signaling the end of summer.

I pulled off my brogans, tied the laces together and slung them over my shoulder. My overalls were so short there wasn't much chance in them getting wet in the shallow creek. Still, I rolled up my britches legs a notch or two to disguise the length. With a handful of smooth river rocks gathered from the creek bed, I filled my pockets and trekked down the middle of the shallow stream, tossing the stones one at a time. My toes squished into the cool sand beneath the water. Top minnows nipped at my ankles.

I had a funny feeling in the pit of my stomach. Not so much

funny as strange. Like something gnawing at my insides. My heart pounded against my chest and I could hardly catch my breath. I broke out in a sweat. Never had I experienced such a peculiar malady. I concluded that either I'd contracted a serious disease or else…else I was in love. Yet, I wasn't sure which evil to wish for.

A lump the size of a frog formed in my throat. Just as I figured. She wasn't coming. It was a stupid idea in the first place.

I must have thrown a dozen or more pebbles, attempting to get at least one to skip on top of the water. Yet, each one went 'plunk' and immediately sank to the bottom. I couldn't count the times I'd repeated this action before, each time with the same results. But there was nothing I hated worse than defeat, so when I'd emptied my pockets, I reached down and picked up more rocks. I'd never give up—not until the day I'd see a little stone go pop, pop, pop, sending out ripples as it danced on top of the water. Mama said I was as stubborn as a three-legged mule, and I reckon she was right.

After wading several hundred feet, I stopped and spun around when I heard Zann yell my name from atop the gorge.

"Kiah, wait, I'm coming down."

With my hand, I shaded my eyes from the sun and looked up.

She stood on the rickety old bridge, flashing pearly white teeth and waving. She jerked off her shoes and stockings but I turned away when she commenced to tie the tail of her dress between her legs. When I glanced up, she'd magically turned her skirt into a pair of knickers. My Adam's apple bobbed.

"Stay up there, Zann. You'll scratch your legs on the briars."

She proceeded down the embankment and yelled back. "I'm not afraid of a few little scratches. I'm halfway there, already."

I gasped as she half-walked, half-slid down the steep ravine, overgrown with scrub-oaks and thick blackberry vines.

She stopped to pick beggar lice from her clothes. Then tripping through the underbrush, she hollered, "Hold on, I'm coming. I want to wade with you."

"No you don't!"

Her smile faded. "Why not?"

I took long strides, stomping the ankle-deep water as I splashed toward her. "Because." That was it. No explanation. It wasn't much of an answer and it didn't suffice, for her smile returned and she slowly inched her way down to the sandbar. Flustered, I felt a desperate need to stop her.

"You don't want to wade today, Zann," I blurted. "The water's freezing. You'll catch pneumonia."

I don't know what prompted me to make such an idiotic statement. Sure, it was cool, but freezing? I grimaced. The water in the creek at Pivan Falls never freezes, and especially not in mid-September in Mississippi but it was the first thing that popped in my mind. I couldn't have her prancing around barelegged in the water with me, her skirt all twisted between her legs. Jeepers, how could a girl so smart in some things, be so dumb in other ways? Didn't she know she had no business walking further into the dense woods with a fellow? Any fellow?

"Corn shucks! I'm not afraid of a little cold water. If you can stand it, so can I." She kept running toward me, giggling all the way.

I laughed. Partly because I was nervous, partly because her laughter was infectious, and partly because I'd never heard anyone say corn shucks . . . or at least not as an expression. Everything about her was different from anyone I'd ever known. My words had not been a deterrent. She came splashing, right smack down the middle of the creek. Just as she got near, she fell and I caught her in my arms. She seemed to think it was humorous, although I saw nothing funny about the situation.

"You may as well turn around and go back to the bridge, Zann."

"Don't be a fuddy-duddy, Kiah. The water's not cold at all. I love to feel the sand between my toes."

I glanced down at her bare feet and felt my face flush. "We're here to work, Zann. Remember?"

"Of course, I remember, but you know what they say about all work and no play." She reached down with both hands, scooped water in my face and snickered.

"Why you little—" She'd caught me off-guard and I laughed. Out loud. I couldn't remember the last time I'd laughed. I pulled a handkerchief from my back pocket and wiped my face. I wanted to splash her back, but I dared not. We were here to study, not to

21

horse around. I stuffed the handkerchief back into my pocket and in a serious voice befitting a tutor, I said, "Sure, I know what they say about all work and no play. It puts a roof over your head and food in your mouth."

She made a cute pouty face. "That's not exactly the way I heard it."

"No, I don't suppose it is."

Zann was too sweet to suspect I was being sarcastic, inferring she wasn't in tune with common people. What would she know about folks having to work for a living? Her father was a preacher.

She followed me as I walked under the bridge. I sat down on an old dead log, expecting her to do the same. Instead, she walked right past me, all the way down to the water's edge. Where was she going? I squirmed. Perhaps I should've waited for her to sit first. If I stood now, would it become even more apparent that I was unaccustomed to being in the presence of a lady? If I didn't stand, would she think me rude?

Before I could decide which of the two scenarios would make me look less like a backwoods' nincompoop, she spoke up.

"Mother fixed us a jar of lemonade."

"You got lemonade?" I flinched, thinking I'd sounded much too eager, but it'd been ages since I'd tasted lemonade.

"Yes. I sat the jar down when I took off my shoes. I'd planned to leave it in the creek and let it stay cool, until we finished studying, but we could have it now, if you'd rather."

I shrugged, trying to appear disinterested, but she scampered off as if she could read my thoughts. I reached up and blotted the corners of my mouth, in case I was beginning to drool.

She walked back with the jar. I watched as she reached in her pocket and pulled out a red-checkered cloth. When she lifted back the edges, I saw a half-dozen cookies, each the size of a moon pie.

"I made the cookies, myself, but Mother wrapped them for me."

Puzzled, I stammered. "Your . . . your mother . . . she wrapped the cookies and made the lemonade for you to bring *here*?"

She shrugged as if it were no big deal. "Just as I got home, a neighbor stopped by and said the cow got out of the fence, so I went to find ol' Bessie. When I returned, Mother had squeezed the lemons and had everything ready for me."

To stand or not to stand no longer occupied my thoughts. Something more perplexing pressed on my mind.

"Did you tell her you were meeting me? Here?"

Zann's brow furrowed as if she didn't understand. "Of course. That's why I went home. Remember?"

I found it hard to believe. What kind of mother would allow her beautiful young daughter to carouse around with some strange yahoo out in the middle of nowhere? What was wrong with the woman? Not that Zann wasn't safe with me. She was. But her mother didn't know what sort of fellow I was, or what kind of impure motives I might've been entertaining when I chose this particular secluded spot. I got fired up just thinking how this sweet, innocent girl's good name could've been compromised if I had a mind to take advantage of her. Which I had no intention of doing, but I'm just saying—

I pulled at my shirt collar and flexed my jaw when she plopped down beside me, with barely enough room for a centipede to cross between us.

She unscrewed the cap from the jar, took a swallow, then leaned over and handed me the lemonade. I licked my dry lips, held my head back and took a swig. My pulse raced as our shoulders touched. She smelled like those white flowers that bloom in the spring. Gardenias, I think Mama calls them. I slid down the log. Way down.

"The cookies have raisins in them. You like raisins?"

Before I could answer, she stood. I felt my pulse race. Was I supposed to stand, also? She quickly loosed her skirt from between her legs and plopped back down beside me. Close beside me.

Funny, the smell of gardenias had never made me feel this way before. My hand brushed against hers whenever I reached for another cookie. My face felt hot. I hoped I wasn't blushing. I wondered if her mother was really so naïve, or if perhaps she trusted her daughter enough to know Zann would never allow anything improper to happen.

I averted my eyes, when fantasies, which I'm ashamed to admit I initially found entertaining, gnawed at my conscience and left me afflicted with a frightening deduction. Had I inherited more than my father's looks? Perhaps I was no better than the scumbag. My nostrils flared at the ridiculous idea. I was nothing like him. Yet there was something about Zann that suddenly reminded me of Mama. I'd seen pictures of Mama when she was young, and she too, was quite beautiful in her day. But I imagined she'd been as unsuspecting of Will Lancaster's wicked thoughts as Zann was of mine. Yet, there was one big difference between young William Hezekiah and the elder William Hezekiah. No way would I ever dishonor such a sweet girl to satisfy my own selfish desires. I had no control over thoughts flitting through my head, but I did have control over my actions. I may not be able to help it if a buzzard flies over my head, but I don't have to let him make a nest in my hair.

Zann reached over and with her forefinger and thumb, lifted a curl from my brow. Obeying an impulse, I grimaced and shoved her hand away. Was she purposely trying to taunt me? Perhaps she wasn't as naïve as I assumed. After all, it was her idea for us to study together. Maybe a vulture was flying over her head, too, and just maybe she was ready for him to nest. I wondered. Not that I'd act upon it, but judging from the look on her face, I wasn't totally convinced she'd reject my advances if I wanted to pull her close and kiss her. What was I thinking? If I wanted to? I swallowed hard.

"Kiah, do you?"

My heart raced. Could she read my mind? I stammered. "Do I what?"

"I asked if you like raisins. Do you?"

I sucked in a deep breath and chuckled. "Sure. I like raisins."

"Take more than one," she said, shoving the checkered cloth toward me. Not wanting to appear too eager, I hum-hawed for a few seconds before taking a second one.

"Thanks." I bit down. "Mmm . . . good." The cookies were burned a tad on the bottom. Well, maybe more than a tad, but I happen to like crisp cookies.

She cocked her head to the side. "Listen! Do you hear something?"

I shook my head and swallowed. Could it be my chewing she heard? The munching of the brittle cookies grew louder with each bite. I tried to muffle the sound by letting each morsel remain in my mouth long enough for the saliva to soften the cookie.

She shrugged. "Probably a squirrel eating nuts."

"Yeah, maybe."

I hadn't heard a squirrel. If it wasn't my chewing she heard, more than likely it was the beating of my heart. The rat-a-tat-tat inside my chest caused the same thumping sound as wagon wheels, rolling along a corduroy dirt road. My insides jiggled and my teeth chattered. I tried to empty my mind of unwanted images and concentrate on our reason for being here. I cleared my throat and reached for the math book. We were here for only one reason. To study. Here, under an old bridge on a seldom traveled dirt road. Alone. With the tantalizing fragrance of gardenias hanging heavily in the air.

Chapter 2

After two weeks of meeting almost every day, I pondered how anyone as bright as Zann Pruitt could be so dense when it came to solving simple arithmetic problems.

I put away the text book and decided to begin by teaching basic principles. We'd worked for a couple of hours on percentages when the sun lowered. I tucked the writing tablet under my arm and extended a hand to lift her. "I suppose we'd better go."

She refused my hand. Instead, she put her arms behind her and bracing herself with both hands on the ground, she leaned back with her legs extended in front of her. "Oh, not yet, Kiah," she pleaded.

Such tiny ankles. I swallowed hard. Afraid she might read my thoughts, I quickly shifted my gaze toward the sky. "It's getting late, Zann. It'll soon be dark."

"Surely, we deserve a little free time," she pleaded. "All we've done is study. This is my favorite time of day. Look at the sun. Isn't it gorgeous? Big and yellow like a giant moon pie. Let's stay and watch it set."

I shook my head. No way would I be hanging out in the middle of nowhere with the parson's darling daughter, after dark. I pulled at my shirt collar, and reached out to her once more. "Come on. Your parents will be worried."

"Mother knows where I am, and she'll be so proud when I tell her how much we've accomplished. You're a swell teacher, Mr. Grave." She giggled.

"I'm leaving, Zann. You coming?"

With a slight groan, she reached for my hand and I pulled her up.

She brushed off the back of her dress. "Where do you live, Kiah?"

My feet shifted. I coughed in my hand, stalling for time to come up with a suitable answer that would be neither a lie nor the whole truth.

"Not far from here," I mumbled.

"Near Goodson's Grocery?"

"No." Perhaps she sensed I didn't care to elaborate, because she ceased from questioning me further. When we neared her house, I stopped.

She said, "Are you sure you won't walk me to my door and

meet Mother and Daddy? They've heard a lot about you, and they'd love to meet you."

I winced, wondering what they'd heard, but I had no desire to be in the presence of a preacher until they laid me in the ground, and I wasn't dead yet. So, I made a lame excuse and stood at the edge of the road and watched until she safely entered the front door.

The parsonage sat next to the church. The house was small, but neat. There was a white picket fence around it and little shrubs planted near the porch. The yard was swept clean and next to the road was a little flower garden, filled with yellow flowers— chrysanthemums, I believe.

Mama would love to live in such a pretty place. One day she'd get the chance. I'd make something of myself and when I made good, I'd buy her all the things she never had. Instead of being a washwoman for other people, she'd have her own washwoman. She'd have fancy dresses and I'd buy her a bottle of perfume that smelled like gardenias. We'd have meat on the table every night and eat out of fine china at a table covered with a cut-lace cloth. A crystal chandelier with tiny prisms would hang low over our table. I saw such a swell dining room on the cover of The Saturday Evening Post, once.

I burned inside imagining my daddy dining on delicacies fit for a king in a similar luxurious setting, while my mama ate scraps not fit for a dog, by the light of an oil lamp. An oil lamp, which didn't always have oil. The resentment was eating me alive, but I couldn't seem to let it go. Every way I turned, there were reminders.

As I walked, I mulled over Zann's words. Did she really mean it when she said I was a swell teacher? Though I'd never expressed such a notion to anyone, as far back as I could remember, I held to the idea that I'd one day become a famous professor at an Ivy League college.

Zann's praise encouraged me. Perhaps the dream wasn't so far-fetched, after all. I was smart, and I knew it. That's the one thing I had going for me. Learning came easily. I didn't have much to give the world, but if I could impart knowledge to help others, it seemed a worthy goal. It'd also be a way to provide for Mama and give her the dining room I wanted her to have.

Through the cut-off in the woods, Zann's house was about two or two-and-a-half miles from Rooster Run—a squatter camp on the south side of town. Mama and I lived in cabin #4.

If you inquired, folks would tell you the camp was located on the 'other side of the tracks.' Stands to reason if I was in my own yard, looking across the tracks, I'd be seeing the 'other side.' Not so. There's only one 'other side,' and it's also referred to as the 'wrong side.' That's the side we lived on. Rooster Run was so close to the railroad tracks, the house shook each time the train rumbled past. If it hadn't been for Mama I would've hopped that train years ago to ride as far away as possible. But I'd never leave her. Shouldn't that have been proof that I was nothing like William H. Lancaster IV?

A two-rut dirt road led into our tiny village and ended there. The camp consisted of eighteen makeshift shacks, nine on one side and nine on the other, with only two privies on the grounds. Most of the tenants had children, which presented a problem. Due to the lack of facilities, modesty was not always practiced in the squatter camp. When I asked how Rooster Run got its name, I was told a plump, Rhode Island Red, once taunted the residents by sitting on top of the shacks and crowing every morning, and then slyly evading capture when the residents tried to catch him. Since the rooster hadn't been seen in a couple of years, it was rumored he wound up boiled in someone's pot, though no one ever owned up to it.

Mama managed to buy us a mule and wagon, which I kept in a deserted stable down the road a piece. Mr. Farris, who owned the stockyards in Pivan Falls gave me all the hay I needed in exchange for cleaning stables at the yard. Sometimes I felt ol' Dolly ate better than we did. I worried that one day that mule would end up with the same fate as the rooster. Hunger can cause folks to do strange things.

I lived for the day I could leave and let Rooster Run be nothing more than a bad memory, yet I reckon I had no right to complain. Compared to our neighbors, we faired well. I especially felt for families with lots of children. There was hardly room for

Mama and me in our little cabin, and I couldn't imagine trying to live in such cramped quarters with four or five young'uns in tow. If I hadn't had a good reason for not falling in love already, living in Rooster Run would've provided me one. I'd seen the pain on the faces of the men with families. I wouldn't feel like much of a man if I had to watch my children go hungry.

A rusty iron fence about twelve feet high surrounded the tiny settlement I called home. All sorts of wild tales circulated around the camp about why the fence was there, but no one seemed to know for sure. Though there was no lock on the gate, I still had an eerie feeling I was a prisoner within those walls. An education would be my only way out.

It was dark by the time I got back from walking Zann home. As I entered through the gate, the familiar stench of Rooster Run stole my breath. Would I never become accustomed to the smell? Children with dirty faces and matted hair played in the light of the moon. Some were wearing clothes. Some weren't.

I could see light coming from the oil lamp in our little shanty. When I opened the door, I smelled baked apples. Mama sat in the old rocker, reading her Bible.

"You're late, tonight, Kiah. Did Mr. Farris need you to help at the stockyards?"

I shook my head. "Been studying." I preferred to store the events of the day in the private corner of my memory bank, not to be shared with anyone. Not even Mama. I needed time to sort out my feelings. I wasn't quite sure what had taken place.

"Kiah, Lena Blue from #7 brought us a dozen apples today. Said her husband got a job sweeping floors at the grocery, and Mr. Goodson gave him a bushel basket of apples to divide between the folks at Rooster Run. Mr. Goodson didn't charge Dewey a single copper penny for the whole lot of them. Imagine that. Some were rotten, but Lena and I cut off the bad parts. It was mighty nice of the man to do that, and Lena was right proud of being able to have something to share. Bless her heart, she's not had much to give 'til now."

Mama picked the Bible up from her lap and laid it on the apple crate beside her chair. I could tell she had something on her mind, and it wasn't hard to figure out what it was.

"Kiah, you've been coming home later and later every day from school, but you've never stayed out this late. It's plum dark outside. I ain't complaining, because you get your chores done, but I did get a mite worried when the sun went down and you hadn't come home."

"Sorry to trouble you," I mumbled.

I walked over and lifted two soft-baked apples from the iron skillet onto my plate and sat it down on the small kitchen table.

"Where did you say you've been, Kiah?"

"Studying, Mama."

I turned the straight back chair around backward at the table, and straddled it. I briefly bowed my head, knowing Mama would have something to say if I didn't. I should've been thankful for apples, because they were better than nothing—but my mouth watered for something solid to sink my teeth into—something like a pork chop or a big slice of salty fat back. "Amen," I said loudly and opened my eyes.

"We've got some grits in the cupboard, shug, if you'd like me to stir you up a pot."

I shook my head. "Apples are fine, Mama."

"You stayed at school 'til this hour?"

"No ma'am. I was down at the . . . down at the bridge." I could never get anything past Mama. She could always see through me.

Her eyes narrowed. "The old covered bridge?"

I nodded. "That's the one. I like studying while listening to the gentle sounds of the rippling creek." I don't know why I failed to mention I was there with Zann. It wasn't as if I'd done anything wrong, so why did I feel as though I had? Was it guilt, knowing what ran through my mind when I was with her?

"You've always loved the outdoors." Mama smiled. "Your daddy was like that, too."

I bristled. Now was not the time to remind me I was like William Lancaster. I didn't want to hear it. "Mama, why do you have to keep harping on how much I'm like that man? I'm not like him. Can't you get it through your head? Why can't you accept the truth?"

The minute the words escaped, I wanted to pull them back in, but it was too late. The damage was evident in Mama's glazed eyes. I grimaced at the bitterness raging inside me. This wasn't the person I wanted to be, but it was who I was—a boiler about to blow.

"I'm sorry, Kiah. I didn't mean to upset you, but sugar, you have him all wrong. Will Lancaster is a fine man."

I'd made up my mind to apologize, but hearing her call the jerk a fine man made the hair on the back of my neck rise. I would never change my opinion of him, and after all these years, Mama wasn't likely to change hers either.

I pushed the chair back, walked over and knelt beside her. I clasped her hands in mine. "Mama. I'm sorry I snapped at you. And I wasn't exactly truthful about this afternoon, either. There were more sounds than the rippling creek . . . I was there with a girl."

Red blood flushed in Mama's pale cheeks as a look of panic filled her widened orbs. She nodded slightly, and murmured, "I see." No questions, no other comment. "I see." That was it.

What went through her mind? Did she still want to believe I was like her darling Will? Hot anger shot through me like a poisoned arrow but I tried not to let it show. The muscles in my jaw tightened. I sucked in a deep breath and managed to speak in a slow, calm voice.

"No, Mama, I don't think you do see. I was there because a

girl in my class is having a problem with math. She asked me to tutor her. Mr. Thatcher locks the building after school, so we went to the covered bridge to study."

"Oh." The lines on Mama's face slowly faded. "Who is this girl? Do I know her?"

"I don't think so. She's the Parson Pruitt's daughter."

"Oh, my." The lines returned between Mama's eyes. She fumbled with a button on her dress. "The parson's daughter, you say? But . . . but why did you choose such an odd place to study? The covered bridge? It's so . . . so—"

I decided to help her. "Secluded? And dark?"

She blushed. "Well, yes. I think you might have picked a better place, Kiah." Her eyes squinted as she held her frown. "What kind of girl is she?"

I gritted my teeth. My first impulse was to shout, "Not the kind of girl you were, if that's what you're afraid of." To my relief, the lump in my throat prevented the stinging words from escaping. Hadn't Mama paid for her sin, already? The good church folks at Piney Woods had thrust the dagger in her back. Did she need me to twist it? I drew a deep breath.

"She's a very nice girl, Mama. I think you'd like her."

Mama's lips parted slightly and the air seeping out of her made a faint whistle. "I'm sure I will, Kiah. Maybe you'd like to bring her here to the cabin one day. I'll make some applesauce and we can get acquainted. I'd like that. You've always said I make the best applesauce." She made a waving motion toward the table. "Go sit back down, honey and finish your supper."

How could I admit to Mama that I was too ashamed to tell Zann I lived in Rooster Run? No way would I ever bring her to this dump and sit her down to a bowl of applesauce. I glanced over at Mama. The dress she wore was clean, but with so many stains, who could tell? I'd watched as her weight dwindled down to less than a hundred pounds. She was in her late thirties, yet one would guess twenty years older. When I was younger, I asked why she had quotation marks between her eyes. She said it was the marks of a thinker. I later learned the truth. The marks of a worrier plowed deep furrows into her forehead—a gift from my dear dad. Almost overnight, Mama's dark auburn hair faded to a wiry, dull orange. Her complexion paled and her green eyes, no longer open and bright, were partially hid beneath drooping lids. Her shoulders slumped and she walked with an awkward gait. The years had not been kind.

Shame swept over me, when I admitted to myself that Rooster Run was not the only reason I didn't want to bring Zann home with me. I was ashamed of my own mother. My sweet, precious Mama who'd sacrificed so much for my sake. What right did I have to criticize Will Lancaster and call him a scumbag? Maybe heredity truly is a stronger influence than environment.

I don't know at what point I tuned Mama out, but I nodded as if I'd heard every word.

She smiled. "So, tomorrow, then?"

I swallowed. "Uh . . . no, Mama. Not tomorrow." I wasn't sure what she meant, but I didn't want her making plans to use our meager sugar ration to make applesauce. We wouldn't be entertaining visitors. Specifically, not Zann Pruitt, if that's what she had in mind. I shoved my chair away from the table.

"Sure, son. Maybe some other time."

"Yes'm." I mumbled after wiping my mouth with a dish rag.

Mama leaned forward. "Son, I'm thinkin' this is the time to bring up something I've had pressing on my mind for a good long while. There's a little white church, not more'n three or four miles up the road, and even closer, the way the crow flies." She didn't have to tell me how far it was. I knew exactly where the church was located and it might as well be in Timbuktu, because I wouldn't be going.

She paused and squinted. I could see she was studying my reaction. Well, I'd make sure she didn't misunderstand. With clinched teeth, I leaned the chair back on two legs and focused my eyes on the worn linoleum. I stroked my chin and heaved a deep sigh, meant to impart "here we go again."

Mama knew how I felt about going to church and I couldn't understand why she kept needling me. But if there was one thing consistent about my Mama, it was her confounded consistency. She grinned as if she figured she'd finally made headway. I grimaced. There was nothing in my manner to give her the erroneous impression, but Mama often saw what she wanted to see.

She raised her brow. In a cheerful sounding voice, she said, "Maybe we'll go Sunday and I can meet your new friend."

So that was it, was it? She had the mistaken idea I was interested in sparking with the preacher's kid, and she planned to use it to her advantage. I rolled my eyes and chuckled. "She's not my new friend, Mama. I met her when she first moved here. And I don't know why every time we move, you seem to want to bring up the subject of church. You know I'm not going, and I can't imagine why you'd choose to beat a dead horse and expect to hear a whinny."

"But, Kiah, shug if only—"

I didn't want to hear it. I threw my arms in the air. "Don't you get it? Have you forgotten what Mrs. Ola Mae Dobbins told you? We don't have a boarding pass, Mama. There's no room on their big fine Fellow Ship for colored folks, or us po' whites. That heavenly boat is reserved for rich, white hypocrites." I lowered my voice, and mumbled. "I'd rather die than become one."

Mama reached over and patted my arm. "Kiah, Kiah . . . Sweetheart, Miz Ola Mae was wrong. God's a forgiving God. Don't you remember the story of the Samaritan woman?"

Remember? How could I forget? But I didn't respond because Mama wasn't looking for an answer. I couldn't decide which brought her the most pleasure—retelling the story of the sinful woman at the well, or rehashing her own lurid love story. Most kids go to sleep hearing stories about Three Little Pigs or Little Red Riding Hood. As a child, I went to sleep hearing about a loose woman who lived almost two-thousand years ago.

She said, "If you recall, Kiah, accordin' to the Bible, the woman had known more'n a few men, and I reckon she was ashamed of her past, and rightly so. But . . . well, you know the story, shug. Jesus didn't condemn her. He knew everything about her, yet—"

I tuned her out and threw my head back. I couldn't be responsible for my actions if forced to listen to a repeat for the umpteenth time. It seemed Mama treated the story with the same mindset one has when berry-picking. She took the juicy parts that suited her tastes, and overlooked the less flavorful dry parts. No doubt there was more to the incident at the well than she cared to relate. In all the times Mama had spouted that story, I never remembered her saying anything about the woman's little buzzards. Perhaps that was Mama's unpardonable sin. She bore me.

Chapter 3

I'd managed to keep my mouth shut in the past, but I couldn't keep quiet forever.

"Okay, Mama, so Jesus forgave her. But what d'ya suppose the pious folks at the local temple said when the floozy decided if Jesus could forgive her, then she was good enough to enter their sanctuary? You reckon they wrapped their arms around her and said, 'Well, bless your heart, honey, you come on in?' Not a chance. The big wigs in the temple were afraid she'd point them out." I raised my brow and smirked. "Likely, she could call them all by name. And as for their wives . . ." I stopped and rolled my eyes for emphasis. "I'm sure the ugly old hags felt threatened by the presence of a good-looking dame. No, Mama, the woman wasn't welcome among them and neither were any of her little buzzards."

The words plummeted from my mouth so fast, I'm not sure I could've stopped them if I tried. I felt like the forest fire I'd seen as a child. Nothing could hold it back as it forged forward, destroying everything within its path.

Mama glared, occasionally shaking her head in unmistakable disapproval of my heated outburst. I should've stopped. Wanted to. But I couldn't. The raging fire inside me was lit.

I sucked in a lungful of air and blew out, slowly. "Maybe you're right, Mama. Maybe God's forgiven you for bearing me, and forgiven me for being born. But I'll guarantee you one thing: those folks at church go by a different set of rules. They don't want us muddying up their waters. That's just how it is."

Mama rocked back in her chair. "Kiah, son, I know you were wounded deeply by the ladies from Piney Woods Church, but that was ages ago, and they were wrong. Maybe it'll be different at Pivan Falls."

"Fat chance. I think they all use the same Bible." Going to church had become an obsession with her. I didn't want to hurt Mama, but I had to make her understand. We weren't wanted. Why was that so hard for her to grasp?

She said, "Maybe it ain't like you think. Seems to me since the parson sees fit for his daughter to spend time with you, it proves he don't look down his nose at us."

I sneered. "You think not? Don't be so sure. I doubt the good parson knows his daughter went to the woods today with a buzzard, and even if—"

Mama didn't allow me to finish. "Honey, I wish you wouldn't

say such vulgar things. It ain't fittin'.'"

"Vulgar? Would you prefer I use the term the Bible thumpers use?" I paused to reflect on the conversation I'd overheard years ago. "Face it, Mama, those people don't cater to trash."

A frown fixed between her brows. "Honey, is that what you think of your mama?" Her voice trembled. "You think I'm trash?"

I sucked in a deep breath and let out a huff. "Of course not, but I'll grant you that's how the goody-two-shoes view us. Why can't you see it for the way it is, Mama? You gave up everything for the rotten so-and-so. He took what he wanted from you and gave up nothing. If the man cared one iota for either of us, we wouldn't be scrapping for food like a couple of alley cats. I know what it feels like to go to bed hungry. Does he? Of course not."

"Son, you just don't understand. There were circumstances."

Mama was a God-fearing woman and she'd never lie. Not on purpose, anyway. She wanted to believe William Lancaster had his reasons for not marrying her, but she'd gotten herself into a fine predicament because of harebrained, romantic notions.

William Hezekiah Lancaster IV. Mama fixed it so I'd never forget that name. She gave it to me, as if I didn't bear enough shame because of him. Of course, she couldn't give me his last name, since the louse ducked out as soon as he discovered he'd impregnated her. Yet for reasons I found impossible to understand, Mama forgave him. I suppose that's what irked me most.

Mama dried her face with the tail of her apron, then stood and gently touched the side of my face with her calloused hand. "Goodnight, my precious son."

Ashamed, my shoulders slumped. I didn't feel very precious.

She picked up a coffee cup and laid it in the sink. "Shug, you may be all grown up, but you'll always be my little Kiah-Cooter. I love you to the other side of the ocean and back."

"Yeah, Mama . . . to the ocean and back." I smiled at the little phrase we'd repeated so many times during my growing-up years. Mama looked tired and she had every right to be. Times were hard and it hadn't been easy trying to raise a son by herself.

I pulled off my overalls and muslin shirt and hung them across a clothes line, held up by two posts between our beds. It was my own invention, as a way of turning a one-room cottage into a two bed-room house. It worked. A tattered bed sheet thrown over the line separated our quarters, allowing us a semblance of privacy. The cabin came furnished with two rusty iron bedsteads and two cotton mattresses, both so thin you could feel the wooden slats underneath. Mama let me have the bed near the window. I lay on my back, looking at the grungy walls and tried to shut out the yelling, coming from #6. Frank and Cora Bess were at it again. I closed my eyes tightly, but sleep wouldn't come.

I couldn't get the image of Mama out of my mind. I was accustomed to seeing her look tired, though tonight she appeared unusually haggard. Was it my imagination? Was something wrong with her, or was I observing her the way I presumed Zann might see her? A malnourished, worn out woman, whose looks belied her years? But Zann *wouldn't* see her. Mama never left Rooster Run, and Zann would never have an occasion to enter the gate. I'd make sure of it.

I tossed and turned, unable to find comfort on the knotty cotton mattress. My stomach growled. I should've eaten a few grits along with the apples. I tried not to think of food, so I kept my thoughts tuned to more pleasant things. Zann Pruitt.

A knot formed in my stomach. I wasn't sure if it was hunger pains, or sheer panic that I'd dare entertain forbidden notions of love. A girl like Zann could do much better than to fall for a guy like me. I loathed my life. Though I blamed my father for the predicament we were in, too often I took my frustrations out on my dear, sweet mother. I didn't want to. I loved her dearly, but the mule-headed anger bucking inside me was more than I could harness.

I'd barely shut my eyes, before the morning sun struck through the burlap curtains, casting a warm glow over the dreary room. I jumped up, jerked on my clothes and ran outside to bring in more wood for the stove. I trudged back in with my head lowered. "Sorry you had to tote in the wood, Mama. Why didn't you wake me?"

"Weren't no problem, shug. I reckon you needed the rest. I heard you over there tussling in the bed, near 'bout all night long. Something weighin' heavy on you, Kiah?"

"No ma'am." Did she really have to ask? I bit my tongue to keep from blurting my thoughts. Just because we lived in a one-room pig-sty, and I trekked off to school every day wearing ill-fitting clothes, why should I worry? I yanked out a chair and plopped down at the table.

Mama stirred the boiling grits on the wood stove, and ladled the hot cereal onto my plate. She reached in the oven and pulled out a baker of biscuits, and placed it on the table. I sucked in a deep breath. Nothing smelled better than Mama's biscuits, except of course, ham and red-eyed gravy. But I couldn't remember the last time we had fried ham.

"Pass the butter, Mama." Before she had time to answer, I feigned surprise. "No butter?" It wasn't so much a question as a gripe. I knew we had no butter. I never asked for bacon anymore, but was it too much to expect to have a little butter on the table?

Mama frowned. "Honey, you know we ain't had butter for more'n a week. But Mr. Easton owes me for last week's ironing, and if he pays, I plan to buy some butter and eggs. For now, though, I'm afraid this'll have to do. I'm sorry, shug. I wish I had more to offer you."

I slammed my fist on the table. "You're wrong, Mama. This doesn't 'have to do.' I'm not going to sit around and do nothing." Here I was, a one-hundred sixty-five pound muscular male, five feet eleven, and my mama was working her fingers to the nub to take care of me. It wasn't right. She did the best she could do, but it wasn't enough. The alley cats got more protein in a day than we got in a month. I shoved my plate aside and grabbed my jacket.

Mama's brow furrowed. "Where you going, Kiah? It's too early to leave for school."

"I'm not going to school." I shifted my gaze to the floor. I couldn't look her in the eyes. "I'm going to get a job, Mama. There are plenty of men holding down jobs who never finished high school." I glanced up in time to see the panic on her face. With nothing more needing to be said, I trudged toward the door. She leaped from her chair and grabbed my arm.

"No, son. I won't let you go. You can't."

Tears blinded me. "Turn loose, Mama." I pried her bony fingers from my jacket sleeve. "We can't go on living like this."

Mama fell to her knees and grabbed me by the leg. "Use your brain, Kiah. What do you propose to do? Look around you at the grown men here in Rooster Run who haven't been able to find work. What makes you think you can do better?"

I reached down and offered my hand to help her up. She refused, and held tightly to my pants leg.

"Let go, Mama."

She turned loose and took my hand. I lifted her from off the floor. I said, "Maybe I can't do better, but I won't know until I try."

She moaned, "Oh, Lordy. What in this world am I gonna do?"

Her panic-stricken eyes fixed on me, the way someone on a

sailboat might fixate on an approaching twister. My throat ached. I watched her body go limp as she walked over and fell back into the old rocker and squalled like a baby.

I knelt beside her. I couldn't let her tears get to me. I had to be strong. "Mama, you can send me on my way *with* your blessings or without them." I brushed my hand through my hair and tried to reason with her. "Don't you understand? I can't sit here and do nothing. I feel like a louse."

Slowly lifting her head, she took her hands and cupped them around my face. Her voice low and filled with compassion, she said, "Oh, Kiah, my precious son. You've had a tempest brewing inside you for years, but lately the raging storm has taken on a fierceness that frightens me. Sure, times are hard, yet we've made it this far, haven't we? We'll make it, Kiah. We will."

I stood and whirled around. There was so much I wanted to say, but I couldn't, because if I did, it'd give confirmation to her words. Though I didn't want to admit it, she was right. The storm had intensified. My temper had become uncontrollable. I sucked in a deep breath, and tried to appear calm, as she presented her case.

Her voice rose, as I lumbered toward the door. "There ain't no jobs out there, Kiah. We're not the only ones who have it hard, you know. The nation's in the depths of a Great Depression. Don't quit school to go on a snipe hunt. You're too close to a diploma to give up now."

Mama seemed to grope for words, which would make an

impact on me and change my way of thinking. Her comment about the snipe hunt hit the intended nerve, bringing back a painful memory of the night I discovered everyone but me understood that catching an elusive snipe would be as futile as sacking an angel.

She finished by saying, "We ain't by ourselves, Kiah. Everybody's suffering."

I bristled. "Not everyone, Mama. Not everyone." I referred to the man responsible for sentencing us to a life of poverty, while he drove around in a fine car and employed servants to do his bidding. I didn't know him, but I'd met others like him. Self-centered snobs. In '29 when so many fat cats were losing their stored-up wealth in the stock market crash and were jumping out windows, I wouldn't have grieved if he'd been among them. That sounds like a ghastly fate to wish upon one's own father, and perhaps I should be ashamed to admit it. But I never have been one to hide my feelings.

I laid my hand on the doorknob. "Bye, Mama," I whispered.

When she didn't respond, I assumed she'd given up and allowed me to have the last word. I'd won, but somehow I didn't feel much like a winner. She buried her face in her hands.

I turned around, looked at her and froze.

She appeared to be praying, when she wailed, "Please, dear Lord, don't let him ruin his life."

How could I leave her in such a fix? I trudged over to where she sat and stood over her. "Mama," I whispered. "Please don't cry. I'm doing this for you. Can't you understand? It isn't fair for you to work so hard for me. I want to find a job so I can take care of you. Is that so wrong?"

She raised her head. The look of terror in her eyes reminded me of a scared alley cat peering into the face of a hungry bulldog. Her voice quivered. "Kiah, if you want to do something for me, you'll stay in school. After next year, you'll have a high school diploma. We've come this far. If you drop out now, all will have been in vain. Promise me. Promise me, Kiah that you'll complete your education."

I sighed. "Okay, Mama. You win—for now."

There was no more talk of my quitting school. Or at least not that semester.

Chapter 4

I took one look in the cracked mirror at my unruly hair and groaned. If I wet it and held my head over the hot stove and combed it until it dried, the tight ringlets relaxed into gentle waves. Though my locks seemed to garner a lot of attention from the girls, I hated it.

Why couldn't I have inherited Mama's sleek hair? Why did I have to get *his*?

Mama paced the floor while reminding me of the time.

"Kiah, your hair looks fine, son. I wish you wouldn't fret over it. Why, his hair was one of the first things that attracted me to your daddy."

I bit my lip.

Mama stood in the doorway holding a syrup bucket that contained my lunch while urging me to hurry. I didn't have to ask what was in the pail. Same as yesterday. And the day before. And the day before that. Three biscuits left over from breakfast. Each would have a hole, made by Mama's thumb to make a well for the syrup that oozed over the top. I was sick of eating cold biscuits for lunch, but I kept my mouth shut. I'd already hurt Mama enough. I hung the bucket over my arm, grabbed my books and pecked her on the forehead before rushing out the door.

The bell had rung by the time I got to the little schoolhouse. I ran in and took a seat in my desk. I glimpsed across the aisle. My face grew warm when Zann peeked over the top of her book and grinned.

Lucky for me, the teacher had his back to the door. I sat up straight and let out a grateful breath. I'd managed to slip in without being caught.

Mr. Thatcher walked over and stood in front of the blackboard. His wrinkled, gray double-breasted suit would've fit better if the tailor had added enough material for a double-bellied man. It didn't take a fortune teller to know what he had for supper, since he wore it on his tie. The man had a razor-sharp brain, yet he couldn't seem to remember to lace his own shoes. He was a bachelor, and I'd heard it said all he needed was a good woman to take care of him. I groaned, imagining myself in twenty years. Was I destined to become a slob?

He picked up a piece of chalk and commenced to write on the blackboard. Then, turning to face the class, he asked, "How many completed your math assignment last night?"

I raised my hand, glanced across the room and grimaced.

Mr. Thatcher pursed his lips. "Well, I see only two of you were able to finish. I must apologize. Last night I realized we've not covered chapter 12. I only meant to give you chapters 10 and 11." He walked over to Zann's desk and picked up her paper. "Quite remarkable, Miss Pruitt. Did you find the assignment difficult?"

Zann looked at me and grinned. "No sir. I didn't find it difficult, but I didn't fully understand." She giggled.

Mr. Thatcher rubbed his hand over his bald head. "I don't think I follow you."

I attempted to slow my breathing for fear those around me would hear the hassling.

She said, "Kiah and I worked it together, which made it easier, but I'm not sure I could work a similar problem on my own." She turned her whole body around in the desk and faced me. I slumped further down in my desk and buried my face in my math book.

"Kiah's promised to tutor me and I'm confident in time, with his excellent help I'll catch on. He's a swell teacher."

Mr. Thatcher said, "That's very commendable of you, Hezekiah, to give of your time to help Miss Pruitt. She's an excellent student, yet she does struggle with math." He walked up and down the aisle, before he said, "I encourage others of you to follow Kiah's example and volunteer to help a struggling student. Not many of us are proficient in every subject."

Mort Willoughby snickered, when Arnold Evers stood.

Mr. Thatcher allowed him to speak.

"I agree with you, Mr. Thatcher. Kiah's a selfless codger, for sure, to want to spend time *alone* with Zann Pruitt.*"

I grimaced at his sarcasm. Apparently, he wasn't through. With a sweep of his hand and the voice of an orator, he bellowed, "I ask you, my male comrades, how many would be willing to make such a noble sacrifice as our good friend, Hezekiah Grave?" Laughter erupted when every male student's hand shot up in the air.

Mr. Thatcher pounded a ruler on his desk. "That's enough, Arnold. Take your seat, please."

When the lunch bell rang, I picked up my syrup bucket and went to the far end of the school yard. I reached in the pail to pull out a cold biscuit. I let it fall back when I looked up and saw Zann heading straight toward me. She carried a little white wicker basket, which she brought to school every day. Stares from other students bored holes through me. I closed my eyes and hoped when I opened them, she'd be gone. I let out a groan and lifted my lids at the sound of her voice.

"Hi, Kiah. Mind if I join you?"

Studying with her was one thing, but I didn't need her hanging around me in public, giving everyone the idea we were courting.

"It's a free country. Sit where you like," I mumbled and glanced across the school yard to see who might be watching.

Apparently, she was unaccustomed to sarcasm, for she didn't seem to catch it, when flung right between her pretty brown eyes. The wide smile never left her lips. She pulled a red checkered cloth from her basket and spread it on the ground in front of me.

She chirped, "Why don't we share our lunches?"

I couldn't let her see I had nothing to eat but cold, left-over biscuits. I shrugged. "You go ahead and eat. I ate a huge breakfast this morning, so I'm not hungry. "

She smiled. "Oh, drats. I hate eating alone. Have lunch with me. Please? I brought enough to share."

"Sorry. I'm stuffed. Couldn't eat a bite."

She pulled out two china plates and two small cardboard forks. Was she deaf? When she opened a Mason jar and scooped mashed sweet potatoes, loaded down with butter on both plates, I could see she had every intention of sharing her lunch in spite of my protest. My mouth watered. How long had it been since I'd tasted buttered sweet potatoes? I looked away, but then I got a whiff of fried chicken.

"I hope you like dark meat," she said, holding up a drumstick. "Daddy likes white meat, so I packed the breasts and pulley bone in his lunch pail, but I brought two drumsticks and two thighs for you and me."

She thrust the drumstick in my face. The delectable aroma of batter-fried chicken made my nostrils flare

"Here, Kiah, take it."

56

I wanted to refuse. Did she know I'd been eating biscuits for lunch every day? I didn't want her charity, if that's what this was all about.

When I didn't reach for the chicken leg, she laid it on the plate beside the thigh and sweet potatoes. She placed the other two pieces of chicken on the second plate. "Sorry, I didn't bring any bread. Mama burned the biscuits again this morning."

Remembering the burned cookies, I figured Zann took cooking lessons from her mother.

She bowed her head and said a quick prayer. I watched as she took a bite out of her chicken. Never had I faced so powerful a temptation, as I watched her lick grease from all ten fingers. Slowly. One at the time. It took all the will power I could muster to keep from snatching that drumstick from her hands.

That's when I came up with an idea. I reached in my syrup bucket. "You say you have no bread? Mama makes a humdinger of a biscuit. I grabbed a couple before leaving home this morning, in case I happened to get hungry." I pulled out two biscuits and popped one on each plate. Justified, we were now sharing. This couldn't be regarded as charity, could it?

I watched as she took a bite.

She closed her eyes and smacked her lips. "Say! These are delicious . . . and loaded with cane syrup, just the way I like them."

At that moment, I wished more than ever, we'd had butter. They were so much better with fresh churned butter.

"Your Mama makes delicious biscuits, so fluffy and light. My mother's a great cook, but she can't make a decent biscuit. Neither can I." She nodded toward the plate sitting in front of me. "You'd better eat, Kiah. The bell's gonna ring soon."

"Well, I reckon I might can swallow a couple of bites if I set my mind to it." I reached for the drumstick. I don't know if I'd forgotten how chicken tasted, or if that leg was really the best piece of fried chicken I'd ever put in my mouth. When I finished, the bone was picked clean. I eyed the thigh on my plate and pictured Mama, wasting away. Could I in good conscience eat another piece of chicken when my poor Mama needed it worse?

When Zann's head turned, I dropped the thigh into my syrup bucket.

Zann pulled a napkin from the basket and patted her lips. My pulse raced. How could wiping grease from one's mouth look so enticing? My mouth watered as I drank in the luscious sight of full, heart-shaped lips. She reached up and grasped her hair at the nape of her neck, and slung the long, thick curls over her right shoulder. I glanced away when she caught me staring.

The sound of the school bell caused me to breathe a long sigh. Something strange was happening to me, and I needed to put a stop to it before it went any further.

Zann wrapped everything in the checkered cloth and laid it in the basket. "Kiah," she said, "you will tutor me again today, won't you?"

I hesitated. I wanted to do the right thing, but I wasn't sure what the right thing might be. Should I think of myself and put as much distance between me and the object of my frustration as possible? Or should I consider her dilemma and agree to help? Did I have a choice? I'd feel awful if she failed her college entrance exams because of my refusal to tutor her. I had to put these nonsensical feelings of love out of my mind.

She pulled my arm. "Kiah, will you? Please?"

My face burned at her touch. I glanced around to see if anyone was watching. I pressed my lips together and nodded. "Sure, Zann. I'll meet you at the bridge after I run home to see about Mama. She's not been feeling well lately."

"Oh, I'll walk with you. I'd love to meet your mother. Maybe she could tell me her secret to making biscuits."

"No!" I winced at the sharpness in my voice. I tried once more. "Today wouldn't be a good time. I won't be long, I promise."

"I understand. I told Mama this morning not to expect me home after school, but I'll run to the house and pack a couple of cupcakes and a quart of lemonade for us to munch on."

The mention of cupcakes and lemonade made my mouth water, but at the same time, guilt plagued me, knowing how much Mama loved sweets. If only she could have something good to eat—something like cupcakes with frosting and a big glass of Zann's delicious lemonade made with so much sugar one could sop it with a biscuit.

After school I ran all the way to Rooster Run, jumping two fences along the way. Mama had an iron sitting on top of the stove, heating, and she held another in her hand as she pressed down on a man's starched white shirt. Folded ironed clothes were neatly stacked on both cots. Mama smiled, but her eyes looked hollow, like two big sinkholes. The sparkle left them long ago.

She said, "You look as if you're in a fine mood. Did my Kiah-Cooter have a good day at school?"

I groaned. The affectionate term was okay when I was a child, but I was a man now, and I constantly feared she'd slip and say it front of someone. Perhaps I was being paranoid. After all, she never saw anyone except the neighbors at Rooster Run and the snobs who brought their laundry and worked her for a pittance. Why should I care what they thought?

"Mama, I brought you a surprise."

She sat the iron down on a tin plate and smiled. "A surprise? For me?"

"Yep. Sit down, close your eyes and hold out your hand."

"Oh, honey, you're so sweet to want to give me something, but I reckon we'd better wait until I finish ironing. I only have three more garments, and Mr. Easton should be here to pick them up soon. Did you pick your Mama some wild flowers on your way home?"

I placed my hands on her shoulders. "Nope. A heap better than flowers. Now. Sit down and close your eyes. If you aren't finished ironing when Mr. Easton comes, he can wait."

"Kiah, I really . . ." Before she could finish, I guided her to the rocker.

"Sit!" I chuckled at the quizzical look on her face.

When she closed her eyes, I pulled out the chicken and placed it in her hand.

She gasped. "I don't have to open my eyes to know what I'm holding. I can smell it. But where? Where did you get fried chicken?"

"Someone at school had extra pieces at lunch and shared with me."

Mama choked up. "Kiah." She paused. "Honey, was it because you—"

I bristled. "I know what you're thinking, Mama, but you're wrong. She doesn't even know—" I stiffened. I hadn't intended to say 'she,' but it slipped.

Mama looked up at me. "Parson Pruitt's daughter?"

Anger swelled inside me. I wasn't sure why or even who the anger was aimed toward, but it was anger, nevertheless. "Yes, Mama," I grumbled. "Parson Pruitt's daughter. Don't sit there staring at it. Eat. I hoped you'd be grateful."

A tear made its way down her cheek. "I am grateful, son. I truly am. But I want you to eat it. You're a growing boy. I don't need as much to keep my body running as you do." She pushed the chicken toward me.

I shoved it back. "Mama, I couldn't eat another bite. That's why I had a piece left over. You should've seen the spread Zann brought. I've never seen so much food."

Mama's lip trembled. "Kiah, I know how it embarrasses you for folks to know our circumstances. I'm so sorry, sugar."

"Oh, Mama, it wasn't charity. Not at all. I didn't have meat and she didn't have bread, so we shared. Mama, she said your biscuits were much better than the ones her mother tries to bake. I could tell she meant it. I plan to take four tomorrow. Two for her and two for me. She only took one of the three today, but I'm sure she was only being polite and didn't want to take the last one. She didn't even notice they weren't buttered."

Mama's lip curled. For a second, the twinkle seemed to return in her eyes. Maybe I only imagined it. She took a bite of chicken and now I was sure I detected a gleam coming from the sunken orbs.

After wiping her mouth with her hand, she said, "You like this girl, don't you, son?"

My body grew rigid. I'd already explained our relationship. Tutor and student. Why couldn't she leave it at that?

"Of course, I like her Mama, but not the way you mean. She's a swell kid, but that's all she is. A kid."

"I see." She licked her lips. "How old is she?"

I mumbled, "Sixteen."

Mama's smile added to my frustration. "A kid, you say? Why, son, I wasn't much older than her when you were born. Seems to me sixteen is mighty nigh to being a woman."

"Not her. She's . . . well, she's innocent. You know . . . naïve, like a child. She hasn't been exposed to the rough side of life. As far as she knows, life is one big carousel, going round and round to the merry sound of music." Perhaps Zann Pruitt did possess the innocence of a child, but it didn't take 20/20 vision to see she was mighty nigh to being a woman, as Mama had so aptly put it. I made a deliberate effort to clear her image from my mind. Allowing thoughts to linger was akin to taking a second look.

"I need to run, Mama. She'll be waiting for me to tutor her."

Mama wiped her hands on her apron, grabbed a pot holder and picked up a hot iron from off the stove. "I guess I'd better get started if I plan to have the ironing done by the time Mr. Easton gets here. Thank your friend for me and tell her I said the chicken was delicious."

I nodded, to indicate I understood, although I had no plans to tell Zann I sneaked the chicken home because my mama was hungry.

I sprinted toward the bridge. I hoped I hadn't kept her waiting. I won't deny the job of tutor appealed to me, and in time I'd prove her confidence in me was well placed. My goal was to see Zann Pruitt make the second highest grade in the class on the final math exam at the year's end. I was arrogant enough to believe that even with the proper tutelage she'd never rise above me.

As I drew closer to the bridge, I could see she wasn't there. My heart sank. What if she didn't show up? I slid down the embankment and sat on a little patch of grass under the bridge. Minutes later, I heard footsteps on the wooden slats above me. I grabbed my math book, opened it, and pretended to be studying. But the voice I heard wasn't Zann's. I cringed, recognizing Arnold Evers' boorish laughter. Who was he talking to? I slid further under the bridge, hoping I was out of sight.

I heard him yell, "Hey, Zann. Fancy meeting you here. Mort and I came to try our luck. I hear the crappy's been biting. Wanna walk down the branch with us and fish? I'll cut you a pole."

My heart hammered.

Zann's soft voice didn't carry, yet I deciphered enough to know she declined the offer.

Arnold said, "I suppose you'd rather fish with Hezekiah Grave? What do you see in him, anyhow? He's a real chump. I think he came to school in first grade wearing that same pair of overalls."

Mort Willoughby let out a hearty laugh, which sounded more like a mule braying.

If it's true one can feel the blood boil, then I'm sure that accounts for the peculiar stirrings inside my gut. But not wanting to embarrass Zann, I lay low and waited. Surely, Arnold and Mort would leave and go further down the creek where the water wasn't so shallow.

My heart pounded as I strained to hear the conversation above me.

Arnold said, "What's on your face?"

There was a pause, and then he said, "No, not there. Let me get it for you."

Zann screamed, "What are you doing, Arnold Evers. Turn me loose."

I'm not sure if I grew wings, but it seemed I flew to the top of the embankment. I don't think Arnold had time to see me coming, when Mort hollered, "Let her go, Arn. She ain't worth it."

I didn't know which one to sock first, so I laid them both out. Knocked the breath out of Arnold, before shoving Mort over the edge and into the shallow water. I'd had plenty of things to rile me in my life, but I never remember being overwhelmed with such rage as when I saw Arnold holding her while she fought him. Arnold jumped up, brushed himself off and grabbed his pole. I snatched him by the shirt collar. "Arnold Evers, if you ever lay a hand on her again, you'll look like a lone oak at a woodpeckers' picnic. Do you get the picture?"

He glared at me and then looked down at Mort who was crawling up the embankment. "You can have her," he sneered.

His words made me want to hit him again. How could I respond to such a statement? I couldn't say, "I don't want her," even though I didn't . . . or at least I didn't want to want her. Life was becoming complicated. I watched until they were out of sight.

I turned to look at Zann. Her face was redder than a July tomato. "You okay?" I asked.

"Yes, thanks to you."

I ran my fingers through my hair and mumbled, "I'm glad he didn't hurt you. You ready to study?"

"Ready," she smiled. "But first, shall we have a little refreshments? I made cupcakes last night. I hope you like chocolate."

I couldn't recall the last time I had anything chocolate. She pulled out three cupcakes. Chocolate on the inside and white icing on the outside. She called it a devil's food cake recipe, and I could understand where it got its name. Anything that good was surely a sin. We'd both eaten one, when she handed me the third. "Here, I brought you an extra."

"No, you have it."

"Kiah, I made two dozen. There are plenty left at home. I want you to have it."

Refusal to accept might seem ungrateful. I could've eaten the whole two dozen, but I couldn't get Mama off my mind. She'd enjoy a cupcake with icing. "Thank you, Zann. I think I'll save this one and take it home with me, if you don't mind."

She smiled as if she'd hoped I would.

I pulled out the math book and turned to chapter 13. I tried not to focus on the dab of white icing on the tip of her nose, but the more I tried to ignore it, the more prominent it became. "Uh . . . Zann, you have . . . you have icing on your—" I swallowed. What if she were to think I'd taken a cue from Arnold. "I'm telling the truth."

She giggled. "Well, don't just sit there. Get it off, silly." She handed me a napkin and closed her eyes.

I leaned in, and with the edge of the linen cloth, gently wiped the tip of her nose. The mouth-watering smell of chocolate mingled with the sweet, alluring fragrance of gardenias created an enticing aroma, which I imagined smelled similar to the forbidden fruit in the Garden of Eden.

I straightened and cleared my throat. "Did you work the fractions I gave you to practice on?"

She lowered her head and snickered. "I tried. Honest I did, Kiah. I feel so dumb."

"Don't say such, Zann. You're about the smartest girl I've ever met. Someone along the way failed to do their job in teaching you basic math skills. That's all. As smart as you are, it won't take long for you to grasp."

I gave her simple problems to boost her confidence and then proceeded to slide into more complex ones until I found her level. It seemed I could see the light in her head go off as she gained understanding. I enjoyed helping Zann, yet I'm not sure I would've enjoyed it nearly as much if she had a homely face and a squatty body.

In my eleven years of schooling, I'd never made anything below an A in math. Mr. Thatcher, my math teacher said I had a brilliant mind. Even if it was an exaggeration to encourage me, it worked. I entered the math competition at the beginning of the school year, competing against math students from all across the Tri-State area. Winning the trophy was exciting, but my greatest joy came from knowing I'd pleased Mr. Thatcher. Someone besides Mama was proud of me.

We had a pleasant fall. The weather turned cool, although the thermometer hadn't dipped lower than 55, even at night. It was my favorite time of year. The woods in the early October evenings took on a soft orange glow as the sun sank earlier with each passing day. Vibrant goldenrod, yellow daisies and bright purple wildflowers added a touch of warmth to the woods with its barren trees and brown, dry leaves blanketing the earth.

Zann and I met every chance we could, for the next two months. Her math grades improved dramatically.

School let out for the Christmas holidays. Mr. Thatcher handed out report cards at the end of the day and congratulated Zann for making an *A* in math. I should've been pleased. Instead, regret gnawed at my gut. She no longer needed me.

When the bell rang to go home, I grabbed my coat from the cloak room and trudged out the door with a lump in my throat the size of a wharf rat. I dared not look in her direction. I couldn't. If she said anything to me—anything at all, she'd see—and know. I'd never been good at hiding my feelings, and in spite of my staunch resolve not to fall in love, I'd failed.

I was half-way across the school yard when she yelled my name. "Wait, Kiah. Wait!" She ran toward me.

I upped the pace, pretending not to hear, though I heard every single sound she made. I heard the leaves beneath her feet as she drew closer to me. I kept walking. I heard every breath she took. I dared not turn around. If I walked any faster, I'd be sprinting. But she kept coming. I even heard her skirt rustling as she caught up with me and grabbed me by the arm. I heard the beating of her heart. Or was it mine?

I stopped and grimaced. "What do you want?"

Her brow furrowed. "Are you angry with me?"

"Angry? Why would I be angry?" I snarled.

"I don't know, but you didn't seem thrilled when Mr. Thatcher announced my grade." She placed her hand on my shoulder and shook me. "We did it, Kiah. We did it. Aren't you pleased? I could never have done it without you."

I couldn't look at her. I gazed out across a field of dried corn stalks. "I'm happy for you, Zann. I am." The last sentence wasn't meant to convince Zann as much as it was meant to convince myself. I wanted to be excited for her, and I tried. I did.

She said, "I'll meet you at the bridge in thirty minutes. I can't wait to show Mother my report card. This will prove to her and

Daddy that we've been studying."

I picked up a pine cone and tossed it as far as I could throw it. "I suspected as much," I scowled.

Zann lifted her shoulders. "What do you mean?"

I growled, "So your parents didn't believe we were studying. They don't trust me, do they?" I'll bet they wouldn't have worried if you'd been at the bridge with one of the choir boys from your daddy's church."

She reached up and laid her hand on my shoulder. "Oh, Kiah, I was only joking. Mother and Daddy never doubted for a minute we were studying." She brushed her hand over my lips. "Wipe the frown off your face, okay? Your dimples go into hiding when you frown."

I had plenty of reason to frown. With school out for Christmas, I wouldn't see her for two whole weeks and three days. By the time school reconvened, she'd realize she had no need for me.

She said, "Meet me at the bridge in thirty minutes."

I shook my head. "No, Zann. The math lessons are over. There's no reason for you to go there."

Her smile faded. "Okay, Kiah. If that's the way you want it."

"That's the way it's going to be, Zann." I turned and walked away. Had to. If I didn't leave immediately, I'd change my mind.

I wasn't ready to go home. I found an old tin can and kicked it all the way to the covered bridge. I climbed down the embankment and sprawled out on the cold ground underneath. This was our place. The place where I sensed her presence, even when she wasn't with me. Why did I tell her not to come? Didn't she know how I ached when she wasn't near me? How I longed to spend every moment in her presence?

Reality slapped me in the face and set my thinking straight. I told her not to come because it was the right thing to do. As much as it hurt, it was up to me to end things before the situation became more complicated. Our love could never be. Turtle doves and buzzards don't belong together.

I picked up a pine straw and stuck it in my mouth. As I lay on the ground, chewing on the straw, I closed my eyes. I listened to the sounds of water rippling over the rocks, a mockingbird, a train whistle in the distance, and the crackling leaves as birds scratched around in the underbrush, searching for earth worms.

The happiest hours of my life had been the ones I spent with Zann, under the bridge. I tried to picture her sitting beside me. Her hair slung over her left shoulder, her eyes twinkling like black onyx. I sucked in a breath and for a moment, I got a whiff of gardenias, her presence was so real.

"Kiah?"

I opened my eyes, "Zann? What are you doing here?"

She didn't answer. Her rosy lips curled upward.

I couldn't take my eyes off her.

She reached down and pulled the straw from my mouth. My

heart pounded against the walls of my chest when she leaned down and lightly brushed her lips across mine.

Startled, I sat upright and ran my fingers through my hair. I didn't know whether to pull her close or push her away. Then, I remembered Mama and jumped to my feet as quickly as if I had a fire lit under me. In a way, I did. Mama was beautiful and naïve once, just like Zann.

I hoped Zann wouldn't mention the kiss. I didn't want to talk about it. I wanted to pretend it never happened and I hoped she'd do the same.

Is it possible to forget something that occupies every hour, every minute and every second of one's waking moments?

Chapter 5

Idiotic desires whirled in my head like sand in a cyclone. I had to pull myself together. With feelings this strong at the beginning of the battle, I feared defeat was only an arm's length away.

She stood and brushed the back of her skirt. With a soft, pink glow painting her cheeks, she'd never looked more beautiful. "Kiah, I'm sorry if I—"

I placed my palm over her lips and shook my head. "Don't say it."

She nodded as if she understood. But did she? Did she feel what I was feeling? I wanted to say something profound, but there was only one thing on my mind, and I could think of nothing else.

She finally broke the silence. "You like pecans?"

I laughed. There was nothing funny about the question, but I laugh when I'm nervous.

She crooked her neck and looked at me befuzzled like. Her lips parted, then widened. A little chuckle slipped out. Then her eyes met mine and we burst into full blown, side-splitting laughter.

We couldn't stop, though I'm not sure either of us understood why.

I sucked in a deep breath. "I'm sorry, I wish I could quit laughing."

She caught her breath. "Did . . . did I say something funny?"

"I'm not sure . . . what did you say?" My response seemed to ignite the giggles all over again and we laughed until our eyes ran water.

She held her hand over her mouth. "I simply asked if you like pecans."

"Oh!" I took another deep breath, and the laughter died down. "Yeah, I reckon everybody likes pecans."

"What about pecan pie?"

I nodded. "Yep! I reckon it's about my favorite of all desserts. Mama makes a really good pecan pie."

"Well, there's a pecan orchard across the road from the parsonage and Daddy asked me to gather some nuts before supper. Mother always bakes pecan pies at Christmas. Why don't you come with me, and you can pick up a sack full to take home to your mama."

My head dropped. I needed time to think. Mama would be thrilled to get a bag of pecans, but suppose Zann's folks walked over to check me out. What if her daddy took one look and said, "Isn't this the boy the parishioners say lives with his unwed mama in Rooster Run?" Would Zann be shocked? Or did she know already? She wasn't one to pry. At first I'd been glad she hadn't asked many questions about my home life. Now, I worried. I figured the only reason she wouldn't be curious would be because she had all the answers. I couldn't decide which of the two scenarios could be worse.

Zann pulled me by the hand. "Come on, let's go get those pecans."

I had no desire to get close to the preacher's house. The idea of a showdown with her father made me shudder, and if the scenario went as I pictured in my head, it wouldn't be pretty. Yet, I let her lead me down the road. When she smiled, my insides waffled. It would've been easier for me to stack greasy chinaberries than to say 'no' to Zann Pruitt.

Though it was 55 degrees, I broke a sweat, as I considered what I might be letting myself in for. I figured her parents would have plenty of questions for me, and I was confident they wouldn't like my answers.

I offered to wait in the pecan orchard while Zann ran across the road to the parsonage to get a couple of sacks for the nuts.

I leaned against a tree, hoping to fade into the background whenever I heard a jalopy chugging down the dirt road. Apparently, I wasn't as well hid as I'd hoped, for the car stopped, and a man yelled, "Hello, there."

When he stepped out of the car and headed toward me, I didn't have to be told who he was. Pastor Pruitt. He was a big man, at least six feet three and I guessed his weight to be in the 200-225 pound range. His black hair had grayed around the temples, giving him a most distinguished look. Dressed in a black suit, starched white shirt and black string tie, he carried himself with an air of reserve, much like I imagined an Army General, although I'd never personally met a real live General. But I'd seen pictures and read books on the Civil War. If the parson grew a beard, in a few years with a little more gray, he could pass for General Robert E. Lee.

He thrust his hand toward me. "Hezekiah Grave?"

I swallowed hard, hearing him call my name. He had a gentle voice, yet I had the distinct impression, if given cause, the same voice could raise the rafters off a barn. I shook in my brogans and nodded. "Yessir, I'm Hezekiah Grave." Heat rose from my stomach to my face whenever I took his hand. With a firm grip, he squeezed my sweaty palm, gave a hard pump and let go.

A frightful curiosity churned in my belly as he gazed at me and stroked his chin. I assumed he was sizing me up. If his opinion wasn't favorable, at least he was too courteous to let it show.

He grinned. "So you're the young man my daughter appears to be so fond of."

My face burned. Panic engulfed me. How was I supposed to respond to such a statement?

I breathed easier, when it appeared he wasn't expecting a reply.

He glanced around. "Where's my beautiful daughter?"

Like a dimwit, I stammered, "She's gone to get a couple of knacks for the suts." I slapped myself on the side of the head. "What I meant to say sir, is that Zann went to get sacks for the nuts." I grimaced, expecting him to laugh in my face. But he didn't. He didn't flinch.

"Fine, fine. That's just fine," he said. "Supper should be ready soon. Would you care to stay and eat with us? Dora—my wife— she always fixes enough to feed the countryside. We'd be most pleased to have you join us."

I wiped beads of sweat from my upper lip. "Thank you sir. That's mighty kind of you, but I reckon I need to be getting home as soon as I can pick up enough pecans for a pie."

"Take more than enough for a pie. Christmas is just around the corner and if you don't have pecan trees on your place, I'm sure your mother will be mighty proud to have you bring home a good ten pounds or more. Women folks can think of a hundred different ways to use pecans during the holidays."

I nodded. He was right. Mama would be right proud if I stuck around long enough to load up a sack.

Parson Pruitt said, "They're Stewarts, you know. My Dora is partial to Stewarts."

At first, I assumed the Stewarts were friends of the Pruitts, until I realized he was referring to the type of pecans. I suppose the following silence was no longer than a couple of seconds, though it seemed much longer. What could be taking Zann so long? I shuffled my feet and tried to think of something insightful to say, but my brain had taken leave of absence.

The parson spoke first. "You have a fine name, Hezekiah. I suppose you were named after the King of Judah?"

He waited for my response.

My mind raced. History wasn't my favorite subject, yet I'd always made good marks. But in all my years of schooling, I couldn't recall studying about the King of Judah.

His brow raised. "Are you familiar with the story of Hezekiah in the Bible?"

I sheepishly shook my head and figured I was losing points with Zann's father, by admitting I didn't have a clue.

He stroked his chin. "Well, there's a very interesting story in the Good Book about a time when King Hezekiah was dying and he prayed and asked God to lengthen his days."

I waited, but he out-waited me. I finally mumbled, "So what happened?"

His smile was warm. Not accusing, as I'd imagined. "God answered."

I couldn't believe I stood here carrying on a Biblical conversation with a parson. Why didn't Zann come on? Was she watching out the window and laughing?

An uncomfortable silence followed. At least uncomfortable on my end.

Then, he said, "God heard Hezekiah's prayer and saw his tears, and God allowed him to live fifteen more years." The Parson's eyes lit up. "Isn't it rich to know that we have a God who hears our prayers and answers our tears?"

Now, he had my attention. Questions, which I'd never considered before, popped in my head, but I would've cut off my tongue before allowing myself to be suckered in by a preacher. Even so, I did want to know what he meant by 'God answers our tears.' Was he serious? How many tears would I have to shed before God would answer mine? I looked across the road and breathed a sigh when I saw Zann approaching.

"Here comes my daughter now. I'd stay and help you two, but I need to gather a little wood before supper." He turned to walk away. When he reached the road, he looked over his shoulder and yelled, "The invitation for supper still stands. If not tonight, maybe one night soon. It was a pleasure meeting you, Hezekiah."

I threw up my hand and uttered a weak thank-you. Conflicting thoughts fought for space in my head. The conversation proved one thing. He didn't know about my situation. If he had, he wouldn't have referred to pecan trees being on "my place," as if Mama and I might own a plot of ground and live like normal, decent people. I didn't need a college education to look around at the residents of Rooster Run and know there was nothing normal about those of us who lived there. The frightening idea occurred to me that no one in the camp would consider themselves to be abnormal, even though I was quite sure they all were. I felt normal, but maybe I wasn't, and like the others, just didn't know better.

Zann stopped long enough to peck her father on the cheek, and then she ran over and handed me a croaker sack. "I'll bet I can beat you filling up a sack," she giggled.

The sound of her voice caused the tension to leave my body. "No fair. My sack is larger."

After we both had picked a good ten pounds or more, Zann said, "Kiah, I have a favor to ask."

I slung the sack over my shoulder. "Your wish is my command, m'lady."

"Great. I'd like for you to escort me to the church Christmas party on the 20th."

She hardly got the words out of her mouth before I shook my head. "Sorry. I can't go."

Zann had the unique ability to smile and manage to look sad at the same time. I think it was those big brown eyes. They twinkled when she was happy, and looked sort of pitiful like a basset hound's whenever she wasn't pleased. But her lips always curled up at the edges—sometimes slightly, sometimes stretching from one ear lobe to the other.

"But Kiah, you have to go. Mama's made me a gorgeous white gown from a Vogue pattern, and I'll have no other occasion to wear it. It's simply divine and I want you to see me in it. You will go, won't you?"

I shook my head. "I can't go, Zann."

"What do you mean, you can't? Do you have a good reason?"

"Sure, there's a good reason."

She waited. I could tell she expected me to explain. I sighed. This moment was bound to come.

"Zann, you might want to sit down on the grass. We need to talk."

Her brow furrowed. "You're scaring me, Kiah. What's wrong?"

"It's a long story." The moment I said the words, I sensed a panic surge. What was I thinking? How could I explain why I didn't go to church? Why I'd never go? My initial intention was to enlighten her about spiteful hypocrites who crushed a little boy's spirit, years ago. Yet, there was much more to my story than I was at liberty to tell. How could I make her understand my point of view, without explaining what the pious church folks held against us—the humiliating part I hoped we'd never have to discuss.

She laid her bag down, sat on the ground and leaned back on a tree. "I'm listening."

I might as well get it out in the open. I couldn't hide the truth forever. I leaned against a tree and blurted out the words. "Zann, I live with Mama in Rooster Run." I watched for a look of astonishment but her expression didn't change. I waited.

She looked neither impressed nor shocked. Not even a slight gasp.

Bumfuzzled, I asked, "Did you know already?"

She shook her head. "I didn't know where you lived, but I know where Rooster Run is. But what does it have to do with the Christmas party, Kiah? I don't understand. Why won't you go with me?"

Didn't she get it? Go with *her*? "Zann, have you ever been beyond the gate at Rooster Run?" I expected her to say no. Her answer stunned me.

"Sure. Many times. Our maid lives there in #3. You may know her. Dabney Foxworthy. Not only is she our maid, she's also my best friend." She paused. "Do you know Dabney? She's a couple of years older than us."

My pulse raced. "Yes. I know Dabney." I snapped, "I'm quite sure I know more about her than you do." I picked up a pecan and slung it as far as I could throw it.

Zann frowned. "You act as if there's something wrong with her. There's nothing shameful about being a maid."

I smirked. "Yeah? Maybe not, but everyone knows cleaning houses is not the only way she makes a dollar. I imagine Dabney Foxworthy makes more in one hour at night than she makes in a whole week working as a maid."

I expected Zann to at least raise an eyebrow. Instead, she rolled her eyes in disgust. "Kiah, who are we to judge?"

Her remark caught me by surprise. Maybe I had no right to judge, but didn't she realize *her* position? Didn't she understand her elite Christian heritage qualified her to be both judge and jury of the lower class? Surely, such a distinguished pedigree provided her with a non-expiring Fellow Ship boarding pass.

Instead of admiring her for not being critical, annoyance gnawed at me. Maybe because she shot down my notion that all Christians were a bunch of pompous bigots.

"Kiah, when you get to know her as I do, you'll discover Dabney is a really sweet girl. I think she's pretty, don't you?"

What kind of question was that? Besides, I knew more about Dabney Foxworthy than I cared to know. What made Zann think I'd want to get to know her better?

"Well?" Her shoulders lifted. "I asked you a question. Don't you think she's pretty?" She grinned as she waited for my answer.

Heat rose from under my collar. "I reckon," I mumbled. She was right. Dabney *was* pretty, but until now I'd never stopped to think about it. Her golden hair was a mass of long curls, which she sometimes secured with a barrette on top of her head, with a few loose tendrils framing her sun-kissed face. Her eyes were the color of the ocean—sometimes more green than blue—and at other times more blue than green. Perhaps I'd paid more attention to Dabney Foxworthy than I wanted to admit to myself. I scratched my head, as I captured her image. The girl was stacked like a brick outhouse. I glanced at Zann and hoped she couldn't read my thoughts. Then, I shrugged and said, "Aww, I reckon she's pretty. Or at least she could be, if she'd take a rag and wipe off the war paint."

Zann smiled. "What do you mean, you reckon she's pretty? You know she is."

I went from being slightly annoyed to being riled. It wasn't fair to be grilled about some painted hussy who prissed around like her hip was out of joint. Aware of Dabney Foxworthy's reputation with the boys, I resented Zann trying to get me to see her in a false light. "She wears too much make-up," I snipped.

Zann nodded.

I let out a breath, glad she saw fit not to argue.

"I agree, Kiah. I've told her she's beautiful without all the paint, but Dabney has a low self-image. It's hard for her to believe she's pretty."

Zann's eyes widened as her brow shot up. "Kiah, I've just had an excellent idea. If you were to talk to her and convince her she's a natural beauty and doesn't need all the make-up, I'm sure she'd listen. She needs to hear it from a fellow. I think it might be the esteem booster she needs."

I stiffened. "Oh, no, not me. If having a man tell her she's beautiful will boost her confidence, then I can assure you Dabney Foxworthy has more confidence than the law allows. I'm sure she hears it over and over every Saturday night." I smirked. "It's a known fact, the line forms in front of her door on the week-ends." I grimaced, ashamed, as the raw words spewed from my lips. It was crude and uncalled for.

"Kiah Grave, what's your problem?"

I winced. Maybe I'd been too hard on myself. Apparently, I hadn't been as explicit as I supposed. "If you don't get it, I don't know if I can explain it to you, but I'll try. Zann, if flattering words could change Dabney, she'd be changed already. She's heard the words. Many times. But she's what she is, and neither you nor I nor anyone knocking on her door at midnight can say anything that will turn her into an untarnished angel."

Zann's eyes squinted.

I scratched my head. "I'll try to make this as simple as I can. Zann, you can't turn a mule into a race horse, simply by entering it into the Kentucky Derby."

I saw nothing humorous in my illustration, so when Zann chuckled, I was irritated. The visual was clear-cut and to the point.

"What are you saying, Kiah?"

"I'm saying fine race horses are bred. Take you, for instance. You're a race horse. You're greatly respected for your style. You live in a fine stable, and have plenty of fresh grass to graze on. All you have to do is bow your head and partake of the bounty before you. On the other hand, Dabney and I are mules. We're burden-bearers. We know how to carry our load, because we've had plenty of practice. We find shelter anywhere we can, and we expect no one to lead us into the green pastures."

Her jaw dropped.

When I blinked, I envisioned a big question mark tattooed on her forehead. I blurted, "Zann, what I'm trying to say is you'll never be able to turn Dabney into a girl like you, because she was born on the wrong side of the tracks." I dropped my head. "And so was I."

"So what?"

I grimaced. Now she was getting on my nerves. "You want to know 'so what?' I'll tell you 'so what.' Your daddy's a preacher." I'd gone too far to stop, though I didn't like the hole I'd dug for myself. I blurted, "I don't have a daddy. There! Have I answered your question?" I gently massaged my chin. Grinding my teeth together always made my jaw ache.

Her expression softened. "So your mama's a widow?"

"I wish." I jumped up and turned my back to her to keep her from seeing tears welling in my eyes.

She stood, reached up and placed her hand on my shoulder. "I don't understand."

I jerked around and faced her. "I'm saying I wish the man *was* dead."

Her eyes widened. "Kiah, you don't mean it."

I lashed out. "Oh, yes I do. I've never meant anything more in my life."

When Mrs. Pruitt yelled for Zann to go eat supper, I was relieved.

She reached for my hand and squeezed it. "We'll talk later. I'll be at the bridge tomorrow at four o'clock, if you happen to show up," she smiled.

Disgusted with myself for being vulnerable, I tapped my fist against my lips. What had happened to loose my tongue and cause me to bare my disgrace with the one person with whom I wanted to shield the truth?

Maybe I'd show up tomorrow. Maybe I wouldn't. I didn't answer.

She turned and waved at me when she reached the road.

I waved back. I wanted to muster a smile, but my face refused to cooperate. I felt naked.

Chapter 6

Since the first of October, I'd been working at the stockyards every Friday afternoon and all day on Saturdays. Mr. Farris said he might use me during Christmas break, and I tried to prove I could work as hard as any man he'd ever hired.

I did odd jobs, such as clean the stalls, and help load livestock for the auctions. I didn't make a lot of money, but every penny I earned was one more than we would've had. Sometimes the farmers would slip me a few coins for helping them load or unload their stock. I had my eye on a blue plaid shirt in the window of Watson's Dry Goods Store.

Tuesday morning I awoke to the sizzling sound of bacon frying. I savored the smoky aroma as it permeated the tiny cabin. With the money I made at the stockyards, I bought eggs, bacon, a round of bologna, and some hoop cheese. Mama needed protein worse than I needed a shirt.

During the winter months, her diet consisted mainly of starchy foods: biscuits, corn bread fried in hog lard, corn meal mush, grits and hominy. When we had a little extra money, she'd buy a pound of fatback, Vienna sausages or a can of tripe, but she wouldn't eat any of it. She gave it to me, insisting she didn't have a taste for it. I could've eaten the feathers off a duck and I was sure she could've, too—but only if she was convinced there were enough feathers for two.

I figured her health would improve if she had protein, and lately I'd insisted upon it. But to my sorrow, I saw no improvement. She continued to dwindle away. If she persisted in losing weight, I was afraid I'd be able to reach around her waist with one hand.

I crawled out of bed, dressed and walked over to the stove. "Smells good, Mama." One look at her drawn face told me nothing smelled good to her. She looked green. I made a pot of coffee and poured us both a cup. I pulled her chair out from the table. "Sit down, Mama."

"In a minute, sugar. I've got grits boiling on the stove."

I reached for the spoon to stir the pot. "I'll watch the grits. You sit down and drink your coffee."

The fact it didn't take much prodding signaled she was sicker than she wanted me to know. I turned in time to see her shuffling across the linoleum floor, her hand over her mouth. Then, the screen door slammed and I could hear her throwing up outside the back door. I ran out and pleaded with her to let me go for the doctor, but she was adamant. The harder I tried to convince her she needed medical help, the more stubborn she became.

I managed to get her to lie down, while I washed the few dishes. At lunch I made some corn meal gravy and fried up a slice of bologna. I coaxed her to eat, but she insisted she couldn't hold it down. Said she wanted to sleep, and I figured she needed the rest as much as she needed the meat and gravy.

I walked over to Goodson's Grocery and bought a bottle of Warburg's Tincture, which Mr. Gus guaranteed would cure anything that ailed her. The information on the back of the medicine bottle claimed the tonic was not only a sure-fire remedy for all types of fevers, including malaria and typhus, but it was also a 'treatment for incipient consumption, chronic bronchitis cough, want of appetite, delirium tremens, morbid digestion, scurvy and every disease of a scorbutic character.' Two bits seemed a small price to pay for such a powerful drug.

I arrived back home and Mama took one look at the medicine bottle and shook her head. "You can pour that down the toilet, shug. What I need is a good hot cup of sassafras tea. I reckon you wouldn't mind seeing if you could fetch me a good root, would you, Kiah?"

"Mama, there's no sassafras anywhere near here."

"Shucks, I reckon you're right, son. Law, I sure do wish I could get hold of a good root to boil. Sassafras tea cures near 'bout any ailment you can name."

I poured the Warburg's Tincture in a small cup. "Well, Mama Mr. Goodson says Mr. Abner was on his deathbed, when he took a few swallows of this, and the next morning he was up plowing his field. Mr. Goodson swears by this stuff."

She crossed her arms over her chest and scowled. "He has no call."

She wasn't making sense. Maybe it was the fever. "What do you mean, Mama? No call to do what?"

"Gus Goodson ain't got no call to swear. Bible warns against swearing. You don't swear, do you, son?"

I rolled my eyes. "No, Mama. I don't swear, but I might start if you don't take the medicine. I went to a lot of trouble to get it for you and it wasn't cheap, so all I'm asking is for you to swallow it."

"I know you mean well, shug, but ain't no tellin' what's in that bottle. It ain't natural, and I don't aim to take it."

I looked at the clock. Three-twenty. In forty minutes, Zann would be waiting at the creek. Nausea welled inside me. Maybe I needed a dose of Mama's medicine. But it'd take more than a swig of Warburg's Tincture to cure my ailment. As much as I wanted to see her, I couldn't go face her. Not now. I'd known all along she was too good for me. Now that I'd spilled my guts, she knew it, too.

After cajoling Mama into taking the horrid smelling brown liquid, she closed her eyes and went sound asleep in less than five minutes.

I trudged outside and sat under a mimosa tree. Nineteen-year-old Dabney Foxworthy opened her back door and sloshed a pan of soapy dishwater on the ground. As soon as she saw me, she walked over.

She smiled and said, "It sure don't seem like Christmas is only a few days away. Too hot. I lived in Detroit one winter, and I'll never forget how pretty everything looked, all covered in a blanket of snow. It must be near 'bout 75 degrees out here. It don't seem right, does it?"

I didn't say anything, but if I had, I would've remarked the reason it didn't seem right was because it wasn't right. A thermometer nailed to the side of the shack clearly showed 68 degrees. However, I was in no mood to participate in a conversation with someone of her reputation about anything, including idle chatter about the weather.

Pretending to be hot, she yanked up the tail of her dress and fanned her legs. She didn't fool me. Not for a second. I saw what she was up to, but I wasn't in the market for what she had to offer.

I stood and walked toward the road. She cupped her hands over her mouth and yelled, "You don't have to be such a snob. I was just trying to be neighborly. Besides, you might want to come back, Kiah Grave, 'cause I've got something to give you that you're gonna want."

I bristled. "Yeah, well give it to some other fellow. I don't want anything you've got to offer." How could she be so brazen?

As I trudged through the woods, I felt my heart would burst. I couldn't separate the feelings stirring within me. Maybe I was bitter...or disappointed...or sad...or lonely...or maybe I was filled to the gills with the anger bubbling inside me. That was it. I was angry. But angry at whom? Zann? Mama? Dabney?

I cringed at the answer. I was angry at myself for the rude way I talked to Dabney. She called me a snob, and for good reason. It's the same word I used to describe folks who looked down their noses at me and Mama. Who was I to judge Dabney? I regretted my nasty words, but if I went back and apologized, she might get the wrong impression. I'd think of a way to make it up to her, but not now. I wanted to see Zann, but pride stood in my way.

As I walked along, I kicked at the black walnuts, which lay scattered along the edge of the road. My mouth watered, remembering the delicious black walnut cake Mama made last Christmas, but I hadn't forgotten how hard it was to hull out those cantankerous nuts. I was thankful for the pecans, which would be much easier to crack.

I rounded the bend in the road near the bridge and stopped. Conflicting feelings stirred within me. I wanted to see her, but what was the point? She no longer needed a tutor. She'd been a good student. My job was done. We had no business meeting at the bridge over the holidays. To do so would only invite trouble. Trouble, which neither of us needed. I couldn't get the kiss out of my mind. I couldn't allow it to happen again. I stopped and leaned against a hickory nut tree. I needed time to think. Zann Pruitt would never marry someone like me. Would I want to spend the remainder of my life like Mama, moaning over what might have been? No siree. Not me. I slowly slid down to the ground and buried my face in my hands. I was afraid. Afraid if I went to the bridge, love would eat away at me like a cancerous tumor, robbing me of a decent life, the way unrequited love robbed Mama. I rose to my feet, turned around and made my way back to Rooster Run.

I walked through the gate and groaned at the sight of Dabney hanging clothes on a line. I didn't want to face her after the vulgar way I spoke to her, but I'd prove I was no snob. I wasn't sure whether I needed to prove it to Dabney, or to myself.

Though she saw me coming, she pretended not to notice. I walked up beside her. She didn't so much as cut her eyes my way. She reached in a small canvas bag hanging on the clothes line, lifted out two clothes pins and stuck them between her teeth. I watched as she reached into a hamper and pulled out a white bed sheet.

"Here, let me help." I volunteered, thinking it a perfect way to prove I was no snob.

"No thanks," she mumbled. It wasn't difficult to see she hadn't changed her mind about me. She had every right to be sore. My bad-mannered behavior called for an apology. I watched in silence as she folded the sheet, gave it a few pops and hung it on the line. Her long, slender fingers smoothed out the wrinkles, before she pulled the pins from her mouth and secured the edges of the sheet to the clothesline.

I sucked in a breath of air and mimicked the words I'd heard Mama say, when she hung out clothes. "I don't reckon anything smells better than fresh washed garments hanging on a line." I'd hoped for a response.

With no comment, Dabney reached in the hamper and pulled out a towel. Now, she was getting on my nerves. Who was being a snob? She could at least acknowledge my statement with a nod. I decided to take one more shot, and if she didn't answer me this time, I'd leave her be.

I tried to muster a smile through clinched teeth. "Dabney, you like pecans?"

She shot me a quick glance. "I reckon."

I sensed victory. I'd broken through her cold, dark shell. "Well, I picked up more than we'll need. I'll go to the house and get you some."

She lifted her shoulders in a shrug. I took it to mean, "Don't care if you do, don't care if you don't."

I felt like getting a whole sack full of nuts and throwing them one by one in her face. Couldn't she see I was trying to make up for my behavior? "I'll be right back," I said.

Mama was still asleep. I tiptoed over to the cupboard and filled my pants pockets with pecans.

I hurried back outside. Dabney looked up, and for a moment, I saw a fleeting smile. "Got something to put them in?" I asked.

She held up the canvas clothespin bag. "Drop 'em in here," she said.

I ran my fingers through my hair, trying to decide how to word an apology. My mind went blank. "Dabney, I want to say—well, what I mean is, I wish—"

She interrupted. "Kiah, I don't blame you for thinking what you did. I know what folks say about me. Some of it's true. But Zann gave me a note last evening and asked me to give it to you. That's what I was referring to when I told you I had something I thought you'd want." She reached in her apron pocket and pulled out a folded piece of paper.

What a louse I'd been. I closed my eyes and slung my head back. "Dabney . . . what can I say? I'm so sorry. I had no right."

She shrugged and handed me the letter. "I'm used to it."

The hurt in her eyes made me feel smaller than a chigger. "I suppose it's too much to ask you to forgive me."

"Shucks, ain't your fault that folks say I'm white trash. Maybe I am." She whirled around, but not before I caught her lifting her apron to brush away the tears.

While I clamored for a suitable response, I heard her door slam. I looked up and she was gone. But her sad words continued to clang in my ear like an out-of-tune piano.

I walked next door, sat down on the stoop in front of our shack and pulled out the letter. I could smell Gardenia Perfume.

Monday

Dear Kiah,

I didn't want to leave you tonight, when Mother called me to supper. I could tell you were hurting.

Kiah, I'm sorry you've missed out on the blessings of having a father in your home, but he's the one who's missed out. You are such a warm, caring person. Why did you think it would make a difference if I knew your situation? Can't you understand that I don't care where you live or who brought you into this world? All I know is that I love you very much. I can't wait to see you at the bridge tomorrow.

Love,

Zann

I read the lines again and again. My heart turned cartwheels. I let out a loud yee-haw, prompting Granny Griffin from across the road in #5 to stick her head out the door to see what the commotion was all about.

She hollered, "What's going on out yonder?"

I laughed. "Zann Pruitt loves me, Granny, She loves me very much."

She cupped her hand over her ear. "What's that?"

I chuckled. "I said Zann Pruitt loves me."

She grumbled. "Zat all?" She slammed the screen door without waiting for a response, although I shouted it out, anyway.

"No, Granny. That ain't all. I love her, too. Yes'm, I sure love that girl." A sense of freedom overpowered me as the words from my mouth hit my ears.

According to an old Arabian proverb, there are three things, which one can't hide: smoke, a man riding a camel, and love. I don't know about the smoke or the man on the camel, but there was no way I could hide my feelings for Zann.

Call me naive, but love had sneaked up on me. I find it hard to understand how someone so dead set against becoming romantically involved could've fallen so hard, so deeply, so totally and irreversibly in love.

There was no turning back. Love crashed into my heart like a cyclone. Hurling, swirling, and flinging all my good attentions to who knows where. I don't know the minute, the hour or even the day it happened. I was swept up, sucked out and carried away. And from that moment, I understood my life would never be the same.

Zann and I had never spoken the word 'love' before. Not even when she kissed me. If a brush of the lips could have such an effect, I couldn't imagine what it'd be like to hold her in my arms and plant a doozie on her. Of course, I wouldn't. She was the preacher's daughter. But one day . . . one day after I received the college scholarship and landed myself a high-paying job, I'd marry Zann Pruitt and fill my days loving up on her. How quickly I'd changed. Love no longer sounded like a dirty word. I was in love, and I didn't care who knew it.

I crammed the note in my pocket and stuck my head in the door. Mama was sitting in her rocker with her Bible.

"Mama, how you feeling?"

"Much better, son."

"You're looking better. Mind if I run down the road for a spell? I'll be back in a jiff."

"Go right ahead. I'll be fine."

I sprinted across the field and through the woods as fast as I could go. I hoped she'd still be waiting, but it was after five o'clock. What was the chance she'd be there? If only I'd read the note sooner.

Fallen leaves crunched beneath my feet as I ran. The cold air made my nose water. I crammed my hand in my back pocket. No handkerchief. I never left the house without my pocket knife and a handkerchief. Now, today of all days, why did I have to leave it behind? I cringed, imagining myself sniffling, as Zann and I shared our true feelings. I pulled the tail of my flannel shirt to my nose, and hoped the warmth would stop the constant drip.

My heart sank when I reached the bridge and she was not in sight. I scrambled down the embankment and caught sight of a small scrap of cloth. Blue gingham. I smiled. She'd been there. Of all her dresses, and she had several, the blue gingham was my favorite. I supposed she tore off a piece of the hem and left it for me to find, to prove she'd been there. I instinctively held the material to my nose, as if I'd be able to smell her sweet scent lingering. There was no hint of the smell of gardenias but my vivid imagination could almost conjure up the familiar fragrance.

I wanted to see her. I wanted to see her bad. I didn't think I could stand waiting another day. I remembered the words in the letter. She loved me. At the moment, nothing else mattered. Not even the fear of going to the parson's house. I wanted to tell her I'd be tickled to take her to the church Christmas party. The bitterness I harbored toward church folks had vanished. Mama was right. They weren't all like the folks from Piney Woods.

I jogged all the way to the parsonage, sprinted up the steps and knocked on the door. Parson Pruitt cracked it open and peeked his head out. I waited for him to invite me in, but the creases on his forehead told me an invitation wasn't forthcoming. His voice was stern. Not light-hearted and friendly, the way he sounded in the pecan orchard.

"Zann can't come out."

So, he was having a bad day. We all have them. I said, "I understand. I'll wait on the porch, sir," thinking perhaps Zann was eating supper.

He glared at me and bellowed, "Stay away from my daughter." His face reminded me of a chameleon's throat the way it changed from a rugged tan to pomegranate red.

He thrust a clinched hand in the air. "Young man, you'd better be making fast tracks before the devil wins this war I'm fighting. Now, get off my porch." The door slammed.

His fist in my face couldn't have stunned me more. I turned and ran. I was angry for being so stupid. I should've known better than to think the good Parson would allow me to see his daughter after he found out the truth about me. I'd shed more than a few tears in my lifetime, but I'd never sobbed the way I wept on the way home. I stopped in front of the iron gate at Rooster Run and waited until there were no tears left. I couldn't let Mama see me in such a fix.

I walked in the house, and found Mama asleep. I was glad. I didn't feel like being questioned. Though I hadn't eaten, I wasn't hungry. I wanted to crawl in bed, pull the covers over my head, sleep and never wake up. Why did I have to tell Zann my life history? Maybe her father could've forgiven me for living in Rooster Run, but as a Reverend, it'd be impossible for him to look upon the shameful result of Mama's sin. Meaning me, of course. The disappointment was almost too much to bear. I wouldn't be escorting her to the Christmas party or anywhere else.

I tossed all night, angry at myself for breaking both vows. I did the unthinkable. I fell in love, and then I made things worse when I brazenly tromped up the steps to the parsonage and spoke to the parson. I buried my face in my hands and groaned. I'd let down my guard. Why was I surprised at how things turned out? All I wanted to do now was to forget her. That'd be easier said than done. How can you forget someone who has the ability to make your heart beat by the touch of her hand and with a sweep of her lips cause it to stop?

Chapter 7

I came home from working at the yard, dog-tired. I looked at the calendar above my bed. Saturday, December 20th, the night of the church Christmas party. My stomach wrenched.

Too exhausted to eat, I walked over and fell across my bed. I looked in the corner of the room and groaned. "What's that supposed to be?" A scraggly pine limb was stuck in a foot tub.

Mama's head dropped. "I wanted a Christmas tree, so I broke a switch from off a tree in the woods. It didn't turn out to look the way I'd hoped. I'll throw it out tomorrow." I saw her lips tremble and her eyes fill with tears.

What was wrong with me? Why did I choose to hurt the one person who loved me more than life itself? How could I be so cruel?

Ashamed, I stood and wrapped my arms around her. "You want a tree? Don't you fret. We'll have a tree. We'll have the best Christmas you've ever had in your life." I meant every word of it.

I grabbed my jacket from off the nail.

Mama's eyes grew wide. "You going somewhere?"

"Well, I can't cut down a Christmas tree if I stay in the house, now can I?"

Her face lit up. "I reckon not."

Christmas was her favorite time of the year, though I hadn't always shared her enthusiasm. Especially when I was in grammar school and the teacher would go down the row, asking all the kids to tell what Santa Claus brought. I hated having to make up the lies.

I could usually count on getting a piece of fruit, but it was never from the jolly old man or his elves. As a child, I decided the reason Santa Claus never stopped at my house was because Mrs. Ola Mae ratted.

I went to #8 and asked Mr. Newsome if I could borrow his ax. He was the only one in the camp with tools. He was particular about lending them out, but he took a liking to me when we moved in, and said I could borrow anything he had.

I walked out to the edge of the woods and spotted a short-leaf pine with full branches. The kind Mama liked. After cutting it down, I made a stand and drug it home. The look of awe on Mama's face when she saw the tree was worth more to me than a bag of money. I threw the pine limb out the back door.

"Kiah, you think we might buy some popcorn to string on it?"

"Well, it wouldn't be a Christmas tree without decorations, now would it, Mama? If you want popcorn, it'll have popcorn. We'll decorate it Monday night when I come home from work, and it'll be the prettiest tree in all the county."

The fresh scent of evergreen filled the room. Mama thanked me more times than necessary, before crawling in bed.

It was only eight o'clock and I couldn't sleep. I had to get out of the house. I didn't start out knowing where I was going, but somewhere between Rooster Run and the church, I figured out my destination. I'd stay out of sight in the pecan orchard and wait. If I was lucky, I'd get a glimpse of her walking home from the party. I tried to envision her in the white sleeveless gown she'd described so enthusiastically, yet I knew my imagination could never equate such beauty.

I stepped up my gait when I came to the edge of the road leading to the church. My heart beat faster as I sprinted down the lane. Hiding in the orchard, I waited for the party to end, and when it did, I scrutinized every person leaving the building. Zann wasn't among them. Her father, the last to leave, locked the building. But where was Zann? She'd looked forward to the Christmas Party for weeks. I wanted to run ask Parson Pruitt if she was ill, but I couldn't. He hated me.

Would I ever be able to get her out of my mind?

Sunday morning I woke to the sound of Mama's off-key

humming. "You sound chipper, Mama. Feeling better?"

"I do, Kiah. I reckon it must be the Warburg's Tincture."

I sat down at the table and smiled. She could credit the tonic, but I knew better. The Christmas tree standing tall in the corner was the medicine that did the trick. She sat down and sipped on a cup of coffee. There was something different about her. Something besides the smile on her face. "Your hair . . . you've done something different . . . and you're wearing lip rouge."

She lowered her head and blushed. "I didn't think you'd notice. You like it?"

"I do. You look . . . well, you look real nice, Mama. Real nice." I could tell she was pleased.

She reached up and patted her hair. "I haven't worn it up in a long time. I wasn't sure I could find my combs, but they were tucked away in my carpet bag."

"Did you get all spruced up for a special occasion?" The question was asked in jest, but her answer stunned me.

"As a matter of fact, I did." I watched her suck in a deep breath and slowly let it back out. She had a peculiar look on her face. She sat a bowl of oatmeal in front of me. Without so much as drawing a breath in between her sentences, she quipped, "I wish we had some raisins. My mama liked to put raisins in her oatmeal. You like raisins, honey?"

I had a sudden rush of adrenalin. I remembered the day Zann asked me the same question. Though I hadn't wanted to admit it at the time, but that was the day I fell in love.

"Do you, Kiah?" Mama asked.

I laughed. "Yes, Mama, I love raisins, but the oatmeal is good without them." What had brought about the sudden change in Mama? She looked alive for the first time in months. Where was *her* rush coming from?

Maybe the Christmas spirit was responsible for her gaiety. Had she got all gussied up, hoping I'd take her to Goodson's to buy popcorn for the tree? Of course. That was it. Had to be. I dreaded giving her the news, but nothing would be gained by putting it off. "Mama, if you were hoping we'd go to Goodson's this morning to buy the popcorn, he won't be open today. It's Sunday."

She nodded. "I know what day it is, Kiah. The popcorn can wait."

I scratched my head. "But . . . but you look—"

She laughed. Not a little snicker, but a side-splitting hee-haw. "I declare, Kiah, you must've thought I was sweet on ol' man Goodson, if you believed I went to the trouble of getting all gussied up, just to go to the grocery store."

I wanted to deny it, though the notion had crossed my mind. "Then what's the occasion, Mama? You aren't wearing lip rouge for me and I know it. What are you up to?"

"Not up to nothing, son. I'm going to church and I want you to go with me."

The breath left me as if someone had socked me in the stomach. Of all the things she could've asked, that was the one thing I couldn't do.

I sat stirring my bowl of oatmeal, and the longer I sat, the madder I got. Why would she do this? What was the point? For the first time in months, she was feeling like a human being again, and now she wanted to spoil it by setting herself up for ridicule by a bunch of pious do-gooders. It didn't make sense and I was quick to let her know how insane I considered the idea to be.

For years, I'd ached, seeing the hurt in her eyes when women shunned her and crossed over to the other side of the street, just because she bore a child out of wedlock.

Out of wedlock. That was the decent way of putting it. The more offensive way was to call me a nasty name and act as if Mama and I deserved punishment for breathing their air.

Her shoulders drooped when I refused to go with her. Apparently, all my rantings and ravings didn't discourage her ridiculous notion to go, because she picked up her purse and said, "Well, if you won't go with me, you can at least hitch up the mule and take me."

I ran my fingers through my hair and grimaced. "Mama, I don't think you should."

"Kiah Grave, since when do you get off telling your mother what she should or should not do. I'm going to church even if I have to walk every step of the way. Dabney said the little young'uns are having a Christmas Pageant this morning and I want to see it."

My jaw dropped. "Dabney? Dabney goes to church?"

"I didn't know you knew Dabney that well."

I smirked. "I don't know what you mean by 'that well,' but I know enough to shock me that she'd have the nerve to darken the doorway of a church." I rolled my eyes. "Mama, there's things about Dabney you may not know. I really wish you wouldn't get so chummy with her. Haven't we given folks enough fodder for gossip, without you hanging out with the likes of Dabney Foxworthy?"

Mama glared at me as if I'd suddenly sprouted horns. I didn't know what she was thinking, but my gut told me it would be best not to ask. She stood in the doorway with her arms crossed. "Are you coming or not? I don't wanna be late."

"Hold on, Mama. I'll hitch up Dolly and take you, but don't expect me to escort you into church. I'll be waiting outside for you when it's over."

"Suit yourself."

I could tell she wasn't happy with me. But I wasn't too thrilled with her, either. Dabney walked through the gate, as I lifted Mama onto the wagon.

Mama hollered, "Dabney, wait and you can catch a ride with us."

I lowered my head and groaned. Didn't Mama know what

people said about the girl?

I sat in the wagon, holding the reins, until Mama popped me on the arm. "Where are your manners, Kiah? Help the lady up."

Dabney's face turned red. "I can manage."

Mama's eyes told me I best not keep my seat. I jumped out of the wagon. My fingers almost touched, when I reached around her tiny waist and lifted her up. I flinched when Mama slid over, putting Dabney right smack in the middle. Humiliated, I popped the reins and Dolly lit out like her tail was on fire. The wagon jerked and bolted over the bumpy clay road. Mama grabbed her hat, leaned across Dabney and shot me a look which I'd learned to interpret at a very early age. I pulled back on the reins. "Whoa, Dolly. Whoa, Babe." I looked at mama. Neither of us said a word. We didn't have to.

I didn't pay much attention to the female chatter as we rode along until I heard Mama ask about the Christmas party. My ears perked.

Dabney said, "We had a good turn-out. I 'spect there were fifty people or more there. It was a shame that Zann and Mrs. Pruitt weren't able to go. Zann had a pretty dress her mama made for the occasion—it was white with baby blue netting on the skirt and a wide, satin cummerbund. I ain't never seen nothing to beat it."

"Sure sounds pretty, all right," Mama said. "I once had a pretty white dress made outta satin. Made it myself, but things didn't turn out the way I planned, so I never got to wear it. But that's all water under the bridge, as they say. Too bad Zann didn't get to wear hers."

Dabney giggled. "The parson didn't take too kindly to it being sleeveless. I think he thought it was scandalous, but Mrs. Pruitt convinced him it was nothing of the sort."

My irritation mounted. I wasn't interested in a silly old dress. I wanted to know why Zann wasn't at the party.

I tried to sound only casually interested. "Too bad she was sick." I cut my eyes to the side and observed Dabney's reaction. She worked for the Pruitt's. If anyone knew what was wrong with Zann, she'd know. When she failed to comment, I tried once more. "Uh, I reckon she was sick. Why else would she have missed a chance to wear her new dress?"

Dabney frowned. "Yeah. Sick." There was something strange about the way she said it. I could think of no other reason Zann would've missed the party, but why was Dabney acting so mysterious?

I pulled the wagon up to the end of the lane and helped the ladies down. "I'll be waiting in the pecan orchard across the road, when church lets out." I recognized a couple of boys from school, walking toward the church. I swiftly looked in all directions to make sure no one had seen me driving up with Dabney Foxworthy.

Mama's never been one to give up easily. "Kiah, you're likely to get cold sittin' here in the wagon with the wind whipping through the trees. Don't you wanna come with us, shug?"

"I'll be fine, Mama."

"But won't you get bored? The Pageant's likely to last longer than an hour."

"No problem."

Dabney thanked me for the ride and commented she was glad they arrived early so they could sit on the front. Was she serious? I figured the gossipy old ladies would certainly have plenty to talk about next week with Fendora Grave and Dabney Foxworthy sitting shamelessly on the front pew. There was nothing I could do about it. Mama had been bound and determined to go to church. When she made up her mind to do something, a pack of wild wolves couldn't stop her.

I parked the wagon directly across from Zann's house and watched the door. I too, was glad we were early, but not for the same reason as Dabney. I watched for Zann's mother to walk out the front door of the parsonage, on her way to the church. If Zann was still sick, she'd be home alone. I'd sneak over and explain to her that I went to the bridge as soon as I read her letter, and how sorry I was to have missed her.

I heard the piano playing. Church had already begun, yet Mrs. Pruitt never left her house. Maybe Zann was sicker than I imagined. I could stand it no longer. I didn't care if her mother was with her. I had to see her—talk to her. I tied up the mule and darted across the road to the parsonage.

Her mother answered the door. "Ma'am, my name's Kiah Grave. I'm a friend of your daughter's. Is she home?"

The pupils in her eyes darted back and forth. She whispered, "Yes, but she isn't seeing anyone. You'd better go, young man."

"Will you tell her I'm here? I'd really like to see her."

"That's not possible. Please leave."

"Yes'm, I'll leave if you want me to, but can you tell me what's wrong. She doesn't have . . . scarlet fever . . . does she?" My heart pounded as I waited for her answer. I'd heard of a couple of cases in Tylertown, which wasn't too far from Pivan Falls.

She clenched her lips together.

My question was a simple one. Why couldn't she give me a straight answer?

She mumbled. "I'm sorry. You'll have to go."

"Yes, ma'am. But will you tell her I came?" The door slammed in my face. I stormed back across the road and climbed in the wagon. I don't know which emotion stirred the most pain. Was it sorrow for not being able see Zann? Or the intense anger I felt toward her snooty mother who'd apparently learned of my background and decided her daughter was too good for me.

The last Christmas carol was sung, and the parishioners filed out the door of the little white church. I flinched, seeing Mama and Dabney come out of the building, holding hands. Mama waved at me with her free hand. I crouched down, pretending not to see them. I didn't want folks looking toward the pecan orchard to see who Mama was waving to.

When they crossed the road, I jumped out of the wagon and helped them up, before Mama had a chance to scold. I asked all sorts of questions about the pageant—questions for which I had no interest in learning the answers, but I stalled for time, waiting for everyone to leave. I didn't want to get on the main road and risk being seen with Dabney Foxworthy sitting beside me in my wagon.

Mama was quiet as we made our way home. Had she been given the Rules of the Fellowship? Served her right. I wanted to punish her for not listening to me. "So, Mama, you finally got your wish. Tell me, did the good Christian folks welcome you with open arms?"

Her face lit up. "Kiah, they were wonderful. Such a sweet bunch of folks, and the pageant was adorable. You should've seen the tyke who played Joseph. When the Innkeeper forgot his lines, sweet little tow-headed Joseph helped him out."

Dabney chimed in. "Though I felt sorry for the cute, pudgy kid as he stood stone-faced trying to remember, I couldn't help giggling when Joseph stepped up to help him. He said, 'Well, Mister Innkeeper, you ain't said, but I don't reckon there's no room in your Inn, so where you gonna put us?'"

Mama could hardly speak for laughing. "Kiah, you would've loved it. It was precious."

I suppose I had a quizzical look on my face, because I still didn't understand what was so funny about a kid forgetting his lines.

Mama shrugged. "I reckon you just had to be there, son. I'm so glad I went, but I'm feeling a mite wore out, after such a big day. Kiah, would it be asking too much for you to fix your lunch when we get home? I think I'm fixing to lie down for a spell."

"Sure, Mama. That's a good idea. You do look a little peeked."

Dabney glanced at me and nodded in agreement. "Fennie, I put on a mess o' turnips before leaving this morning. I'll bring you a bowl full with some pot liquor and a couple of corn pones soon as I can fry up the bread."

Maybe Dabney caught me drooling, for she said, "Kiah, the butcher gave me some ham hocks, so I'll fix you a plate and make sure you get plenty of meat. Your mama told me you like meat."

Mama patted Dabney's arm. "Bless yo' heart, that's mighty neighborly of you, sugar. I've had me a real hankerin' for some greens, lately. But no need in you having to bring 'em over. Kiah can go get 'em."

I winced. Since when did Dabney Foxworthy start calling Mama by her first name? This relationship had gotten a bit too chummy. But I couldn't deny the sound of turnips, ham hocks and cornbread could turn a man's head and change his way of thinking. Dabney was looking better all the time.

After putting Dolly in the barn, I ambled over to #3 and

glanced about to see if anyone was looking. I could smell the turnips, even before Dabney opened the door.

"Come on in, Kiah. It's almost ready."

I entered and looked about. She walked over, closed the door softly behind me, and mumbled an apology for the disarray. I saw no reason for her to be embarrassed. The room was spotless. A pretty lavender crocheted bedspread covered the cot. I wondered if she made it. Somehow, I'd never considered Dabney to be the domestic type. White ruffled curtains hung over the window. The cabins were all the same size, but hers looked spacious. Maybe because it was less cluttered. Mama stayed too busy washing and ironing for other folks, to fret over how our house looked. And I had to admit, I wasn't much help when it came to prettying up the place.

Dabney went back to the stove to tend to the greens. I popped my knuckles—a nervous habit I couldn't seem to break.

"Have a seat," she said. "I'll only be a minute."

"I'm fine," I muttered, shifting from one foot to the other. I wanted to get the turnips and get out as fast as I could. Why she frightened me so, I really can't say, but I was as nervous as a cat staring into the mouth of a burlap bag.

The ticking of the Grandfather clock on the mantle seemed to grow louder and louder, shattering the uncomfortable silence between us.

My eye caught sight of a one-armed baby doll with molded

hair propped on the mantle next to the clock. In a pathetic attempt to initiate a conversation, I walked over and picked up the toy. "Whose doll? Got a kid stashed away somewhere?" I pretended to be looking under the cot.

She whirled around. Hot darts couldn't have melted the sharp icy-stare she shot toward me. "Please. Put her back." Though her voice was soft, there was something in her tone, which told me I'd hit upon a sore spot.

The girl was weirder than I thought. I shrugged and laid the toy back where I found it and sat down in a high-back rocker with a cowhide bottom. The chair squeaked as I rocked back and forth, faster and faster as I nervously waited. How long did it take to fry a few corn pones?

I jerked at the neck of my flannel shirt. Here I was, sitting inside Dabney Foxworthy's cabin. What would the guys think if they got wind of this? They liked to make up tall tales about their trips to visit #3, as if it were something to brag about. Yet, here I was inside her cabin and scared out of my gourd someone would find out. Maybe I was the weird one.

Her back was to me, as she pumped water into a dishpan and washed her hands. I had a chance to stare without being noticed. She wore a white bib apron, with a sash tied tightly around her trim waist. Her hair was the color of golden rods and today, it fell loosely around her shoulders. She wasn't bad to look at. Not bad at all. It didn't take much imagination to conclude that for a good-looking dame like Dabney, peddling her illicit brand of wares would be a cinch. I wondered how much money she made in a night. I'd heard tales, but I couldn't believe half of what I'd heard. I sat biting my nails and staring at her fine form. Yep, she was quite a looker. I felt my face flush, as if she might turn around and read my thoughts.

Dabney dipped the turnips into a bowl and then reached in a box and pulled out two yellow onions. "You can't eat turnips and corn pones without a juicy onion to go with it."

I popped my knuckles and mumbled a brief 'Thank you.'

"Shucks, it ain't much." Her face turned scarlet which stunned me. I hadn't considered that anything might embarrass a girl of her reputation.

The hot bread lay on newsprint to soak up the grease. I watched her pick up the pones and wrap them in white cheesecloth.

I grappled with a question, which gnawed away at my gut. There was no one else to ask. I swallowed and blabbed it out. "Dabney, what's wrong with Zann?"

Her brow furrowed and her eyes shifted away from me. For a minute it appeared she wasn't going to answer.

"She's sick, Kiah."

I jutted my jaw forward and winced. She was being as evasive as Mrs. Pruitt. But why? Rolling my eyes, I said, "Well, I figured she was sick. Is it anything serious? There are all sorts of things that can make a body ill. She could have something as simple as the sniffles or as serious as smallpox. But you know what's wrong with her, don't you? I know you do. You see her every day."

She turned her head.

Her peculiar reaction made me more curious than ever. "Dabney, I went to see her today while I waited for you and Mama to get out of church, but ol' lady Pruitt came to the door. She acted like I had a transmittable disease, and slammed the door in my face. Wouldn't let me see her. I don't think she'll tell Zann I was there. Will you tell her? Will you, please, Dabney?"

Dabney shoved the bowl of turnips in my hands, as if she were holding a hot iron. Then, acting as if she hadn't heard a word, she said, "Kiah, tell your Mama I hope this makes her feel better. She wasn't up to par this morning, but I could tell she enjoyed the pageant. I'm glad she got to go." She held the screen door open. "Bye, Kiah."

I didn't have to be hit over the head with a two-by-four to figure out she was trying to get rid of me. Maybe she didn't want to answer my questions. Or maybe she was expecting company and needed me out of the house. Whatever her reasons, it was apparent I wasn't going to get the information I wanted. Not out of her. Not today, anyway.

When I walked in the house, Mama was stretched out on the bed. "You go ahead and fix you a plate, Kiah. I'll eat d'rectly. I'm just a mite wore out right now. Think I'll rest."

I sliced the onion and sat down to a big bowl of turnips and fried bread. It had been a long time since I'd tasted anything so delicious. Not only was Dabney a great housekeeper, she was a fabulous cook. Too bad she wasn't the marrying kind, because she could've made some man a good wife. I chuckled at the amusing thought as I took a bite of a crispy corn pone. I glanced around at our unkempt cabin and made a new resolution. We couldn't help being poor, but after seeing Dabney's place, I knew we didn't have to live like slobs. Mama, being sickly, had more on her than she could handle alone. The blame belonged to me. After Christmas, I'd buy a can of paint and spruce up the place. I cringed when I looked at the ratty cotton quilt slung over Mama. Maybe I could ask Dabney how much she'd charge to crochet two bedspreads.

Monday morning I awoke early. I brought in the wood for the stove, started the fire under the wash pot, and after breakfast, I hitched up the wagon. "Mama, I've got some running around to do, so I'll pick up a few groceries and get the popcorn while I'm out. Anything special you'd like me to bring home?"

"The popcorn is special enough, shug. I'm glad you didn't forget."

Mr. Farris, my employer at the stockyard, had taught me to drive the hauler so I could transport hogs to the out-of-town buyers for him. He said I could make more money as a long-distance driver on week-ends than I could make in a month as a stable boy. I'd managed to save thirty-nine dollars and sixty-five cents, though Mama didn't know it. That was the most money I'd ever had in my pocket at one time. But I didn't plan to hold on to it. I made Mama a promise and I was out to keep it. This was going to be a Christmas she wouldn't forget.

I stopped at Goodson's and bought the popcorn. I took care of that first, to make sure I didn't forget, since Mama was counting on it. I bought a half-dozen Florida oranges, a few sweet potatoes, some dry lima beans, a bottle of Karo syrup, five pounds of Domino sugar, a sack of flour and a pound of butter. The popcorn was for Mama, but the syrup, sugar, flour and butter was for me. I wanted to make sure she had everything she needed to make a pecan pie.

Then I rode over to Pascagoula to do a little Christmas shopping. The day started out rather warm, but the temperature was dropping fast. It was beginning to feel more like Christmas.

As I rode into town, I admired the many wreaths, which hung from windows and doors of the stately Victorian homes lining the Avenue. I turned onto Main Street, and the spectacular Nativity display in the square made me wish I'd brought Mama along. The town was gaily decorated with rows and rows of colored lights strung from one side of the street to the other. Huge boughs of greenery graced every street lamp. I was fascinated by the number of automobiles. People honked and waved as they passed on the street. For the first time in my life, I understood what it meant to get into the Christmas spirit. I took Dolly over to the livery stable and walked around the corner to the Five and Dime. With money in my pocket and a full Christmas list, I could hardly wait to shop.

I bought a bag of gum drops, a box of shiny Christmas ornaments, and a large bottle of Evening in Paris perfume for Mama. I considered giving her White Gardenia, but changed my mind. It didn't seem right somehow, my Mama smelling like my sweetheart. Evening in Paris came in a pretty blue bottle, and I knew she'd be real proud. I didn't reckon she'd ever had any perfume, or at least not since I'd been born. The nice sales lady told me to take it to the back of the store, and they'd wrap it for me. I could hardly wait for Christmas day to see the look on Mama's face.

The next item on my list wouldn't be as easy. I wanted to buy something really nice for Zann, but I couldn't find it in the dime store.

Not knowing what I was looking for made the task difficult. I walked down the street, looking in every window. Then I spotted it. Displayed in the drugstore show window was the perfect gift. I had to have it. A miniature cedar chest with shiny brass hinges and filled with fine linen stationary. The druggist pulled it out of the window for me, and when he opened the lid, it played a pretty melody. He called it The Blue Danube Waltz.

It was the most beautiful cedar box I'd ever seen. A picture of a shallow stream lined with weeping willows was painted on the lid. The scene reminded me of the creek in Pivan Falls. I hoped Zann would think so, too.

The druggist smiled. "Son, what's her last name? The stationary is monogrammed, and I think I have every letter in stock except *M* and *Q*."

I hesitated.

He reached under the counter. "Her last name?"

I didn't want to say 'Pruitt,' since he'd know for sure it was for the parson's daughter. Everyone for miles around was acquainted with Pastor Pruitt, so I said, "Her last name begins with a *P*."

My pulse raced when he fumbled around, shoving boxes aside. It appeared he couldn't find the right monogram. I had my heart set on the cedar chest, so I sensed relief when he rose from behind the counter, holding up a small packet of stationary.

"This gonna be all for you, Sonny?"

"I think so," I said, reaching in my pocket for the four dollars and fifty cents.

He handed me the stationary to inspect. It was neatly tied together with a thin, pink satin ribbon. I held the packet to my nose and sniffed. The paper was scented and had the initial *P* embossed in gold script in the right hand corner. The outer edge of the linen paper had a gold border, which the druggist informed me was 24K gold. He pointed out the tiny brass lock on the lid and showed me the key taped to the underside.

He gave a chuckle and said, "Your little lady can lock up all those sweet nothings you write to her and her pappy won't be able to read 'em."

I'm sure I blushed.

"She must be special to rate such a fine gift," he said.

"Yessir . . . yessir, she's sure special all right."

After he wrapped it in green paper and tied a big red ribbon on top, I unhitched Dolly and started home. About three miles out of town, I turned around and headed back to Pascagoula.

I tied Dolly up at the end of the street, walked in the dime store and told the clerk I wanted another bottle of Evening in Paris. I had it wrapped also, but before I left the store I was questioning whether I'd done the right thing.

I looked across the street at the marquee above the theatre. I knew I needed to get home, but the temptation to stay was too great. Johnny Mack Brown was starring in *Billy the Kid*. I'd never been to a picture show in my whole life and it only cost a dime to get in. Mama had entertained me for hours with wonderful stories about the famous cowboy. According to Mama—and I believed every word she said—Johnny Mack was sweet on her when they were fifteen. That was the summer she went to Dothan, Alabama to pick cotton on her Grandpa's farm and the Brown's lived down the road a piece.

But the courtship ended when she went back to Oklahoma. Johnny, as she called him, later moved to Tuscaloosa and played football for the University of Alabama, before becoming a famous movie star.

I paid for my ticket and followed some fellow through the big double doors, when a man wearing a red jacket and a funny little cap shined the light in my face.

"Hey you! Where you think you're going?"

He got my dander up the way he smarted off, but I held my temper for fear he had the authority to throw me out if I caused trouble. "Just want to find a seat."

"You colored?"

"Colored? Me?" My complexion was dark from working in the sun all summer at the Stock Yards, but no one had ever mistook me for colored before.

He motioned to my left. "Colored folks sit upstairs."

I shrugged. "Fine." I figured the view was better from up there, anyway. The picture show had already started, when I took my seat.

The fellow next to me leaned over and whispered, "Hey, you ain't s'pose to be up here. Peckerwoods sit downstairs."

The story of my life. I didn't fit in anywhere. I watched Johnny Mack riding tall in the saddle, and wondered what it would've been like if Mama had married him, instead of getting herself messed up with Will Lancaster. I'll bet Johnny Mack would've done the right thing, and married her. I fantasized the kind of life I might have had, if my name was Johnny Mack, Junior.

When I walked out of the theatre, it was dusk and the

Christmas lights lining the street were turned on. I wanted to stay longer and enjoy the sounds and sights, but knowing how Mama worried, I left.

On the way home, I stopped at a meat rendering plant and bought a ham. With only twenty-three cents left in my pocket I headed for Rooster Run, but I'd had a wonderful day, bought everything on my list . . . and a very special gift, which wasn't on the list.

Heavy clouds hung in the sky. I hoped I could get home before the bottom fell out. Mama was standing in the doorway when I pulled up to unload the wagon.

"Where in the world have you been, Kiah Grave? I've been out of my mind with worry. I expected you back hours ago."

"Sorry, Mama. Didn't mean to worry you, but I had some business to tend to."

She watched curiously as I carried the bags into the house.

"Whatcha got, shug? What's in them sacks?"

I laughed and gave her a hug. "Don't you know you shouldn't ask questions at Christmas, Mama?"

She gave a childlike snicker. "Well, I'm just tickled you showed up ahead o' the rain. I was afraid it was gonna come a gully-washer before you had a chance to get home."

I placed the groceries on the kitchen table. Mama's eyes filled with tears when she unwrapped the packing from around the ham. "My, my. A smoked ham? This must've cost a pretty penny."

126

"It's paid for, Mama. You don't worry about the cost."

"I do declare it's been 'coon ages since I've tasted ham. Thank you, sweet Jesus," she said, lifting a hand in the air. "I can't think of anything I'd rather have, Kiah. This is setting out to be the best Christmas you and I have ever had. Ain't God good, sugar?" She threw her arm around my shoulder. "I said, ain't He good?"

I could believe this might be our best Christmas, but why was she giving Jesus the credit? Wasn't I the one who brought home the ham? Why should I care? If she was happy, did it matter who got the praise? She got what she wanted. All I wanted was to see my girl and know she was all right.

I placed the sacks containing the Christmas presents on my bed and pulled the curtain. I hid two gifts under the bed. Mama followed me with her eyes, when I pulled down a pine bough on the tree and tied her present near the top. I'd never been able to buy her anything really nice, and I wasn't sure I could wait one more day for her to open it.

Though it looked as if it might storm at any minute, I went into the woods back of the house in search of a mock orange tree. Pulling out my pocket knife, I cut off a branch and took it home. I remembered a Christmas long ago when I was a youngster and we lived on the Poor Farm. An elderly lady invited all the kids into her cabin. She had a small mock orange branch, with brightly colored gum drops stuck on every thorn. She recited a poem about little children having visions of sugar plums dancing in their heads, and she called the gum drops 'sugar plums,' and told us all to pick three. It was such a treat. I still remember the colors I chose—a purple, a green and a yellow one. I never forgot the gumdrop tree and this year, we were going to have our own.

When I returned to the cabin, Mama had the corn popped. I mixed up a batch of flour, water and salt to make a base for the sugar plum tree. I'd wait for it to dry, then sink the mock orange branch into the dough.

After putting the groceries in the cupboard, Mama poured the popped corn into a large bowl, and brought two needles and a spool of thread to the table. "Kiah, you gonna help me string the corn like we did last Christmas?" Her brow furrowed. "Or was it the year before, sugar? I can't recollect."

"Sure, Mama. We'll do it together." I didn't want to remind her that it couldn't have been last Christmas. Surely, she remembered how I balked at the mention of a tree, because I didn't want anything to remind me it was a season to be joyful when I had nothing to be joyful about. In fact, I couldn't remember the last time we strung popcorn together. It was selfish of me to deny her such a simple pleasure. But when one is so self-absorbed in his own wants, nothing or no one else seems to matter. This year, I'd try to make it up to her.

Mama and I sat at the table and strung the corn. When we finished, I pulled out the colored balls. She squealed with delight.

"Land sakes, I haven't had a Christmas tree this pretty since the year I worked at the bank in Goat Hill and—" She stopped abruptly, and appeared to be shocked by her own voice. "I'm just saying it's been a mighty long time since I had a tree with real ornaments."

I knew she was thinking of the Christmas when that no-good yahoo she called my daddy walked out on her and got himself engaged to another woman. To my delight, though, she didn't commence with the trip down memory lane. I'd spent a lot of money to make this a special Christmas, and I didn't want it ruined.

Chapter 8

Tuesday morning, Mama trimmed the ham and stuck it in the oven. "I'll bake the sweet potatoes and the pecan pies tomorrow," she said proudly.

I checked the base of the gumdrop tree with my finger. The dough was dry and hard as the shell on a mud turtle. The branch leaned to the left a tad, but one would hardly notice once I loaded it down with all the candy. After lunch, I heard the children playing in the yard. I carefully picked up the candy tree, walked outside and before I could place it on the old oak stump, dozens of curious little eyes were surrounding me and my tree.

Dabney Foxworthy must have been watching from her window, because she came tripping outside. "What's that for?" She asked.

I told her the story behind the gumdrop tree. "I wish I could recite the poem," I said. "But all I remember is the line about the sugar plums, and the ending, 'Merry Christmas to all and to all a good night.'"

She giggled. "Oh, you're talking about *'Twas the Night before Christmas.'* I know that one."

By now, every kid in Rooster Run had gathered around us. Dabney recited the childish poem while I counted the kids. There were enough gumdrops for every child to have three. Why it would make a grown man want to cry, I couldn't say. All I know is that I struggled to keep my composure.

The kids were awed by the poem, just as I'd been. I suppose like me, they chose to dream of a jolly old man who delighted in making dreams come true. Before going in, I managed to mumble a quick "thank you" to Dabney for such a great performance. I'm not sure who was most embarrassed. Her face glowed. She murmured something and though I didn't understand, I didn't ask her to repeat it.

After supper, I walked outside. The moon was full and the thermometer was dropping. There was no chance in a white Christmas, but I was glad it was getting a little cooler. There was something not right about warm weather at Christmas time.

Though it was late, I put a saddle on Dolly and rode over to the pecan orchard. I tied the mule to a tree and ran across the road to the parsonage, carrying a pretty green package tied up with a big red ribbon. The card simply said, "Merry Christmas, Zann." Though I didn't sign my name, I hoped she wouldn't have to guess where it came from.

With my pulse racing, I made a mad dash for the porch, where I quickly deposited the package next to the front door. I knocked and then took off like a scared rabbit, hoping I could hide before someone answered the door. I squatted down behind an oleander bush and waited. If Zann came to the door, I'd sneak from behind the shrubbery. But if her father opened it, I'd wait until he went back into the house, and then I'd dart across the road and jump on Dolly before the preacher would have a chance to see me.

I bit my lip when the porch light came on. Parson Pruitt moseyed out and glanced around. With a stoic expression, he strolled over to one end of the porch and then walked to the other side, scratching his head. For a second it appeared he wasn't going to see it, but as he turned to go back into the house, he stumbled on the gift. I almost let out a yelp when it appeared he kicked the box. What if he broke the mirror? He reached down and picked up the package. I watched as he opened the card. There wasn't much to read, so I couldn't imagine why he stared at it long and hard.

"Who's out there?" He yelled in a gruff voice, sounding more like a warden stalking an escaped convict than a parson retrieving a Christmas present addressed to his daughter. Why was he so all-fired upset? He stomped back inside the house and I waited for over fifteen minutes before I came out of hiding, for fear he might be peering out the window. When the lights went out, I took off, jumped on Dolly and lit out for Rooster Run as fast as that ol' mule could trot.

I was disappointed I didn't get to see Zann, but glad the parson didn't catch me. I'd always considered preachers to be somewhat soft and mealy-minded. However, I decided I'd sooner wrestle with a crocodile than to face off with the parson, in his frame of mind. The man looked mad enough to chew roofing nails in half.

Christmas eve I went to bed with the smell of baked ham and sweet potatoes filling the air. I lay wishing everyone in the world could anticipate waking up on Christmas morning to such a grand feast.

It felt swell to know I'd been able to do something to brighten Mama's life. I could hardly wait until morning. I smiled, imagining her surprise when she'd awaken and open her gift. She'd have something wrapped for me. Perhaps a crocheted bookmark or . . . I cringed. Hopefully, she hadn't stitched up another handmade muslin shirt. I suddenly chuckled at the possibility of having to feign delight if such a gift should appear under the tree. But for Mama's sake, I could. And I would.

I closed my eyes tightly, but sleep wouldn't come. There were so many questions and so few answers. Why had Mrs. Pruitt slammed the door in my face? I had the strange feeling Dabney was keeping something from me. But what? If only I could see Zann, even for a few minutes, all would be well in my world. The girl loved me. She said so. She was on my mind every waking moment, and returned in my dreams when I slept.

For years, I'd held to a false notion of what it meant to love

133

and to be loved. I presumed love to be nothing more than the body's response to a physical attraction and I convinced myself if I could keep my eyes from looking twice at a good-looking dame, then the possibility of falling in love would be nil. Since getting to know Zann, I'd discovered love was much more than the eye could see.

I lay in bed, remembering the first day Zann Pruitt came to school. She had a yellow ribbon in her hair. I smiled, recalling how my pulse raced at the sight of her. Her irresistible beauty frightened the daylights out of me. Determined not to follow the path of my father, I viewed her as the enemy. I pulled out all the artillery when she showed an interest in me. Yet my rudeness failed to deter her.

Ah, but she wasn't my enemy. She was my other half. The missing part of me. She brought a joy to my life, which I'd never known. She taught me how to laugh . . . to live . . . and yes, thanks to her, I'd learned how to love. Really love.

If there'd been nothing more to Zann Pruitt than a pretty face and a fine figure, I could've walked away and never looked back. But as lovely as she was to gaze upon, her outer layer wasn't the magnet that drew my heart, or the strong vice that held it there.

I was in love, but I was in love with the inner Zann. The Zann who refused to reject me, even when I rejected her. The one who lifted me up, though I put her down. The Zann who treated me with kindness and made me laugh when there was nothing to laugh about. The Zann who made my heart sing. The Zann I wanted to spend the rest of my life with.

If any girl had reason to be proud and full of herself, it would've been her, but I'd never met anyone who demonstrated such sincere humility. Such warmth. Not only was she the most beautiful girl in Pivan Falls, she could sing like a bird, play the piano like a concert pianist and she received the highest marks in school—well, in every subject except math, of course. Yet she wasn't puffed up. She was a lady in every sense of the word. She never had to fret over birds making a nest in *her* hair. No sirree. The fowl of the air, which circled over my noggin on a daily basis, dared not fly over her sweet, innocent head. Full of compassion, she hurt when others hurt and was an advocate for the down-and-out. This was the real Zann. I was in love and my world would never be the same again. I pulled the quilt over my head, turned over and fell asleep.

I awoke Christmas morning to the sound of rain pounding on the tin roof. Mama was sifting flour from the bin and singing *Away in a Manger*. Though she couldn't carry a tune in a flour sack, the off-key melody hit a chord with me. I'd heard the familiar carol all my life and had even sung it myself; yet, until now, I'd never paid much attention to the lyrics.

The words swirled in my head. 'No crib for a bed?' I tried to imagine Jesus Christ being born in such an humble setting as a stable, and his mama laying her sweet, newborn infant in a cow trough.

I chewed my lip and mulled over the account of my own birth, which Mama had related to me on many occasions. Said I was born under a chinaberry tree . . . which meant I didn't have a crib, either. A lump formed in my throat. All my life, I resented being poor, fueled by the knowledge that my wealthy father owned a mansion and lacked for nothing. I viewed life as grossly unfair and through the years, the anger inside me burned like a hot fever, affecting every cell of my body. Every facet of my life.

Did Jesus hate being poor, while his father owned the cattle on a thousand hills? Did He have to deal with ignorant gossips while growing up in Nazareth? Did the neighbors do the math and whisper behind Mary's back? I wasn't comparing my mama with the mother of Jesus, nor did I dare compare myself to the Son of God, yet I couldn't help wondering.

After breakfast, I washed the dishes and tended to the beans cooking on the stove, while Mama rolled out the dough for the pie crusts.

I dried my hands against my overalls, and while the beans simmered, I pulled the curtain that separated our quarters. I slipped a small wrapped package from beneath the bed and stuck it under my coat and tried to sneak out the door without being seen.

"What you fixin' to do, Kiah?" Mama asked as I eased open

the door.

"Just need to run outside. I'll be back before the pies come out of the oven."

"Is it still raining?"

"Just barely drizzling. I'll be back in a jiff. You watch the pies, Mama. Don't let 'em burn."

She didn't question me further. I suppose she figured I was headed to the outhouse.

I hurried over to #3, placed the gift behind the screen door and ran back home as fast as I could run.

The meal was prepared, and the delightful smell of hot, buttery syrup and parched pecans sifting from the oven filled the cramped little cabin. "Merry Christmas, Mama," I said. "Your gift is hanging on the tree. Go get it."

"We'll open them at the same time, sugar." She reached in the bottom of the Hoosier cabinet and pulled out a present, neatly wrapped in funny papers. I wondered where she found the Sunday funnies, since we didn't subscribe to a newspaper. She handed me my present, and I ran my fingers over the outer edge, probing, in an attempt to guess. But I was stumped.

"Merry Christmas, son. I hope you like it."

I liked it already, though I had no idea what it was . . . I only knew it didn't feel like a shirt.

"I think I know what it is." I teased.

Mama laughed. "I declare, Kiah, you act like a little young'un." I loved making her laugh. She said, "Go ahead and shake it, if you want to. You won't ever guess what's in there."

Mama seemed delighted at my excitement but the real joy in my heart was brought on by the anticipation of seeing her open her gift.

With my fingers still probing the wrapped gift, I feigned a frown. "Hmm . . . it feels like a cracked mirror with acorns glued on top. Did you make it yourself?"

She threw her head back and cackled. "I declare, Kiah Grave, if you ain't a sight. A cracked mirror with acorns? I told you you'd never guess. Go ahead, shug. Open it."

I carefully pulled away the tape, not wanting to tear the paper. I had an idea the funnies would be as fine a gift as anything that might lie inside.

Mama tore into her little package and oohed and ahhed over the perfume. She dabbed a few drops on her neck and the inside of her arm.

Thrilled when I pulled back the paper on my gift and found seven large blocks of Peanut Brittle, I jumped up and gave mama a big hug. "Oh, Mama, you couldn't have given me anything I'd rather have. But where did you get the peanuts?"

She beamed. "With all the pecans you picked up, I had more'n enough, so I swapped Myrtle a quart of pecans for a quart of peanuts. I thought you'd like the brittle."

In jest, I made what I considered a casual comment. "Have I died and gone to Heaven? Pecan pies and peanut brittle all in the same day?"

Mama's expression changed. Something in her eyes told me I'd said the wrong thing, though I couldn't figure why she'd appear to be troubled. "What's wrong, Mama?"

"Nothing's wrong. Just thinking about what you said, sugar. You been having thoughts about Heaven, lately, have you? Maybe the little Pruitt girl been talking to you about the Lord?"

I rolled my eyes and grunted. "For cryin' out loud, Mama, I was only funning."

Maybe she wasn't upset to begin with, but my last comment lit her fuse.

Mama shook her finger in my face. "Well, it don't seem right to fun about such matters. I ain't sayin' God don't have a sense of humor. Maybe He does, maybe He don't. I'm just sayin' it don't set right with me for you to make light of such things."

Sometimes Mama's mixed-up theology made me want to sneak her Bible and search the scriptures, if for no other reason than to prove her wrong. But now was not the time to argue. Not today, of all days.

With my arm resting on her shoulder, I gave her a hug. "Mama, I'm sorry if I offended you, but if God loves us the way you say He does, then I'm sure He didn't mind me being thankful for the pie and candy. And that's all I was saying."

Relieved to see the lines on her face diminish, I breathed easier when she said, "Well, I hadn't looked at it in that light, sugar. Maybe I was being a bit overwrought."

When the rain started back, she pulled the burlap curtain away from the window. "Would you look at how it's coming down in sheets? If this keeps up, we'll have to pack some garments in front of the door to keep out the water. We've certainly had our share of rain."

Didn't bother me. No sound on earth could comfort me like the sound of rain pounding on a tin roof.

A streak of lightening lit up the room, just as someone knocked on the door.

Bad weather made Mama skittish. She looked at me wide-eyed. "Now, who could be out in weather such as this? Quick, Kiah let 'em in."

I snatched open the door and my jaw dropped when I saw Dabney standing there dripping wet. I stood gaping. Did she know I was the one who left the perfume? Maybe she came to bring it back. I wouldn't blame her for not wanting to accept a gift from me. Not after the way I had talked to her.

If she didn't already know I was the donor, she'd know soon, because Mama would want to show her what she got for Christmas. I cringed. I could imagine the jokes that would surface as soon as word got out that I gave Dabney Foxworthy perfume. What was I thinking? If I had to give her something, why of all things did I have to choose something so personal?

"Who's at the door, Kiah?" Mama asked.

I swallowed hard. "It's Dabney, Mama."

"Well, for goodness sake, don't leave her standing out there in the rain. Invite her in."

She had a newspaper draped over her head. The mystery of the Sunday funnies was solved. I stepped aside and motioned her in with my hand.

She giggled. "The bottom fell out of the cloud, just as I shut the door behind me. I tried to run fast to keep from getting drenched, but I'm too wet to come inside." She shoved a plate covered in tin foil toward me. "I brought you something." Her face turned red. "I mean I brought your mama something."

I was fine with that. Fine she was too wet to come in and fine she didn't bring me anything. I would've been finer if only she'd left before Mama had a chance to invite her inside.

Mama yelled, "Come on in, sugar."

Dabney cut her eyes toward me, and blushed again. Why did she keep blushing like there was something between us? If she had a notion I'd given her the perfume because I was sweet on her, she was as nutty as Mama's brittle.

She crooked her neck and looked past me. "Fennie. I wanted to bring you a little something. Merry Christmas."

Mama walked to the door and her face lit up, seeing the plate. "Why bless your heart, honey, what do we have here?"

Dabney lifted her shoulders. "Shucks, it ain't much. Really. Just a fruit cake. I used my Grandma's recipe. I couldn't afford the candied fruit. I don't much care for it anyway, so I added lots of nuts and raisins. I hope you like it."

I groaned. What was it with women and raisins? "Yes!" The word shot out of my mouth as if it had been sitting on the edge of my tongue, waiting to escape.

Mama looked at me strangely and I could tell she was waiting for an explanation.

My face burned. "I mean yes, I like raisins. That's what you were about to ask, wasn't it, Dabney?"

Dabney shook her head and blushed again. "I'm sorry. I shoulda asked." She shrugged. "I reckon since I like them I assumed everybody else does."

How could I have been so stupid? I swallowed hard, knowing the worst was yet to come. She hadn't mentioned the perfume.

Dabney placed her hand on the doorknob. "Well, Merry Christmas, folks."

Mama walked over and put her arm around her. "Dabney, sugar, you got kin joining you for the holidays?"

I groaned, fearful of what Mama was up to.

"No ma'am."

"Well, then Kiah and I insist you spend the day with us. Don't we, son?"

What could I do but nod?

Dabney shook her head. "Thanks, Fennie. You're sweet, but Christmas is for families. I don't want to butt in."

Mama chuckled. "Butt in? Why, you're practically family, sugar. It'll seem more like Christmas, with an extra plate set at the table. Ain't it the truth, Kiah?"

I feigned another smile. My mouth was beginning to hurt from the stretch.

Mama said, "Kiah, stoke up the fire and pull a chair up to the hearth so Dabney can dry off. She's soaked to the bone."

I swallowed when Mama said, "Dabney, shug, you'll find a bathrobe hanging on a nail beside my bed. Get off those wet clothes and wrap up in my robe before you catch your death o' pneumonia."

"I'm okay, Fennie. Really."

But whenever my mama got a bee in her bonnet she couldn't be reasoned with. She took the gray flannel robe from off the hook and handed it to Dabney. "Now, you get out of those wet rags, sugar. Your teeth are chattering."

I rushed over and pulled the curtain. "You can dress over on the other side."

"Thanks," she said in a hoarse whisper.

I stoked the red embers with a poker, though my mind wasn't on the fire in the hearth. What was Mama thinking? The anger inside me burned hot. What if someone should have reason to come calling . . . and find Dabney Foxworthy inside my house, wearing a housecoat. Though the thick flannel robe covered her completely, I still couldn't get it out of my mind that she wasn't properly dressed. Didn't seem decent. Didn't seem decent at all.

Worried about Dabney's wet head, Mama coaxed her to stand near the fire. I groaned when she backed up to the fireplace, and lifted the back of the robe, exposing her lower legs.

"Ah," she said. "Don't you love a fire? The way it pops and crackles, and sends a raw, ruddy glow about the room?"

I rolled my eyes. If there was a raw, ruddy glow in the room, the ruddy could've been coming from me and the raw from her, seeing how her clothes were hanging on *my* curtain and she was prancing around in *my* living room in nothing but a housecoat. It was hard to believe the robe was the same one I'd seen on Mama, day in and day out. Sure looked different on Dabney.

Dabney helped Mama get the food on the table. The rain stopped, and when she saw we only had two tea glasses she told Mama she needed to run home and would be back shortly.

If I'd been in good standing with God, I would've prayed hard for her not to return, but she was back at the door before I had a chance to slice the ham. She was wearing a dress, and had Mama's robe in one hand and a flour sack under her arm, although I could tell it wasn't flour in the bag. Her wet hair was brushed out, and hung over her shoulders. With the make-up washed from her face, she didn't look a day over sixteen.

Mama said, "I declare, sugar, you didn't have to go to the

trouble to fix up for us, but you look plumb pretty. Don't she look pretty, Kiah?"

I pretended not to hear and Dabney handed the flour sack to Mama. "I brought you another present, Fennie."

Mama reached in the bag and pulled out four jelly glasses. She carried on over them as if they were fine crystal.

"Dabney, honey, I declare if these ain't the prettiest glasses I believe I've ever seen. Ain't they pretty, Kiah?"

They looked like all the other jelly glasses I'd seen at Goodson's Grocery. I flinched, seeing four eyes on me, waiting for my response. I nodded in agreement they were super-duper jelly glasses.

We were halfway through lunch, when Mama said, "Dabney, you won't believe what my sweet son gave me for Christmas. I've never been so surprised in all my life. Guess. Just guess."

I sucked in a deep breath, and waited for what was about to come. Dabney appeared nervous.

"Talcum powder?'

Mama smiled and shook her head. Guess again.

"Stockings?"

Mama grinned. "Nope."

"A handkerchief?"

"Shucks, you won't ever guess. I'm telling you what's the truth, Dabney, you coulda knocked me over with a tail feather, when I saw what was in that box." Mama slapped her hands on either side of her face, as if shocked all over again. "Honey, he bought me a bottle of Evening in Paris perfume."

I squirmed in my chair.

Mama beamed. "You know the kind I'm talking about, Dabney? Comes in those fancy little blue bottles. You've probably seen 'em in the store."

I closed my eyes tightly, wishing at the moment I knew how to pray.

Mama said, "I told him he ought not to spend his hard-earned money on frivolous things for me." She pointed to her neck and leaned over toward Dabney. "Smell."

Dabney leaned in and sniffed. "Smells lovely. That was very sweet, Kiah."

I didn't want Dabney Foxworthy calling me sweet. I wasn't sweet. Sweat popped out on my brow as I waited for her to tell Mama about *her* gift. Mama wouldn't have trouble guessing where it came from.

Needless to say, I was stunned when Dabney said, "Fennie, your perfume smells so good, I just may do something frivolous myself. Would you be offended if I decided to get me a bottle of Evening in Paris?"

"Goodness, no. I think you should, sugar. You'll be surprised how it lifts your spirits."

"Well, that settles it. We'll be the envy of every woman in church next Sunday, when they get a whiff of the two of us." She glanced my way, though her gaze didn't linger.

That was the day I gained a real respect for Dabney Foxworthy. She was a swell kid and I was a dope for not recognizing it before now.

Chapter 9

The week after Christmas was the longest week of my life. Eager for school to begin again, I was waiting on the school steps thirty minutes early, our first day back.

I hoped I suffered from a mild case of paranoia and there was a simple explanation for why Zann's parents didn't want me to see her. Maybe her father wasn't angry at me, but worried because his daughter was ill. That being the case, I could certainly understand his concern. I tried to convince myself that if it was anything serious, I would've heard. Word travels fast in little towns.

When the bell rang and her desk was empty, my fears returned with a vengeance. Something terrible must've happened for her to miss the Christmas party, the pageant and not be back for the first day of school.

Mr. Thatcher called the roll. "Zann Pruitt? Zann?" He glanced over the top of his spectacles. Almost as if he were pondering her absence, I heard him mumble, "She's had perfect attendance, until

148

now."

Mary Alice Jenson spoke up. "She wasn't at the pageant Saturday night, Mr. Thatcher, and Mama asked Parson Pruitt if she was sick. He nodded his head but I don't think he ever said what ailed her."

"Thank you, Mary Alice. We have four absent this morning. Perhaps the weather has brought on colds." He reached in his desk drawer and pulled out a math book. "Please turn in your workbooks to Chapter Fourteen. I'd like to start where we left off before the holidays."

His words expressed my feelings exactly. That's precisely what I wanted to do. Start where we left off. She loved me. And I loved her. So why did I feel so anxious?

The next twenty-four hours were long. I arrived at school early and waited by the door for Zann to arrive. When the bell rang, and she was not in sight, I lumbered into the room and slumped down in my desk.

Mr. Thatcher stood and went through the usual "Good morning students," routine.

Maybe for him. I wasn't in the mood for such cheerful chatter. I looked up, when I heard him say, "Welcome Parson." I jerked around in time to see Zann take a seat at her desk. She cut her eyes at me, smiled faintly, then quickly looked away. What was going on?

Mr. Thatcher walked to the back of the room where Zann's father stood, leaning against the wall near the door.

I watched out of the corner of my eye. Mr. Thatcher held out his hand. "Parson, did you need to confer with me?"

The parson's response was so low I couldn't hear it. Moments later he left, and Mr. Thatcher commenced with the lesson for the day.

I couldn't keep my eyes off her. I could tell she'd been sick, for she looked a mite peaked, though I determined it wasn't anything serious, else she wouldn't be back in school. I watched the big clock above Mr. Thatcher's desk, counting the minutes until lunch.

When the lunch bell rang, I went into the cloak room and took my syrup bucket from the shelf. I couldn't wait to share my ham biscuits and peanut brittle with her. I walked back into the school room in time to see her heading out the door with her father. Confused, I decided she was sicker than I realized, and her father had returned to take her home. Disappointed, I lumbered over to the big live oak, where Zann and I shared lunch so many times.

I'd almost finished my lunch, before I noticed the parson's car never left. Zann sat in the front seat of her daddy's jalopy, eating a sandwich. After months of coming to school alone, why did the parson now feel it necessary to escort his daughter to school? And why had he returned to have lunch with her? But the question troubling me most had nothing to do with Parson Pruitt. Why was

Zann treating me as if I were a leper? Was she angry because I didn't meet her at the bridge the day school let out? If she'd only give me a chance to explain.

The following day, she showed up several minutes after the bell rang. Her father walked her to the door, left, then returned at lunch. My curiosity turned to anger. What a sap I'd been. She was no different from all the other goody-two-shoes who felt they were too good to wipe their feet on me. I had no one to blame but myself. I knew better than to fall in love. And with a preacher's daughter, no less. If he considered it necessary to bring her to school to protect her from me, he could forego his trouble. I was through. Through with Zann and through with the whole female race. Zann Pruitt could jump in a big fat lake.

For the next two weeks, her father continued to act as a body guard. I had an urge to tell him he had no need to worry. I wouldn't touch her with a six-foot hoe.

But two weeks after school began, I saw her walking to school alone.

I sat on the school steps, waiting for the bell to ring. I held my head down to keep from looking at her. Then I felt her hand on my shoulder. Shivers sneaked up my spine.

Her voice was barely audible. "Kiah, we need to talk."

"Ha! After giving me the cold shoulder for two weeks, you now feel we need to talk? I'm not sure I have anything to say to you, Zann Pruitt."

151

"I don't blame you for being angry, Kiah, but you don't understand."

"Oh, I understand, all right. I learned the facts of life early. At the tender age of eight, to be exact, when three church ladies came to our home to explain to me and Mama what the Bible has to say about good Christian folks like yourself associating with folks like us. So if you're here to teach me that Bible lesson, you can forget it. I know it by heart."

Her face reddened and her eyes filled with tears. Before she could respond, the bell rang.

I rushed out the door with my syrup bucket at lunch. I didn't want her to think I was lollygagging around, waiting for her. I sat down and leaned against the oak tree. I reached down for a biscuit when my eyes focused on two dainty feet, next to the syrup bucket.

"Mind if I sit down?" She asked.

"Suit yourself."

"Kiah, the music box is beautiful. I love it. Thank you."

I made a puny shrug. I've never known how to handle compliments, I reckon because I haven't had much chance to practice. I reached in the bucket and pulled out a pint jar of buttermilk and a biscuit.

She unwrapped a sandwich. "You like bologna and cheese?"

I liked bologna and cheese but it riled me when she had the gall to wave it in front of my nose. I wasn't some starving mutt, looking for her to toss me a bone. I had plenty to eat. Good stuff. I figured if the Mississippi State Fair ever added a biscuit category, Mama would win the blue ribbon. Yet, I won't deny the bologna and cheese sandwich smelled better than a rib-eye steak.

Zann's beautiful arched brows lifted. "Well? Do you? Like bologna and cheese, I mean."

"I reckon," I muttered.

"Good. I brought an extra."

I bristled. One part of me wanted to reach for it, yet another part wanted to give her the what for. I barked back at her. "Zann, I don't need your charity. I have a good job and enough money to buy all the bologna and cheese I want. So quit feeling sorry for me, okay?"

She began to blubber and I wanted to kick myself. "Aw, shucks, Zann, stop crying. I didn't mean to hurt your feelings." I winced at my words. She was a girl. How did I expect her to react? I reared my head back and closed my eyes. I sucked in a deep breath and in a low, calm voice, I said, "Zann, I'm sorry. It's just—"

"Kiah, you have every right to be angry. But if you'd listen, I think I can explain. It's not like you think."

Determined to remain calm, I sucked in a heavy breath. "What am I supposed to think? Your father refused to let me see you, and then he got the notion you needed an armed guard to protect you from me."

"Kiah, you have it all wrong. Daddy won't be escorting me to school anymore. Mama convinced him he can't guard me twenty-four hours a day. I know you don't understand, but trust me when I say it has nothing to do with you."

"And you expect me to believe that?" I bit my lip and waited.

She turned her head, as if she couldn't look at me when she said, "I can't let you go on thinking it has something to do with you."

I watched as tears filled her eyes.

"Kiah, a fellow . . . well, he made improper advances toward me and Daddy went berserk when he found out." She dropped her head and sobbed.

I wanted to believe I'd misunderstood. As the words sank in, I broke out in a sweat. "Who? Tell me who he is, Zann, and I promise you the sorry rascal will never bother you again. Who is he? Was it Arnold? It was, wasn't it?"

"Kiah. Forget it. Please."

"How can you ask me to forget it? Did he . . . did he hurt you, Zann? Because if he did, tell me and I'll pulverize the big galoot and spread him out for rat poison." It was a good thing Arnold was absent, because all I could think about was the day he grabbed her at the bridge.

She shook her head. "I can't tell you who he was. Please don't ask. I shouldn't have told you. Can we not talk about it? I just want to forget it ever happened."

So maybe I was wrong. Maybe it wasn't Arnold. Whoever he was, even if he hadn't hurt her physically, the creep scared her. If only she'd tell me his name, I could guarantee her she'd never have to worry about him bothering her again.

I recalled Mr. Thatcher's words when he said, "Let's start where we left off." Starting over sounded good. My chance had come and there was no gain in letting it pass me by. I winked and said, "Got another one of those bologna and cheese sandwiches in your basket?"

A broad smile spread across her face.

Zann and I no longer met at the bridge. Her father insisted she go home after school. Although I didn't like it, I understood why he felt the need to be protective. Maybe he had more reason than he realized to demand she go straight home after school. The little bird circling my head had become harder and harder to shoo away.

In the coming weeks I kept getting horrid images of a faceless boy taunting Zann to let him kiss her. Though I tried not to think about it, the mental pictures tormented me both day and night. Did he merely make an attempt, or did he hold her tight and kiss her? Would she tell me if I dared to ask? For her sake, I needed to let it go and stop dwelling on things I couldn't change.

Although we could only be together at school, it was better than nothing. I dreaded summer coming, thinking I wouldn't be able to see her at all, but she came up with a grand idea.

"Kiah, Mr. Hogan, who owns the drugstore, goes to our

church. I'll apply for a job as a soda jerk, and maybe you can stop in and see me there."

"That's a swell idea. The men at the stockyard eat there often. They say they can buy a hot dog for a dime and a coke for a nickel. You get that job, and I'll eat there every day this summer."

She laughed. "I have a feeling you'll be tired of hot dogs by fall."

When Mr. Thatcher called me up to his desk and said, "Kiah, scholarships are available for bright students who can't afford college, and I've never had a student more deserving than you," I thought my heart would leap out of my body. He said, "I've sent in applications to both state schools. I'm sure you'll be accepted and will have the option of choosing your preference."

I wanted to run home and tell Mama the good news, but what if he was wrong, and I didn't get accepted? I decided to wait and surprise her after I received confirmation.

On April 1, we were standing outside the school building when I asked Zann if she applied for the job at the drug store. If it hadn't been April Fool's Day, I might have taken her response seriously. But I assumed she was jesting when she said, "Kiah, I won't be in Pivan Falls this summer. I'm going to Louisiana. I'll be spending the summer there until school resumes."

I laughed. "Oh, you are, are you? Well, have fun. I'm taking a European Cruise."

She didn't crack a smile. "I'm serious . . . I have an aunt who lives there. I'll be staying in New Orleans until fall."

This was no longer funny. My jaw tightened. "So you have an aunt in New Orleans. Why do you have to spend the entire summer with her?" I suppose I growled, though I didn't intend to sound so gruff.

Tears streamed down her rosy cheeks.

I bristled. "Your daddy's idea, I presume."

She nodded. "Don't be mad, Kiah. I can't stand for you to be angry with me."

I pulled out a handkerchief and wiped her face. "I'm not angry with you, Zann. I'm angry with the situation. I'll miss you something awful."

Her lip trembled.

I tried to sound upbeat to lift her spirits. "Maybe it's for the best, sweetheart. If you were here, I'd want to be with you every minute of the day. With you away, I'll work all the hours I can get at the yard this summer. Next year we'll apply at the same college. Mr. Thatcher's confidant I'll be offered scholarships to both state colleges, so I'll let you pick the one we should attend. I want to be where you are."

The bell rang and we walked back into the little school house. It was going to be a long summer.

Chapter 10

School let out for the summer on May 3rd. My stomach tied in knots, knowing it would be the last time I saw Zann for three-and-a-half long months.

I wanted to plead with her not to go, but I knew it wasn't her idea to leave. What right did I have to cause her more grief?

I took the long way home, by way of the bridge. I'd miss her - terribly but she'd be returning in the fall and she was worth waiting for. I leaned against the rickety wood railing and looked down below, where Zann and I had shared our innermost thoughts. I'd told her things no one else in the world knew about me. I chuckled aloud as I recalled the first day we met here and the funny way she yanked off her shoes and tied her skirt between her legs. I relived our first kiss. My heart ached. I missed her already and she hadn't yet left town.

I never fathomed that love could be so grand. I pictured her wearing the blue calico dress—my favorite. Her hair down, blowing in the breeze. My lips parted in a wide grin, as I envisioned her smiling back at me with eyes sparkling like jewels. I'd hold the image in my mind until she returned to me. Though I'd miss her terribly, three-and-a-half months wasn't so long, when compared to a lifetime. That's how long we'd have together. I wanted to grow old with Zann Pruitt. I would, too. As soon as I finished college and got a job, I'd put a ring on her finger.

The world had never looked as beautiful. I couldn't remember the sky ever being so blue, or the water so sparkling clear. The plum trees were budding and the grass was green velvet. Gray Spanish moss hung gracefully from the large live oak trees. The fresh, invigorating scent of evergreen needles filled the warm air. All was quiet except for the bubbling sound of water, rippling over rocks. I looked up on the rise and imagined a beautiful house with tall columns. Our house. Mine and Zann's. We could sit on our veranda and look down at the spot where we first fell in love.

I couldn't fathom what Zann Pruitt saw in me, but I reckoned I was about the luckiest man alive. I'd spend a lifetime with one goal and one only. My life's ambition was to make her happy. I'd work hard and care for her the way she deserved to be cared for. Our children would never wear rags from a rummage sale. No siree. We'd buy them new outfits every fall, and they'd be the best dressed kids at school. And the smartest. At night, we'd gather the children at the kitchen table and help them with their homework. They'd be top in their class. Zann would teach our little girls how to dress and act like ladies and I'd practice being a gentleman so I could properly train up our boys. I'd want them to have a good role model. And no one—no one would ever call one of my kids a little buzzard. If I could prevent it, they'd never know the meaning of such a ghastly word. My pulse raced as I recalled my own childhood, but I quickly erased it from my mind. From now on, life would be different.

I'd need to start going to church after we married, for Zann's sake—her father being a preacher. The idea didn't trouble me so much, anymore. I'm not saying I was ready to be dunked in the creek, but lately, I'd been slipping around, reading Mama's Bible and pondering. I made sure Mama didn't catch me. She'd jump to conclusions and I didn't want to disappoint her. There were questions I needed to settle in my mind, but the last thing I wanted was for Mama to get all excited, thinking I'd done gone and got religion. I was curious. Not stupid. I hadn't forgotten that I didn't have reservations on the big fine Fellowship.

I marked the long days off on the calendar above my bed. Dabney and Mama had become close friends. No, it was more than a friendship. Mama looked toward Dabney as the daughter she never had and it appeared Mama was the mother Dabney had always wanted. I no longer worried about what ignorant people thought about her. She was a sweet girl. Maybe she'd made a few bad decisions in the past, but who hasn't? Since getting to know her better, I learned Dabney followed in her mother's footsteps out of desperation, making money the only way she knew how.

One Sunday night as we sat on her front stoop and she commenced to tell me about the parson's sermon, I asked why she wanted to waste her time going to church. Surely, she'd heard what people said about her.

"Kiah, Parson Pruitt is about the kindest man I've ever met. I was sitting outside on the doorsteps one day, when he drove up, got out of his car, walked over and knelt right there at my feet, like he thought I was a Princess, ya know? Just between me and you, though, it did kinda scare me, him being a preacher. Then, he reached up and took my hand in his and said he wanted me to know that God loved me and that he loved me too. And I knew he meant it, Kiah. Don't ask me how I knew, but I did."

Jeepers, how dense could she be? How many times had she heard that old line before? I raised my brow when she commenced to tell me about the parson's visit. No doubt, he wasn't worried about being seen, for who'd accuse him of being there for any other reason than to see a sinner saved? Not those brain-washed holy-rollers, that's for sure. Folks have a tendency to forget that preachers are mortals walking around on two legs like the rest of us, and not angels with wings tucked neatly beneath their frocks.

"Dabney, I just don't want you to be suckered into listening to the lies of any man, even if he does have the title Parson in front of his name. A man is a man is a man. Remember that."

She stood and stretched. "My foot's gone to sleep."

Was she even listening to what I said?

She held her foot up and wiggled it in the air. With a full moon outlining her silhouette, the thin cotton dress failed to hide the beauty of the feminine curves to which it clung. When it appeared she'd caught me staring, a strange sensation I attributed to a blush crept from my neck all the way to the top of my head.

Suddenly, I felt the need to reemphasize. "Yep, Dabney, you just remember what I'm telling you. Any man will say whatever it takes, and you're plain stupid if you haven't learned that lesson already."

She plopped her hands on her hips and spoke rapidly, her chastising words firing out like hot lead from a Gatlin gun. "So Kiah Grave, you're telling me you're all alike? That you don't care a hoot about me? That you're only pretending to be my friend so you can get a cut-rate on what I have to offer? Well, why didn't you come out and say so, sooner, instead of tip-toeing around the subject."

I looked twice, after imagining smoke billowing from her flared nostrils. I stammered. "Don't be silly. You know I don't think of you in that way. I like you, Dabney, and if I had a sister, I'd give her the same advice I'm giving you."

"Parson Pruitt ain't like all the others. He looks at me with gentle eyes." She glared at me and threw up her hands. "It's no use trying to explain to you. I can see your mind is made up about him."

162

"Dabney, I don't know why you feel the need to take up for him. I'm not saying he's any worse than any other man in town. I'm just saying he's not any better, either."

"Kiah, you're wrong. He's different. No other man has ever stopped to talk to me whenever I'm sitting out in broad daylight. I was on the doorsteps around noon, and he stopped his car right in front of the shanty. And another thing—no other man has ever brought his wife when they paid me a visit."

Was she serious? "You mean . . . you're saying Mrs. Pruitt came with him?"

"She did and they treated me like I was somebody. Not Rooster Run trash." Her mouth flew open. "Oh! I'm sorry, Kiah. I didn't mean to suggest everyone living here is trash, but—"

She didn't need to explain. I was privy to what folks in town called those of us who lived in the camp and at the moment it was at the end of my worry list. If she'd bothered in the beginning to mention the parson's wife was with him, my mind wouldn't have tumbled down such a dark path. I'd hurt her feelings and it wasn't my intent. Still, I was curious. Attempting to sound less accusing, I said, "I suppose they came to welcome you into their fellowship?" Even though in my heart I knew the real purpose of their visit, I was simply curious to know how the subject was approached.

"No, I'd never been inside a church—theirs or any other—not even when Mama died. The undertaker laid her out in the back of the Hardware, and from there she was transported to Potters Field."

"That's tough kiddo." I suppose I should've backed off, seeing the hurt in her eyes as she spoke of her mama, but we could talk about that later. "So what *was* the purpose of the Pruitts' visit?" Naturally, I knew the answer, already. For her own good, she needed to acknowledge the truth. They'd gone for the supreme purpose of familiarizing Dabney with the highly regarded Fellowship Handbook, which states that without exception, only purebreds are allowed to board the Gloryland vessel. What puzzled me was the fact that she'd been attending church lately on a regular basis. Was she so dense she didn't get their message?

She sighed. "Kiah, you know how folks like to talk." She wrung her hands and paused.

I shrugged. "Yeah, Dabney. I know."

"Well, the parson, he got wind of my reputation."

"Oh?" I feigned surprise.

"I reckon you might say Parson Pruitt and Mrs. Pruitt came to teach me right from wrong. Maybe they felt I didn't know no better than to let the men have their way with me in exchange for a little pocket money or a dozen eggs or a chicken. But I knew better. I can't explain how I knew it was wrong, but I knew. I knew it before I was knee-high to a grasshopper. Mama would lock herself up in the house with some strange codger and tell me to play outside on the porch 'til she called me. When I turned thirteen, she started locking me up inside, while *she* sat on the porch. I always said when I got grown, I'd never let a man near me

164

again. But if you get hungry enough, you'll do things you never imagined you'd do."

When I saw her eyes glistening, I wanted to wrap my arms around her and tell her I was sorry she'd endured such a hard life. But I didn't. I just listened. Naturally, she wanted to believe the Pruitts had her best interests at heart. However, all I could think about was the day Mama and I had the unforgettable visit from the religious do-gooders who threw us out of their "Fellowship," without so much as a raft to keep us afloat.

Without opening my mouth, I spoke through clinched teeth. "So I suppose after Parson Pruitt took you by the hand, he tactfully explained the reason for his visit."

"Yes, he did. They were worried about me. I understood what they were saying, but I told them I had to eat and no one in town would hire me."

I smirked. "Oh, I'm sure he put on a most sympathetic face, moments before suggesting you find somewhere else to go on Sundays other than to his church."

"Somewhere else? Why would he say that?"

Was she serious? Seeing the surprise on her face, I decided she really didn't know what I was talking about. I couldn't make sense of it all. Curious, I wanted to hear the rest of her story and I told her so.

Dabney looked right pretty when she smiled. In fact, I reckon she was down-right beautiful, in her own backwoodsy sort of way.

The corner of her mouth lifted in a soft smile and her moistened eyes glistened. She said, "I won't never forget how Mrs. Pruitt put her arms around me. Shucks, no need to confess something you already know, but Kiah I've had a lot of arms around me before. But none ever made me feel the way Zann's mother made me feel. Like a human being and not a play toy to be thrown out the back door after it was no more good. I don't 'spect you to know what I'm talking about, though."

I nodded. "Yes, I do, Dabney. I understand more than you realize." I understood because that's exactly how I believed my daddy had treated Mama . . . like a toy he'd outgrown. I waited for Dabney to tell me if the good parson had a solution for her dilemma.

Her face lit up, as if she were reliving a special moment in her life. "As soon as I told the preacher I didn't like what I was doing, but I had no other way of making a dollar, he took Mrs. Pruitt by the hand and said, 'Dear, didn't you say you could use help around the house?'"

I swallowed the hot anger rising inside me, knowing I'd never get the whole story if I didn't hold my tongue. "Well, now that was mighty considerate of the parson. So what did his wife think of the idea?"

Dabney's brow furrowed. "I know what you're thinking Kiah Grave. It wasn't like that at all. These are good folks. I love the parson, and I believe he loves me . . . but not in a bad way. Not the way you're thinking."

I was embarrassed that I'd not been as subtle as I'd hoped. "Sorry. It wasn't meant as a reflection on you, Dabney. I won't deny, though, the notion did cross my mind that the parson might've wanted to hire you for a purpose other than to clean his house."

She shrugged. "I'm not offended, Kiah. I understand why you'd wonder, knowing my past, but honest, he ain't never been nothing but a gentleman around me. He treats me the way I'd think a daddy would, if I had one. And Mrs. Pruitt is the sweetest woman alive . . . well her and your mama, of course. I love your mama to death."

Dabney managed to convince me all church folks weren't like the ones I'd had the experience of knowing, and in time, I stopped being suspicious of the parson, even though he drove her home every evening. Alone.

But just as I began to trust him, something happened to make me feel I'd been right about the man all along.

Chapter 11

Dabney didn't have fine clothes, but what she had fit her nicely. Almost too nicely. She had three dresses. She had a red one with ruffles, which left little to the imagination when she leaned over. My favorite was a yellow polka dot blouse with a matching tight skirt, even though it hiked up above her thigh when she tried to sit down. And then there was the green striped dress she wore to church every Sunday. I was positive if she sneezed while wearing the green one, she'd pop every button down the front.

So when she stopped wearing those dresses, I assumed she was trying to dress less provocatively out of respect for her employers, the Pruitts. Personally, I didn't like the new look. She looked drab and sloppy with clothes three or four sizes too big for her. I didn't want to hurt her feelings, so I tried to be subtle. "You don't ever wear your polka dot blouse and skirt. Why not?"

She dropped her head. "It doesn't fit me, anymore. I bought me two skirts and a couple of shirts at the rummage sale a few weeks ago."

I tried to dismiss my suspicions, but soon it was impossible to deny, when her stomach protruded from underneath the oversized men's shirts she wore. I felt sick inside.

Knowing her past, I figured there was no need in asking who the father was. Whoever he was, he needed to be hung. But what if—

I tried to dismiss the crazy notion that I could've been right about the parson. But the nagging, unanswered questions pestered me. Dabney had worked for the Pruitt's since Thanksgiving. She'd led me to believe she gave up her former life whenever she went to work for them, and I had no reason to doubt her. Why would she lie to me? My imagination went wild. Was this why Zann was sent away? Had Mrs. Pruitt discovered her husband's infidelity and sent Zann away to keep her from hearing nasty rumors? Zann liked Dabney and the feeling was mutual. They were near the same age and talked about a lot of things. Zann had told me of their conversations. Was the parson afraid for Zann to stick around town? Afraid Dabney might let the bee out of the bucket?

I grew sick every time I looked at Dabney's protruding abdomen. I understood firsthand the kind of life this baby was in for. If I hadn't been so in love with Zann Pruitt, I would've married Dabney myself. I wasn't in love with her, yet I couldn't stomach the idea of another little boy being subjected to the kind of life I'd had. Funny, how I assumed the life growing inside her to be a boy.

I couldn't sleep nights for worrying about her. She'd made a horrific mistake and now she'd have to live with it. The child wasn't responsible, and yet he'd have to pay. Perhaps of the three involved, he'd pay the most. I recalled with a bitter heart, all the years I yearned for just one little store-bought toy at Christmas, and the nights I went to bed so hungry I cried myself to sleep. But even so, I was lucky in a way, because I was born smart. I had that going for me. I'd always held to the notion that if I could survive childhood, when I grew up I'd be able to rise above my circumstances. But what about this little fellow who had not yet been introduced to the world? What if he was like his mother? Dabney was a sweet girl with a lot of wonderful traits. She was prettier than most, no doubt about it. But in spite of her outstanding qualities, no one would ever pick her for the brightest rose on the bush. She said she dropped out of school in the sixth grade, and I could believe she wasn't at the head of the class when she made the decision. How would she be able to take care of a baby by herself? I told myself it wasn't my concern. Still, I worried.

I continued to mark off the days, waiting for Zann to return. School was scheduled to start September 24th. When we lived in Oklahoma, classes began the first Monday after Labor Day, but school always started later in Mississippi. Farmers were busy getting the cotton ginned and needed their children to help pick.

Zann had promised to write, and in the beginning she did. But her letters became shorter and then fewer. I had a bad habit of jumping to conclusions and I tried to shove plaguing thoughts to the back of my mind. Still, I wondered. Had she found someone new? Maybe she only fell in love with me because her choices were limited in Pivan Falls. There'd be lots of fellows to choose from in the big city. And it didn't matter how many girls were there, none could compare with Zann Pruitt. She'd be swamped with admirers. I consoled myself with the belief that even if she found someone in New Orleans to turn her head, she'd have to come home and then I'd do my dead-level best to make her forget him. I'd been so sure when she left that she really loved me, yet time and distance was messing with my mind. Sometimes the fears were so troubling, I wanted to hitchhike to New Orleans and have her reassure me of her love.

Would Zann be devastated if she came home and heard nasty rumors about her father and Dabney Foxworthy? I'm not saying I'd heard any such rumors, but it wouldn't take long for tongues to start wagging. Poor Mrs. Pruitt. I'd only met her once, briefly, although Dabney spoke highly of the woman and she appeared nice enough to me. Too nice to be married to a rotten, two-timing hypocrite.

But could I really justify excusing Dabney's part in this lurid affair? The parson wasn't the only guilty party although he was the only hypocrite and if there's one thing I can't abide, it's a low-down hypocrite. Dabney never pretended to be anything other than

171

what she was. Still, I couldn't understand how she could betray Mrs. Pruitt, who according to Dabney's own admission, had always treated her with utmost kindness. How could Dabney betray her? Didn't she care that if the truth came out, she'd be responsible for breaking up the woman's marriage? Who would take care of Mrs. Pruitt and Zann if it came to a divorce?

Here I was, practically sending the Pruitts to see a divorce lawyer and I had no proof Dabney's child was the parson's offspring.

I worried about Dabney. Her baby was due in a couple of months and she was working too hard for a woman in her condition. Not only did she continue to work full-time for the Pruitts, she hired on as a picker at the Elmore Farms. Mr. Elmore was a truck farmer, and hired folks to pick vegetables in the summer. Several residents from Rooster Run worked for him every year. They went to the fields at five o'clock in the morning and picked for about three hours. Then they went back at five in the evenings and picked another couple of hours. I didn't get off work at the stockyard in time to pick in the evenings and Mr. Elmore wanted workers who could work both shifts. But Mama hired on, and she affirmed my fears that Dabney was working too hard.

But now there were two of them I worried about. Mama's health seemed to improve in the spring, and I told myself all she needed was a little sunshine. But lately, she'd started going down again. She tried to relieve my mind by telling me she'd never felt better in her life, although I found it hard to believe.

Dabney proved my fears to be unfounded. She could out pick anyone in the fields, work all day at the Pruitts, and still have more energy at the end of the day than I started out with. I was glad her pregnancy was going smoothly. Mama's health continued to decline, though she tried to pretend all was well. She now walked with an unsteady gait, and I wasn't the only one who noticed. Dabney confided she'd been worried about Mama for several weeks. Said Mama passed out in the field on two separate occasions. Naturally, Mama failed to share the information with me. I begged her not to go back to the fields, but it was like trying to convince a rooster not to crow.

As much as I complained about Dabney working in her condition, I can't deny I was glad she was there for Mama.

Saturday, September 17th is a day I'll never forget as long as I live. I'd hauled a load of cattle to Biloxi and didn't get back into Pivan Falls until almost nine o'clock. I ate a bite of supper and went straight to bed.

I woke up in the middle of the night and heard a car pull up next door. I almost threw up when I looked out and saw Parson Pruitt's car in front of #3 at ten o'clock. My window was open and Dabney came running out the door.

I heard him say, "I feel like we're sneaking around. I'm not sure this is a good idea, Dabney."

"It's the only way. It'll all work out. You'll see," she said.

I'm not proud to admit it, but I think I hated her at that moment. And I know I hated him. How could they? Had he no shame?

Sunday morning, Mama was frying bacon whenever I crawled out of bed. I grabbed my jacket and headed toward the door. Mama's eyes widened.

"Kiah? Ain't you gonna eat? Breakfast will be on the table in less than five minutes."

"I'm not hungry, Mama." I growled.

She scooped up the bacon and laid it on a clean rag to soak up the grease. "Are you sick, shug?"

"Yeah. Sick of being stupid."

"Land sakes, what kinda stinking thinking is that? Didja get up on the wrong side of the bed this morning?"

I huffed. "No. Someone else crawled in on the wrong side last night."

Mama rolled her eyes and let out a little chuckle. "You ain't making a lick of sense. What you talking about?"

"Nothing Mama. Forget it."

I walked over to #3 and knocked. I figured she was still sleeping, after such a late night rendezvous. Well, she could get up. With both fists, I pounded on the door as hard as I could.

Mama heard the racket and opened our front door. "What's wrong, Kiah? Is Dabney not home?"

I walked back toward the house. "I don't reckon she is, Mama." I didn't have the courage to tell her what I saw and heard the night before.

Mama's eyes lit up. "Oh, my! You reckon she's done gone off to have the baby?"

I shrugged. "I doubt it. Where would she go?" I think deep down I wanted Mama to know the truth. I didn't want Dabney to get away with her little charade, and yet I didn't want to be the one to tell Mama, knowing how it would break her heart.

Mama dried her hands on her apron. "Dabney told me she talked to a midwife in town who don't charge but two-dollars to deliver. I told her when it got time that you'd hitch up Dolly and take her to the midwife's."

Mama's brow furrowed and she clicked her tongue. I couldn't tell if she was disappointed or just aggravated Dabney didn't come to her for help.

"I declare, she hates to put anybody out. I s'pose she didn't want to wake us in the middle of the night. Well, I hope the little thing gets along okay. I wish I'd known. I woulda gone with her. Law, I hate she had to walk. Her in her condition."

I smirked. "Oh, no need to worry your head over Dabney Foxworthy. She's a big girl, Mama, and I got a feeling she was well taken care of last night."

Mama's always been slow to catch on to sarcasm. "I'm sure you're right, son. She'll get along fine. Midwives know what they're doing. It's just she ain't got nobody and I sorta feel responsible for her."

The knot in my stomach tightened. "Oh, I wouldn't say that, Mama. She got pregnant, didn't she? Doesn't that give you a clue she has *somebody*?"

"Well, she's never let on about the baby's father, and it ain't my place to snoop. What I'm sayin' is she's got nobody to look after her besides us. And the Pruitts, of course. They've been mighty good to her . . . treat her just like one of their own, she says. But still, bless her heart, it ain't the same as having blood kin with you when you're having a baby. That's all I was talking about."

"She'll manage. You did, and you didn't have anyone to care about you." I bit my tongue the minute the words came from my lips.

Mama's eyes glistened. "I reckon that's what's been weighing heavy on my mind. I know how it feels. If only I'd asked the whereabouts of the midwife, I'd get you to drive me there. But I ain't got no inklin' where to find her."

I bit my lip to keep from blurting what I'd witnessed the night before. I would have too, if I hadn't been afraid of breaking her heart. She loved Dabney. And she loved the parson and Mrs. Pruitt. The bitter truth would crush her. Not that she'd set herself up as judge. My mama never judged anyone, but she hadn't made many friends in Pivan Falls and Dabney was special to her. She'd find out sooner or later, but I wouldn't be the one to deliver the dreadful news.

I cringed whenever she said, "Kiah, get the wagon. I think I'll go to church. Maybe the parson knows where the midwife lives. If Dabney's delivered, we might need to bring her back home."

I drove Mama to church, parked in the pecan orchard and told her I'd wait for her in the wagon. I'll admit I always felt a little guilty sitting outside when it would've meant so much to Mama for me to go inside and sit on the pew with her. But when I saw Dead-eye Dan and his ol' lady walking up the church steps, I felt justified. Dead-eye was the biggest moonshiner in all of Mississippi. According to rumors, he lost his eye from buckshot when the revenuers shot at him back in the early twenties. I figured if they really wanted to shut him down, they could have. It was no secret where the still was set up. Hypocrites. They were all a bunch of hypocrites, though they'd tell you in a flash they were bound for Gloryland. If they couldn't fool me, how in the name of Dixie did they think they could fool God?

When it was about time for church to be over, I heard the organ playing. I leaned forward and tried to listen to the words they were singing. I soon caught on they were singing the same tune over and over. The words rang out, "*Just as I am . . . I come to Thee. Oh, Lord, God I come.*" I rolled my eyes and smirked. If God accepted that bunch of hypocrites into his heaven—just as they were—I surmised I'd get the red carpet rolled out for me. I wasn't half as bad as a few of the folks I saw darken those doors. Mama excluded, of course.

I saw Mama walking out the door. When she waved, I ducked my head, pretending not to see. She walked across the road and I jumped out and helped her up. "How was church, Mama?" I always asked. Not that I cared, but she was going to tell me, anyway, so I might as well make her happy and appear interested.

"The services were good, honey, but Parson Pruitt wasn't there today. Brother Granger brought the message."

I could see the handwriting on the wall, as Mama used to say. My jaw tightened. The parson and Dabney had run off together. I felt sorry for poor Mrs. Pruitt and Zann. They deserved better. I got hot under the collar knowing the parson had kept such a tight rein on his daughter, and yet he was out carousing around himself.

I didn't care what happened to him or Dabney, though I couldn't help being relieved Dabney's baby would have what every child deserves to be given when brought into the world. He'd have his father's name—his last name. Something I always wanted. If there was anything good coming from this mess that had to be it.

I reckon Mama sensed there was something bothering me because she said, "Kiah, what's wrong?"

"Wrong? Nothing's wrong, Mama."

"You've been quiet all the way home. You haven't even asked

why the parson didn't preach."

Obviously, Mama didn't know the truth, or she wouldn't be grinning like a cat eyeing a milk bucket. But I knew why he didn't show up for church. He'd skipped town with Dabney and it'd only be a matter of time before the whole town would know his dirty little secret. It stood to reason if the church ever learned the parson was the one who impregnated Dabney Foxworthy, he'd have to find another way to make a living, and I couldn't picture him behind a mule.

Mama reached over and rubbed my back with her palm as I popped the reins. "He and Mrs. Pruitt have gone to New Orleans to get their daughter. I 'speck they've missed her something awful. I figured you'd be glad to hear she's coming home."

My thoughts were as scrambled as if they'd been sent through a hay press. If the parson was with Mrs. Pruitt, then what did he do with Dabney? My stomach turned. What if she were lying out in the woods somewhere, with her throat slit? The last person she was seen with was the parson. Had he found a way out of his predicament?

Mama said, "Well, sugar, you don't look very excited. Ain't you still kinda sweet on the Pruitt girl?"

As much as I missed Zann, how could I get excited? I couldn't imagine what the news would do to her.

Mama was full of chatter as we sat down to eat lunch. I was glad she felt better, although a little peace and quiet would've been welcomed. At first, I faked interest, but at the mention of Dabney's name, she had my full attention.

My shoulders fell. "What? What did you say about Dabney?"

"I said I was disappointed I didn't bother to find out where the midwife lives. I'm sure she's had her young'un by now. I 'spect she's boarded up with the midwife, 'til she gets back on her feet. Doctors, nowadays don't cotton to a woman getting out of bed for a full nine days after birthing a baby." Mama sighed. "I woulda been more'n happy to take care of her."

"Shucks, Mama, she's full-grown. Stop worrying. I'll bet you didn't stay in bed nine days after I was born."

She chuckled. "Goodness, no. I had you under a chinaberry tree while working on a tobacco farm in Meigs, Georgia. It was a good thing some of the women there had birthed babies before, because I ain't ashamed to tell you, I was a scared little young'un."

"Georgia? I always thought I was born in Oklahoma."

Mama shook her head. "No, when Papa kicked me out, Mama slipped me enough money to buy a bus ticket to Georgia. She wrote her sister, and asked if she'd take me in. Aunt Maude said she couldn't, me being pregnant and not married, but she did help me get the job on the tobacco farm. She just didn't let nobody know I was kin." Mama smiled, as if the memory was a pleasant one. I can't always understand Mama. With a little chuckle, she said, "You were born on Friday and I was back under the shed tying up tobacco leaves the following Monday, while you lay on a blanket under the same tree you was born under. But I can tell you, I don't recommend it. I hope Dabney can take better care of herself."

I swallowed hard. I hoped so too. For as long as I could remember, Mama had been sickly. There never seemed to be one particular thing wrong with her, but as soon as she overed one ailment, another seemed to latch on. I reckoned it all began the day she gave birth to me.

Mama reached over and poured me another glass of sweet iced tea. She was proud of the small ice box I'd managed to buy for her with the money I made trucking. One would've guessed I'd given her one of those General Electric monitor type refrigerators, the way she carried on. But my motive wasn't entirely pure. Nothing tasted better than a big glass of sweet iced tea on a hot day. The ice truck didn't come to Rooster Run, so I met him at Goodson's Grocery every Saturday to buy a block of ice.

Mama sat back down, and picked up the conversation where she left off. "It's a good thing Dabney landed a job with the Pruitts. There ain't many places what would allow her to sit out for nine days."

After lunch, I sat near the window and read. When the sun went down, Mama lit a lamp and said, "Kiah, that must be a mighty interesting story you're reading. You haven't budged since you sat down."

Maybe it was. I couldn't say. I couldn't concentrate. I'd been watching Dabney's door, through the window. Where was she? How long should I wait before notifying the sheriff? I wasn't even sure we had a sheriff in Pivan Falls. Maybe I'd have to go all the way into Pascagoula to report what I'd witnessed.

Chapter 12

Sunday night I lay in bed and worried. If Dabney was dead, I'd have to testify. But what would my words do to Zann? Would she blame me for coming forward with the truth? All summer I'd longed for the day she'd return. Now, for her sake, I dreaded it. If only I could take her away and help her to escape the gossip which was bound to follow.

Afar off, the lonely sound of a whippoorwill chanted, "whip-o-will, whip-o-will." Exactly when the little bird's message changed, I can't say, but as I listened, the monotonous chant seemed to switch to, "if-u-will, if-u-will."

"Marry me, Zann," I whispered in the darkness. "Marry me, if you will. If you will." I smiled, hearing the whippoorwills echo my sentiments . . . "If you will, if you will."

Every Monday morning my job was to get up at five-o'clock and build a fire under the iron washpot so the water would be hot enough for Mama to wash by the time folks dropped off their dirty clothes. She washed for three families. Three big families. She washed all day on Mondays, and ironed on Tuesdays, charging a dollar per family to wash and a dollar to iron.

She garnered only six dollars a week for a hot, back-breaking job. Lately, the loads had become much larger, though the pay remained the same. I suspected her clients included clothes belonging to folks outside their immediate family. I tried to get Mama to put a limit on the number of garments, but she was afraid of losing their business.

Now that I'd begun to make a little money working at the stockyard, I begged her to give up her job as a washwoman. I could see the toll it was taking on her. I worried. Mama hadn't been well for a long time and lately she'd been having some fainting spells, which I attributed to fatigue. But if my mama had a fault, it was her stubbornness.

After breakfast, I grabbed my cap from off the nail by the door. "The water should be hot by now, Mama."

"You going somewhere, son?"

"Yes'm. Mr. Farris wants me to deliver a load of cattle to the Marler Farms in Alabama, over near Mobile. It'll be late when I come home, so don't wait supper for me. I'll pick up a can of Vienna sausages and crackers on the road."

I didn't like to leave Mama alone at night, but the money I made hauling made her life easier, for sure. We didn't have much, but at least I'd been able to help put food on the table.

Sitting behind the wheel of the truck gave me plenty of time to ponder. I tried not to dwell on things I couldn't change, but I didn't seem to have much control over my thoughts. All my life I wanted to get a good education and be able to give Mama the things she'd never had. The first thing I'd buy her would be one of those new-fangled ringer washing machines like I saw in a wash house in Mobile. But what if she were to die before I could get a college degree? The 'what ifs' and those worrisome 'buts' were driving me crazy.

It must have been after nine o'clock when I returned and parked the truck at the stockyard. I walked home. I could see the oil lamp burning through the window, and Mama waiting up for me. There was no light coming from #3. A lump formed in my throat. Dabney never went to bed early. She wasn't there. I wanted to believe Mama was right and Dabney was recuperating at the home of the midwife, but wishing it to be true wouldn't make it so. I blew out a heavy breath. Dabney was dead. I knew it as sure as I knew my name was William Hezekiah Grave.

Mama was sitting in her rocker in her gown. "Kiah, we have plenty of ice left. Can I pour you a glass of tea? Have you had anything to eat, sugar?"

"No thanks, Mama. I ate a can of Vienna sausages and a pack of crackers in Mobile, and then I stopped on the way home and bought me a cold drink. I'm not hungry. You shouldn't have waited up for me. I told you I'd be late."

"Sugar, don't you know it don't do me no good to go to bed while you're out on the road? I worry about you."

I rolled my eyes. "Mama, I'm not a little boy. I'm a man. Seventeen. I wish you wouldn't fuss over me." I cringed. I'd done it again. Me and my big mouth. I could see the tears welling in her eyes.

I put my arms around her. "I'm sorry. I didn't mean to snap at you. It's been a long day. You have every right to worry. You paid a big price for me, and I'd be upset if you weren't concerned. Forgive me?"

She smiled through the tears. "There's nothing to forgive, honey. It's true I worry about you, but I had a special reason for waiting up tonight."

I pulled off my sweaty shirt and walked over to the sink. I pumped water into a dishpan and reached in the window for a bar of lye soap. I lathered my upper body and said, "Well . . . what was it, Mama? The special reason?"

"I figured you'd want to know the little Pruitt girl is home. They got back this afternoon."

I tried to swallow. I felt I couldn't breathe. Leaning over the dishpan, I sloshed water in my face and with a rag, tried to wash off the soap. There were so many questions, yet I didn't know what to ask first.

Mama handed me a towel and a night shirt. I saw her flinch as I grabbed the towel.

She lowered her head. "I'm sorry, Kiah. I know I should've let you get it for yourself." Her lip quivered. "I don't mean to fuss over you, son . . . but if I didn't have you to fuss over, I'd go slam crazy. Without you, I'd have nothing. But I'll try harder from now on. You're right. You're a man, and a fine one, too."

I reached over and planted a kiss on her forehead. "Don't you dare stop fussing over me. Even if I jump up and down, scream and holler and tell you to stop, don't pay me no mind, you hear? Sometimes I get on my high horse and say things I don't mean. You know it's the truth. You're the greatest, Mama."

She grinned. "I declare, Kiah, you are so much like—"

I playfully popped her with the towel. "Whoa! Don't say it, Mama. Don't say it." I tried to hold my smile, but the idea of me being like my daddy made it most difficult to keep a pleasant expression.

Now that the news had sunk in and I could breathe without panting, I asked, "How do you know Zann's back?"

"Dabney told me."

My knees turned to jelly. I pulled out a chair and sat down. "It sounded like you said Dabney told you."

"Yeah. I did." She reached down and picked up the shirt, which I'd thrown on the floor. Sometimes my mama could talk the ears off a mule, and now when I wanted her to explain, it was like trying to pull hens' teeth.

I sucked in a deep breath. "Are you saying Dabney . . . Dabney was *here*? Here in this house?"

Mama shook her head.

I growled. "Then where was she, Mama?" My mouth felt dry. "Are you sure it was her?"

"Well, for land sakes, Kiah, why would you ask if I'm sure it was her? Of course, it was her."

I threw my head back and moaned. "Mama, just tell me where you saw her."

"I saw her at her place."

I felt my brow lift. "Her place? You mean #3?"

Now, Mama was the one with the furrowed brow. "Honey, are you okay? You're acting very peculiar. Did you stand out in the heat today, unloading them cows? I hear folks can get what they call heat strokes if they get overheated. Older folks can die from it, but if it don't kill you, it can affect you in other ways . . . like talking out of your head."

My blood boiled. I gnawed on my bottom lip and silently recited Little Boy Blue, afraid I'd say something I'd be sorry for. That was a little trick Mama taught me years ago. It worked whenever I'd bother to put it into practice. However, too often I was so angry I spouted off and couldn't remember a single nursery rhyme. As soon as I reached, "He's under the haystack, fast asleep," in a calm, rational-sounding voice, I said, "Mama, I'm not suffering from heat stroke, and I'm not talking crazy. I have a perfectly logical reason for wondering why Dabney would've been at #3 today."

She smiled. "Well, it is where she lives, you know. But I reckon you were surprised she'd be up and around so soon, since I'm the one who told you she'd more'n likely be laid up for days. But she came back to get her things."

I waited. I didn't want to say anything, which could be construed as crazy, but why did Mama get that far and stop? If I wasn't already crazy, she'd drive me there, with all the riddles. I spoke slowly. Deliberately slow. "Why . . . did . . . she . . . need . . . to . . . get . . . her . . . things, Mama? She lives there. Where was she going?"

"Oh." Mama said it like she hadn't realized I might wonder. "She's going over to stay with the Pruitts." Mama let out a big yawn, and walked over to her bed. "Good night, sugar. See you in the morning."

No. She couldn't do this to me. I winced, knowing Mama had no idea the questions whirling inside my head. She stayed up to tell me Zann was back in town. She expected I'd be happy to hear the news. And I would've been, too, if it weren't for the fact I was privy to sordid information to which Mama had no knowledge. I needed to calm down and let her go to bed.

Tired as I was, I was unable to fall asleep. I tossed and turned all night. Mama hadn't mentioned Dabney's baby. Maybe he didn't survive. It was no wonder, the way Dabney worked right up until her time. Poor little creature, I reckoned he was better off, if he didn't make it. There'd been plenty of times in my life I'd wished I'd died before I was born. But my logic didn't keep me from feeling a bit sorrowful for the little fellow.

I wanted to see the light of day so I could grill Mama in a tactful way. I had to keep in mind that regardless of how frustrated the situation made me, it wasn't her fault. I'd remain calm. Couldn't have her thinking I was a candidate for the loony bin.

Tuesday morning I tried to sound chipper when I sat down to the breakfast table. "Yum! These flapjacks look wonderful. How did you know I'd wake up craving flapjacks?"

Mama's smile stretched across her face. "Well, I'm glad. But they seem a little heavy this morning. I don't know why, unless I got a bad batch of flour. At times, I can get a bag of flour that'll make the fluffiest biscuits and the lightest pancakes . . . and then another time I'll bring home a bag that won't produce a decent biscuit. Reckon why that is?"

My resolve to have patience was being tested, as I had absolutely no interest in discussing flour. "I really can't say. Does seem peculiar, though." I feigned a smile. "Pass the syrup, Mama." I poured cane syrup on my pancakes, took a bite, then picked up my napkin and wiped my mouth.

Mama's eyes squinted. "Are they all right? The flapjacks?"

I rolled my eyes and licked my lips to show my approval. "Looks like you got a good bag this time, because these are delicious." Now that I'd taken care of the chit-chat, I worked at turning the conversation around to get her to tell all she'd heard, concerning Dabney and the Pruitts, without it sounding like I was interrogating her.

"Mama, I've been wondering about what you said last night. You know . . . about Dabney going over to stay with the Pruitts. You didn't mention anything about the baby. Did he—"

"You were thinking the sweet little tot didn't make it, weren't you, sugar? I'm sorry. I was dog-tired last night, and it didn't cross my mind you might be wondering. I haven't seen the baby, but when Dabney came back to pick up a few things she said he's a living doll. Says he has a head full of black hair, and he's so alert, he looks like he's a month old. She said the little fellow has the clearest olive skin she's ever seen on a newborn . . . not all wrinkled and red, like lots of babies."

Then Mama changed the subject. "Kiah, you've been so good to me. I hate to ask, but—" She stopped and took a sip of coffee. "Honey, do you think we could afford one of them Singer sewing machines? If you think it's too extravagant, I'll understand. You're better at managing money than I am, but I was thinking if I just had me a machine, I could make you some nice clothes . . . and I'd make me a Sunday dress. I can sew real good, if I do say so myself. My mama taught me how back when I was young. I just ain't never had no machine of my own, although I managed to keep you in hand-made shirts through the years. It'd just be a whole lot easier on me if I had a machine."

I could only remember two store-bought shirts growing up. One was a red flannel and the other was a blue plaid one I bought with my own money. I flinched, imagining Mama with a sewing machine. Did I really want to encourage her raw talent? What if she decided to make me a pair of trousers?

"Of course, if you think it's too extravagant, I'll understand. I just thought—"

"We'll see how much they cost, Mama." It seemed to satisfy her and I was in no mood to talk about flour nor sewing machines, nor anything other than Dabney's baby. Head full of black hair, Mama said. Parson Pruitt had black hair. Zann once told me he was part Indian. I wanted to throw up.

For the next few minutes, the only sounds at the table came from the crunch of bacon rinds and the chink of forks against tin plates. I poured a little hot coffee into my saucer and slurped. "Sorry," I mumbled, knowing how Mama hated it when I did that.

"Mama, what prompted Dabney to want to go stay with the Pruitts, when she has her own place?"

"Oh, didn't I tell you? The Pruitts are adopting her baby, and they want her to be the little tyke's nursemaid. Ain't it wonderful how things work out, sometimes?"

My jaw dropped. "She . . . she gave him away?"

"You mean *her*, honey. Dabney had a little girl."

I ran my fingers through my hair. "But you referred to the baby as he. You said *he* has black hair, *he's* not red, *he* this and *he* that. Did she have twins?"

"Land sakes, no. She never got big enough to have twins. I reckon I have a habit of saying 'he' when it comes to babies. I should've said 'her.'"

My stomach churned. "Well, that takes the cake."

"Whatcha mean, sugar?

"I can't believe she'd give away her own flesh and blood." In my way of thinking, it put Dabney on the same low level as William Lancaster IV. How could a parent walk away from one of their own?

Mama's countenance fell. She reached over and laid her hand on my arm. "Kiah, sometimes it takes more love for a mother to part with her child than it does to keep him . . . or her. There've been times I wondered if I made a mistake by not letting somebody adopt you who could give you more'n I had to give. The way I see it, keeping you was a selfish act. If I'd given you up to some nice family who coulda done for you, you woulda faired better. Oh, but I wanted you so much. I couldn't bear to let you go. So don't feel harshly toward Dabney. I'm sure she did what she deemed best for her little girl. The Pruitts are fine folks and they'll give the baby a good home. It only takes looking at their daughter and seeing how fine she's turned out to know Dabney did the right thing. That baby is going to have a good life."

Mama was right about one thing. Zann Pruitt turned out fine. I'd been bothered by the fact she hadn't written as much as I'd hoped she would, but school would begin soon, and I'd be able to see her every day. I bought a box of chocolate covered cherries for her when I went to Mobile. I wrapped the box in pink paper and tied it up with a green satin ribbon. I was pleased. It looked frilly, like something she'd pick out. I'd saved it to give to her on our first day back at school as a welcome home present.

I waited impatiently for school to begin again, counting the days. But eight days before we were to start back, my world tumbled down like a stack of dominoes.

Mama got up Sunday morning and dressed for church, like she always did. I almost decided to go with her, I was so eager to see Zann. I would have too, except for the fact I didn't think I could stomach sitting on a pew and listening to her father spout off what the good book says with me knowing his evil little secret. I wouldn't want to upchuck in the aisle, which was likely to happen if forced to look at him and listen to his sanctimonious lecture. I put Mama off in front of the church and parked the wagon under a shade tree in the orchard. I hoped to at least get a glimpse of Zann, either going in or coming out of the church.

It was past time for church to begin, and I hadn't seen a single soul come out of the Pruitt's house. Not the parson, nor Mrs. Pruitt . . . and not Zann or Dabney. I wondered why the organ had not begun to play. I swatted gnats, and groaned. Why was it taking so long for church to begin? Were they waiting for the parson? The sooner they started, the sooner I could get back home. The temperature must have reached 100 degrees. Sweat poured from my brow. If Mama hadn't been so frail, I would've driven the wagon back and let her walk home. It wasn't too far to walk, but Mama wasn't feeling herself lately. Why was everything so quiet? It seemed eerie. Though I'd never admit it to anyone, I always enjoyed listening to the singing. My favorite was a tune called "I'll Fly Away." I'd learned that one by heart. Sometimes, waiting for Mama to come out of church, I'd sing with them, but only because there was no one around to hear me.

Finally, the organ begin to play. Not some peppy tune like "*I'll fly away,*" but mournful sounding. Maybe it was a different pianist. Then minutes later, the double doors to the little church opened and I could hear sorrowful moans clear across the road. I watched as men wrapped their arms around their wives in a consoling fashion. What was going on? Why was church letting out early?

Mama trudged slowly toward me, holding a handkerchief to her face. I jumped down and helped her on the wagon. "What's wrong, Mama? What happened? Why is everyone crying?"

I could see she was too distraught to speak.

"Mama, please. Tell me what's wrong."

"Kiah, just take me home, honey, and I'll tell you when we get to the house. I'm too choked up to talk about it right now."

I let her be. The news couldn't be all that bad, but Mama was carrying on as if she'd had a young'un to die. Peculiar how she could be so strong at times and other times she'd fall apart over the least little thing. *The widow Jones.* Sure, that was it. Mama told me earlier in the week the widow had been diagnosed with consumption. No doubt, she'd passed on, which would account for all the tears. The widow was highly regarded in the community. Her late husband served as the preacher until he passed and that's when Parson Pruitt moved to town to take his place.

I assumed church services were called off so the women could go to the widow's home to get her laid out for viewing. Others would need to start preparing the meal for the relatives coming into town, as was the custom in Pivan Falls. Feeling I had my answer, I let it go.

Mama was quiet all the way home, and it suited me fine. I had things on my mind, and didn't feel much like talking.

When we walked in the house, Mama hung her purse on a nail and said, "Maybe you ought to sit down, shug. I have some bad news."

I didn't see a need to sit. Maybe I should've felt more compassionate but I'd only seen the widow Jones on a couple occasions. I expected Mama to grieve. It was in her nature but I never expected the widow's death to hit her so hard.

"Kiah, its just awful, honey. I really wish you'd sit." Her lip quivered. She threw her arms around me and cried on my shoulder.

I patted her back and tried to sound sympathetic. "I know, Mama. I know."

Mama held her head back and with her brow furrowed, she looked into my eyes. "You do?"

"Yes'm. I understand. You thought highly of the widow Jones. I'm sure she'll be missed by the community, but she's gone on to a better place. Right?"

I didn't know how much I really believed about that better place, but I said it, anyway, hoping it'd bring a little comfort to Mama. Knowing she believed all good Christians got to go there when they died, I was stunned when my attempt to bring comfort to her bereaved soul backfired.

Mama's face distorted. She looked at me as if I'd grown a third eye. She shook her head. "No, Kiah. You have it all wrong, son."

I was taken aback. If the widow wasn't going to a better place, I was beginning to feel like the streets of gold weren't going to be too crowded. "What do you mean, Mama?"

The blood drained from Mama's face. "It wasn't the widow who died, Kiah." Then, Mama buried her face in her hands. "Oh, dear Jesus," she wailed. "God bless him. He doesn't know."

Chapter 13

I swallowed. *Dabney*? No wonder Mama was so upset. I fell into the chair and buried my face in my hands. "Oh, Mama," I cried. "No, no, no. She can't be dead. Tell me it isn't true." Bitter tears flowed from my eyes.

Mama leaned over the table and pressed her face against my back. "I wish I could, shug, but I'm afraid she's gone."

"Tell me, Mama. What happened?" Mama reached up and blotted my cheek with a napkin.

Her voice cracked. "Honey, I'll tell you all I know. Deacon Phillips walked up to the pulpit after everyone was seated this morning. He said the sweet little thing died in the middle of the night last night, with the fever. As you can imagine, Parson Pruitt and Mrs. Pruitt are so tore up over her death, they couldn't come to give the news. It's just awful."

I rose to my feet.

"Where you going, Kiah?"

"I need to be alone, Mama."

I hated to leave Mama in the state she was in, but I had to get away to grieve alone. Dabney was the best friend I'd ever had, and yet when she needed me most, she'd not been able to come to me. Maybe she was afraid I'd condemn her for the decision to give up her baby and she would've been right. I would've set myself up as judge and jury. I'd been a lousy friend. Enraged, I wanted to go pound my fist into a wall or kick somebody. Myself, more than anyone else. Who was I to judge her?

Mama said, "I'll have your lunch ready in a little while, Kiah."

"I'm in no hurry, Mama." I walked outside and looked over at #3. I couldn't swallow. Memories flooded my mind. I remembered how beautiful she looked, wearing Mama's old robe, sitting in the fire-light. Poor, sweet Dabney. A special bond had formed between us, but until now, I hadn't realized how much she really meant to me. I longed to be with Zann, to mourn with her. She loved Dabney as much as I did.

I trudged through the back pasture, kicking everything in my path.

I exchanged one emotion for another. Anger boiled up inside me. Why didn't she take better care of herself? I threw my fist in the air and yelled, "Why, Dabney? Why didn't you listen? I told you that you were overdoing and needed to slow down. But no, you wouldn't listen. You pig-headed woman."

I plodded aimlessly through the woods, blaming myself for not preventing such a tragedy. Perhaps if I'd given her the money I spent on the ice box, she could've quit work last month. The guilt gnawed at me like a dog chomping on a hambone.

I recalled how Dabney looked when we were last together. There were no signs. She insisted she felt fine, and she looked healthy enough.

I wanted to blame the baby, but it wasn't fair. Plenty of women had babies and didn't come down with the fever. It wasn't the child's fault, any more than it was my fault for being born. I paused to reflect on my last thought. It was enlightening, since I'd spent years blaming myself for something I had nothing to do with. No. The child was innocent.

Then it occurred to me poor Dabney could've succumbed to a sorrowful heart. Surely, she didn't hand her baby over to Parson Pruitt without regrets. Maybe he forced her to give him the baby.

At dusk, I made my way back to the house. Mama sat in the rocker reading her Bible.

She laid it aside and said, "Kiah, I know how much she meant to you, sugar. I 'spect Mr. Farris will let you take the afternoon off to attend the funeral. Deacon Phillips said it'll be held at the church tomorrow at three o'clock."

Did she honestly think I wanted to sit and listen to a bunch of blubbering females make over Dabney's dead body and act as if they really cared? Didn't none of them care any more about her than they did a mangy ol' yard dog. Mama and Mrs. Pruitt excluded, of course. They loved her, but I wasn't so sure Mrs. Pruitt would have felt the same if she were privy to the information I had concerning the two-timing Casanova she was married to.

Poor Dabney. She never had a chance at happiness. My throat ached. Why? Why didn't I marry her so she could keep her little girl? My heart beat like a jackhammer. Maybe I was the reason she felt pressured to give up her baby. All my whining about the nasty names I was called for not having a daddy. Maybe she didn't want to put her child through the same agony.

I tried to release the guilt by telling myself Dabney wouldn't have married me, even if I'd asked. She understood I was in love with Zann, and that Zann loved me.

But I had a feeling Zann's family had sent her away for a good reason—the reason being to help get her mind off me. Her family would never approve of me, and she'd find herself having to make a choice between us. As much as I loved her, I'd never want to come between Zann and her parents.

Although Dabney hadn't been in love with me, nor I with her, I could now see we could've had a decent life together. She was a good friend and she and Mama got along great together. Wouldn't that have been enough? It was more than a lot of married couples had. I'd think being friends would go a long way in making a marriage work.

I winced. What was I doing? It was too late now to come up with a plan. She needed me six months ago, whenever she began to show.

Mama said. "I've heated up some lunch, shug. You might oughta try to eat a bite."

Mama made liver hash for supper. I didn't feel like putting a single morsel in my mouth, and even if I had, I couldn't have swallowed. I pictured the pious Parson, who'd stand on his soap box next Sunday spouting off religious rhetoric while feeling smug he'd gotten away with his little rendezvous. He was probably glad she died. Now, he wouldn't have to worry about being found out. Maybe he—no, I couldn't go there. Even though he was a scoundrel, surely he couldn't have had anything to do with her death, except in a round-about way. He *was* the one who got her pregnant. And she *did* die from giving birth. But as much as I hated the man, to blame him for her death would be a reach.

If it were not for Zann, I'd expose him in a wink, but to do so would break her heart. And I had to think about Dabney's baby girl. If I exposed him, his wife would leave and take the child with her. Wasn't it better for the baby to have a daddy to provide for her, even if he was a deceitful rascal? As much as I detested my own father, I'd much rather have loathed him inside a nice house with food on the table, than to have loathed him while living in the Poor House with nothing to eat but po' man's gravy.

Monday morning I left for work early. Mr. Farris said one of the drivers was sick and asked if I'd like to make a run to Ocean Springs to haul a load of hogs. I was glad for the chance to get out of town.

It was after eight o'clock by the time I got back home. I walked in the house and threw my cap across the cot. "I'm whooped," I said. "What's to eat?"

Mama said, "I had some hash left over from supper last night. If you don't want it, I'll fry you an egg for a sandwich."

"I'll pass on the hash, but keep your seat, Mama. I'm capable of frying an egg."

Mama rose and whisked her hand. "Oh, no you don't. I'm the cook and don't you forget it. Why don't you stretch out on the bed while I get your sandwich ready?"

"Thanks, I think I will. I'm dead tired. The trip was long, and on the way home, I had a flat. It was good I'd already unloaded the hogs."

Though it wasn't a subject I wished to approach, it was bound to come up eventually and I might as well get it over and done with, "Mama, I'm sorry I wasn't here to drive you to the funeral. I know you wanted to go."

"But I did go, sugar. I walked, but I stopped along the way and rested."

I swallowed the lump in my throat and shut my eyes.

I never even saw the egg sandwich. I guess I went to sleep and didn't wake up until the next morning when the sun came shining through the windows.

Only six more days until school would begin again. I longed to see Zann. I wanted to believe she still loved me, yet hounding doubts rose from the crevices of my mind. Why had she stopped writing?

I reminded myself that I hadn't expected her back home before next Friday, so I tried to pretend she was still in New Orleans. It was the only way I could restrain myself from going to her house and demanding to see her, which I had sense enough to know would be the wrong thing to do. Especially not now. Not when she and her mother were grieving over the loss of a friend, while trying to adjust to a baby in the house. I'd have to wait, and patience was not one of my virtues.

The week drug by. I made my last ex on the calendar above my bed. Tomorrow, we'd be back in school, eating lunch under the big oak. I wanted to believe nothing between us had changed.

Mama got dressed for church, and for once, I was glad to have the chance to drive her there. Maybe I'd get a glimpse of Zann, and maybe—maybe she'd see me, and come over to the wagon. I washed my hair in the sink, and tried to smooth it dry by leaning over the stove. I bought a new pair of dungarees to wear on my first day back at school, but I decided to put them on in case I got to see her.

Mama cried all the way to church. I didn't have to ask what

was wrong. She and Dabney had sat together every Sunday and Mama would miss her. I helped her out of the wagon, then climbed back up and kept my eyes glued on the parsonage. First, Parson Pruitt emerged. Then, five minutes later, Zann's mother came walking out the door. I waited. And waited. But Zann never left the house.

My pulse raced. Something was wrong. Well, I didn't plan to sit there wondering. I waited until I heard the organ, satisfied that the good parson wouldn't be coming back out the church door for at least an hour. I leaped from the wagon, dashed over to the parsonage and beat on the door. I hoped she'd be as eager to see me as I was to see her.

Contrary to what medical science teaches, I learned that day that one can live after the heart stops. I know, because my heart stopped beating when Dabney Foxworthy opened the door to the parsonage, holding a baby.

My mouth flew open.

"Kiah," she said, "What are you doing here?"

My jaw dropped. "Dabney?" I swaggered to the edge of the porch and threw up my breakfast. When I stopped heaving, I turned to see her standing there, as alive as ever.

I murmured, "Fancy meeting you here." My voice was hoarse. "You're white as a . . . yeah, white as a ghost."

"Kiah, we need to talk."

"Yeah, I think you're right. You have a lot of explaining to do." She'd fooled folks into believing a horrible lie, and now I'd caught the whole scheming bunch of them. What a farce. But the bigger question was why? What was the meaning of the charade and how many were involved in pulling it off?

I scratched my head. For a fact, there had been a funeral. Mama went and she came home all torn up inside. Cried for hours. How were the Pruitts able to pull off a fake funeral? And why? Did the casket remain closed so no one would suspect a scam had taken place? Questions whirled in my brain like leaves in a windstorm, but there were no answers. Nothing made sense.

"Kiah, you look awful. Sit in the swing, and I'll go put the baby down and bring a rag to wipe your face." She came walking out minutes later with a wet cloth. When she tried to wipe my face, I slapped at her hand. I didn't want her touching me. All I wanted was an explanation.

When I could speak without yelling, I said, "Dabney, why? Why did you do it?"

Tears flooded her eyes.

"Oh, stop it, Dabney." She'd deceived a lot of people but her tears weren't going to work on me.

"I had to, Kiah. It was for the best." I detected a grave fatalism in her voice. With such acting skills, she could've been on the silver screen. I refused to be swayed by such a little conniver. What a dope I'd been.

I bellowed, "For whose best? His?"

"His?" She raised her brow. "Oh! Haven't you heard? The baby is a little girl."

I nodded. "I know. Mama told me."

"But you said 'his.'"

It was becoming more difficult by the minute to keep my voice down. "You know who I meant. I was referring to the good Parson. I suppose you arranged this little scheme for *him*?"

"Well, I suggested it, but then after mulling it over, his wife came to believe it was a swell idea."

His wife thought it was swell? Were they all nuts? I stood and paced back and forth across the porch. What kind of scam were these people trying to pull? "Dabney, tell me—how did you plan to stay hid?"

"Hid? I don't understand, Kiah."

"Didn't you know people would find out? What kind of saps did you take us for?"

She smiled. I'd never wanted to hit a woman, and I never would—yet I have to admit I wasted no time in shooing that little bird on its way, before it had a chance to make a nest. It frightened me that I could have such thoughts, but how dare she stand there with a grin on her face.

She said, "Kiah, you're getting all steamed up over nothing."

My eyes rolled back in my head. "Nothing?"

"Did you think I was trying to hide from people? How foolish would that be?"

I growled. "Pretty foolish."

"I don't reckon no one was too surprised to learn I was pregnant. So wasn't it logical for them to believe good Christian folks like the Pruitts might be willing to adopt my baby? And wouldn't it seem reasonable I might let them? So why would I want to hide?"

Tired of pacing, I sat down on the edge of the porch. "Dabney, although I couldn't see the logic in it at first, I tried to accept the fact you did what you felt best for the baby. I certainly don't fault you for that. But it's the charade I don't understand. You've deceived everyone who trusted you, including me."

She cried. "Kiah, I didn't want to deceive you. Honest, I didn't. But I promised I wouldn't tell anyone. I did what I believed best for all involved. I'm sorry I let you down. Please, forgive me."

I don't know what made the difference, but the latter tears were more touching than the former. As much as I wanted to punish her for putting me through such guilt and shame, I blamed myself for not being a better friend.

Though Dabney wasn't the smartest girl I'd ever known, I never took her for being an imbecile. What in the name of common sense prompted her to pull such an idiotic stunt? Anger stirred within me. I wasn't ready to let her, nor the good parson get away with fooling everyone into thinking she was dead.

"Kiah, all I'm asking is for you to keep quiet. I should've

known you'd guess, although I don't think anyone else will suspect. I'm not asking for my sake, but I'm begging you to think of Zann."

Her confusing words rolled around in my head like loose marbles. I jumped up at the mention of Zann's name. "Zann?" I screeched. "Where is she?" Having been thrown by the sight of seeing what appeared to be a ghost, I'd completely forgotten the reason I was here. I dashed to the front door and slung it open.

I raced through the parsonage, screaming, "Zann? Zann? Where are you?" I heard the baby crying and saw a bassinet sitting in a back bedroom. Except for the infant, the house appeared to be empty.

I ran back to the porch. Dabney hadn't moved. "Where is she, Dabney? Where's Zann?" I yelled. Horrid thoughts sprouted and took root in my mind. Dabney was crying. I grabbed her by the shoulders and shook her. "Are they hiding her from me? They are, aren't they? You've got to tell me where she is."

Dabney sobbed. I'm not sure if she felt sorry for me or frightened of what I might do in such a state of mind.

"Kiah, you're scaring me. From what you were saying, I thought . . . I thought Fennie told you."

I swallowed hard. "Told me? Told me what?"

"Oh, Kiah. Zann. She's gone."

The cold words dropped like icicles and hung suspended in the air.

I froze. "Gone? What do you mean, gone? Gone where? Back to New Orleans?" I wanted an explanation. Any explanation, other than the one that tried to force its way into my thoughts.

Dabney took me by the hand. "Sit down in the glider, Kiah. We need to talk."

She got that right. We needed to talk, for sure. I buried my face in my hands. "Dabney? What's going on? I feel as if I'm in the middle of a horrible nightmare."

"Kiah, I sat with your Mama at the funeral. She said you were taking it hard, but I had no idea it was this bad. I think you're in denial. I know how much you loved her, Kiah, but you have to accept it. Zann is dead."

The words banged in my head like a loud tune on a player piano. "What are you saying?" I screamed. My breath caught in my throat. "No, no. It's not true. The funeral was—" I was about to say the funeral was for Dabney, but how could that be? Dabney sat beside me, full of life. But there *was* a funeral. Of that, I was sure. Frantic thoughts whirled in my head so fast, I felt dizzy.

"But Mama said—" I stopped short and tried to remember the conversation we had on Sunday before the funeral. Did Mama tell me Dabney died? I couldn't remember. Thoroughly unnerved, I now understood I only presumed the woman standing before me to be dead. Yet here she stood. As much alive as I was. Perhaps even more so, for at the moment, I didn't feel alive. Even if I had, my wish would've been to die for I no longer wanted to live. If Zann was dead, I had nothing to live for.

Dabney's lip quivered. "Oh, Kiah—"

Chapter 14

My head throbbed with pain as if someone had hit me with a hammer. I tried to capture the confusing thoughts swirling aimlessly in my brain.

I jumped up from the glider and sailed off the front porch. I ran . . . and ran . . . and kept on running. Overhead, the sky was changing. Turning dark. Clouds billowed, constantly forming new shapes. The wind blew fiercely in my face. I fought the air, flinging my fists at the gusts whirling around me. Dust filled my mouth as I sprinted down the long, lonesome road, but I kept running. Had to reach the bridge. Had to. Our place. She'd be there, waiting for me.

The run was a picture of my life. Two steps forward, three steps back. Seemed the wind had never been to my back thrusting me onward. Always blowing against me. What did I have to live for? There was nothing left for me. I couldn't go back to school and face her empty desk. If only I had my diploma and could go far away to college. Tears flooded my eyes. Why did I keep fooling myself? Me, a college professor? The dream was nothing more than a bubble and now it had burst. There was nothing left.

Suddenly, I felt a strange sensation. Fear. I'm not sure I'd ever felt fearful before. Angry, bitter, lonely, hurt, yes . . . but afraid? The excruciating agony robbed me of my logic. The trees bent and swayed in an eerie fashion, like giant octopuses hovering over me waving long tentacles, while the wind moaned in sympathy with my plight. How could I go on without her? What was I to do? I trembled when a chilling breeze seemed to answer, as I imagined the wind screeching, "Die, die, die." I wanted to obey the wind. I wanted to die. The thundering echo resounded in my ears.

The muscles around my heart tightened. My knees weakened. My pace slowed. Though strength had left me, I struggled to forge forward, pleading with my weak knees not to give out on me. With determination, I rounded the bend and could see the covered bridge. Almost there. Couldn't breathe. Had to keep going. Maybe if I made it to the bridge, I'd find her. She'd throw her arms around me and we'd laugh together. We'd drink lemonade from a quart jar and eat delicious burned cookies in the safe haven where love had come to us.

I tried to persuade myself I'd been the victim of a nasty hoax, but who'd pull such a hideous scheme? And why? What would be gained? The answer opened up the truth to me. The parson wanted

213

me to believe she was dead, to get me out of the picture. Of course. That had to be it. The whole scenario was a carefully executed fraud. Zann was alive and I'd find her.

I scuttled down the embankment in full-blown sobs, screaming her name. "Zann? Zann?" I stumbled and fell on my face. I listened. There were no sounds. The silence was eerie. Not even the familiar rippling of the water washing over the rocks. Had the stream ceased to run? Where were the squirrels which scampered from tree to tree on any given day? Why weren't the birds scratching for worms? No crickets chirping. No frogs croaking. The world stopped. Why? Where was Zann? Why couldn't I find her? Lying prostrate on the cold, hard clay, I didn't try to get up. Why should I? I had no place to go. No one to see. If only I could close my eyes and die.

I was exhausted beyond belief. Never had I experienced such fatigue. I'm not sure if I went to sleep or if I passed out. I have no idea how long I'd been lying there, when I awoke hearing my name called.

I opened my eyes and squinted. It was dark. Very dark. The image leaning over me slowly came into focus. "Parson Pruitt? What are you doing here?"

"I came for you, Kiah."

He seemed real enough, but maybe this was one big horrible nightmare.

The parson reached down for my hand to help me up. My

pulse raced as I brushed the leaves from the back of my pants

"Kiah, I know how much you loved her."

Past tense. Loved. My lip quivered. I put my hands over my ears. "It's a lie," I screamed. "Tell me it's not true."

The parson's eyes filled with tears. "I'm afraid it is, Kiah." He put his arms around me, and I could fill his body shake in a faint rhythmic pattern as we held on to one another and wept. I had questions, but if I voiced them, it would make it real. I wanted it to be nightmare. "Please, please," I screamed. "Tell me she's not dead. Not Zann. Tell me you're lying."

Moments later, with his arms still wrapped around me, I felt the parson's hand pat my back. His voice quaked. "Let's go, son. Your mama's worried sick. Dabney's staying at the cabin with her until I can get you back home."

I climbed in his car, but neither of us spoke all the way to Rooster Run. I wanted answers, but the words stuck in my throat. I looked over at the parson, and the quiet tears trailing down his cheeks glistened in the light of the moon.

I saw Mama standing behind the screen door, when the parson pulled up in front of our cabin.

She ran out to meet me. "Oh, Kiah, I've been out of my mind. Shug, are you okay?"

I stepped out of the car and jerked away from her touch. My breathing was so fast, I became light headed. Tears blurred my vision. I felt like a trapped 'coon, staring into the eyes of a pack of hound dogs. Though these people meant me no harm, I felt cornered. Alone, and friendless. Berserk, I snapped. "Okay, you ask? You wanna know if I'm okay?" Hideous laughter erupted from my lips. It sounded far away, as if the sadistic sounding chuckles were coming from someone else. "Confound you people. No, I'm not okay." I stepped back and balled my hands in a fist. "What do you expect? I can't deal with this. Scram. All of you. Leave me alone."

The parson held out his hand. "Kiah, let's go in the house."

I looked at the parson, and then back at Mama. Dabney walked outside. They all stared, wide-eyed. I panicked and took a swing at the parson when he stepped forward. The knot in my stomach twisted again. "Leave me alone," I yelled.

My knees buckled and the parson grabbed me. I yelled like a wounded animal. Parson Pruitt slapped me across the face, and I stopped. I mumbled. "I want to lie down. I'm tired."

He held on to me, led me into the house and helped me to the bed. I stretched out. He gently lifted the chenille spread over me, before kneeling down to pray.

In a voice soft and low, he called out, "Father, this is your son, Eddie, here." It sounded strange, the way he addressed God, as if he were a personal friend. Like he really believed Almighty God up in Heaven was his daddy. Even more peculiar, the parson seemed to have the notion his daddy cared about him and his wants. This didn't fit the image I had of a daddy. I didn't want to give the impression I was listening, yet I strained to hear every word.

His calm, soothing words were like salve to my soul, when he prayed, "Father, my little brother here is hurting something awful, and he needs someone to help bear his load."

Then he said, "Remember, Lord, you told your children whenever our burdens got too heavy for us to bear, to ask for help? Well, I'm asking. This load seems too heavy for Kiah to bear alone, so I'd count it a special blessing and a favor to me, if you'd undergird him with your strength." The last thing I heard him say was, "Just between me and you, Lord, I don't think Kiah can rest, 'til he knows the truth, and I'd tell him, if it weren't for the promise I made Dora. If I'm right in my thinking, then Lord, I trust you to work out the details."

I didn't even try to make sense of what he was saying. He was still praying whenever I fell asleep.

The next morning when I awoke, I didn't want to get out of bed. Mama tried to coax me up with the aroma of fried salt pork and flapjacks coming from the kitchen, but I didn't want to eat. I didn't want to go to school. I didn't want to work anymore. In fact, I didn't want to live. I thought of the parson's words. They made even less sense in the morning than they had the night before.

Mama pleaded and cried. "Kiah, I know you've been hurt, sugar, but you can't just give up and die."

Her words infuriated me. "Why can't I, Mama? What do I have to live for?"

"Live for me, honey. For me. Don't you know how much I love you?"

But my heart had grown cold. I had no sympathy for anyone—no one other than myself, I should say. The capacity to love seeped out of my body the moment I finally admitted Zann was gone.

I awoke shortly before noon, and winced at the bright sunlight streaming through the window. I looked outside and saw Mama in the back yard, washing clothes. She had a fire going under the wash pot—a fire, which she built—while I curled up in bed feeling sorry for myself. I didn't want to be like this, but I couldn't turn things around. I crawled out of bed, walked over to the table and picked up a piece of salt pork and poured a glass of buttermilk. There was nowhere I wanted to go. Nothing I wanted to do except to fall asleep and never wake up.

I crawled back in bed and hoped sleep would come soon. Apparently, it did, for I awoke to the sound of voices outside the door and winced when I heard Mama say, "Come on in Mr. Thatcher. He's lying down. I reckon he didn't feel up to par this morning, but I'm sure he'll be back in school tomorrow."

Groggy and disgruntled, I cringed at the thought of having to go through the motions of civility. I ran my fingers through my disheveled hair and sat up in the bed, when I heard Mama and Mr. Thatcher walk through the door.

I slung my legs off the edge of the bed and mumbled. "Hello, Mr. Thatcher." The daggers shooting from Mama's eyes told me I'd better jump to my feet without delay. I stood and grudgingly thrust forward my hand.

With his right hand extended in a hand shake, I couldn't help wondering about the large envelope in his left hand. "Good evening, Kiah."

Evening? I looked out the window, surprised to see the sun had gone down. He said, "Kiah, I have great news. You've been approved for a scholarship to both state colleges. I received the notices last week, and couldn't wait for school to begin to give you the wonderful news. But when you didn't show up at school today, I could wait no longer."

The possibility of getting a college degree had helped me to dream big. All I'd ever wanted was to make it up to Mama for having been born and interrupting her life. Since the age of eight, when I first realized what people were saying about us, I wanted to take care of her and to provide her with the necessities of life. But until Mr. Thatcher came to Pivan Falls, I considered those noble thoughts to be nothing more than hollow dreams. But with a degree, I could make things happen. I could fill those dreams with more than the necessities of life. I'd finally be able to give Mama the desires of her heart. The best of everything. So why wasn't I excited at the news? Wasn't this what I'd been working toward for eleven years?

I pulled both letters from their respective envelopes and read them over a couple of times.

I handed them back to Mr. Thatcher. His brow furrowed. "I must admit, I'm surprised at your reaction. I thought you'd be elated."

Mama frowned. "Honey, it was nice of Mr. Thatcher to come all this way to give you the news, wasn't it?" She was giving me my cue.

I mumbled, "Yes, thank you, Mr. Thatcher."

He nodded and pushed the papers back toward me. "These letters belong to you, Kiah. You need to keep them until you're ready to make a decision."

I didn't tell him I'd already made my decision. I wouldn't be finishing school, nor going to college. I didn't know what I planned to do. I only knew what I didn't plan to do. I wouldn't be going back and sitting alone at lunch under the big oak. I didn't tell Mr. Thatcher because Mama wasn't ready to hear it. Sooner or later, though, she'd have to learn to deal with it.

That night, I sat outside on the stoop and stared blankly at the stars. A car drove up to #3. Parson Pruitt's car. Dabney got out and waved bye. He drove off, and when she spotted me, she walked over and sat down beside me.

I continued to stare at the sky, without acknowledging her presence.

"Wishing on a star?" She asked.

I turned my head and glared at her. "What good does it do to wish?"

She didn't answer. We sat in silence for a long time. Maybe thirty minutes. Maybe longer. But I was glad she was there beside me.

Recovering from an unpleasant tightness in my thorax, my voice cracked when I finally spoke. "What happened, Dabney? How?"

"Are you asking how she died?"

I nodded.

"Kiah—" She spoke my name and then lowered her head and moaned. She began a second time. "Kiah, everyone believes she died of complications from pneumonia."

My body trembled. "What do you mean? Are you saying she didn't?"

She threw her head back and closed her eyes. "Well, she did. And she didn't." Dabney's eyes glassed over. She reached and touched my arm. "Kiah, I want to tell you the truth, but I'll be breaking a confidence if I do."

My jaw tightened. "Dabney, I don't know what's going on, but I can't accept Zann's death as long as I know there are secrets shrouding her demise. You have to be honest with me."

She nodded. "Promise you won't tell a soul?"

Frustration mounted. No, I wouldn't promise. Why should I? I blurted out, "Dabney, why did you do it?"

Her brow furrowed. "I did it for Zann, Kiah. For Zann."

I growled. "That's crazy. Why would she want you to have an affair with her father?"

A heavy flush darkened her face. "What are you accusing me of, Kiah Grave?"

"Don't try to deny it, Dabney. I saw you slipping off with the parson. You think I was so naïve I couldn't figure out why he wanted to adopt your baby?" I scowled. "I guess he got the bright idea from the story of baby Moses." I referred to a Bible story I heard in the Primary Department at Sunday School, shortly before Mama and I got the boot.

"I don't follow you, Kiah."

"Parson Pruitt chose to send for the real mama to come take care of the 'adopted' infant. How convenient for him. It gave him a good excuse to plant you within his palace walls."

Her eyes had a wild look. "You think you have it all figured out, don't you? Well, you're wrong. I can deal with other folks thinking I'm Rooster Run trash, but you—you were different. Or so I thought. Kiah, I could never do what you're accusing me of. Parson Pruitt is a loving husband. How could you even think such?"

Unable to control my tongue, I blurted, "If not the parson, then tell me. Who *is* the father? Or don't you know?" I suppose I would've been forgiven if I'd stopped after the first question. It was the second part that really riled her.

Her jaw dropped. A deep, painful shade of red colored her face. The veins in her neck protruded, when she quipped, "There you go again."

I rolled my eyes.

She snapped, "I can see you don't believe me. You think I've had so many men coming through my back door, I can't keep count. Well, think what you will and see if I care. I don't have to answer to you, Kiah Grave."

"I'm sorry, Dabney, but I do believe you owe me an explanation. You've played me for a fool and I want to know why."

I didn't know how this puzzle fit together, but I sensed Zann's death had something to do with the illicit affair between her father and Dabney, and for reasons I couldn't discern, they were hiding the truth from me. "If it isn't the preacher, then who? If you know the identity of the father, what reason would you have for not telling me?"

She whirled around and blurted, "Because I'm afraid you'd kill him if you knew his name."

I shrugged. "No, I wouldn't, Dabney. Your lovers are your own business." I stopped and mused at the irony. "I won't deny I believed you and the parson had a thing going, and to tell the truth, I'm glad if it's not his." My words must have sounded cold and pitiless.

"Kiah, Parson Pruitt is the most decent man I've ever known, and he loves his wife, dearly. But it hurts me to know what you think of me. I'll admit I've done a lot of stupid things in the past and I've told you I don't do those things, anymore. Why don't you believe a person can change?"

I wanted to yank out a shank of my hair. "Forget it, Dabney," I snapped. Did she take me for a moron? She'd just given birth, for crying out loud, and yet she expected me to believe she was different? Was I supposed to believe she had the baby all by herself, without the help of a man? I didn't have much Bible knowledge, but I had enough to know there'd only been one woman who'd ever done that, and there'd never be another. So who was she trying to fool? I flexed my jaw. "I don't want to haggle with you, Dabney. It doesn't matter what I think. But you've just admitted Zann didn't die from pneumonia. Why the big secret?"

She reached for my hand. "Can we go for a walk?"

My head told me to refuse her hand. But since I hadn't been listening to my head lately, I wrapped my fingers around hers and felt a tinge of comfort as she gave a little squeeze.

I swallowed. "A walk? At this hour?" It must have been nine o'clock or later.

"Yes. I'm going to tell you the truth. The whole truth."

Chapter 15

At long last, the truth.

Dabney Foxworthy and I walked out the gate and down the long dirt road, hand in hand. Neither of us spoke for several minutes. I let go of her hand, when mine began to sweat. I got a whiff of perfume. I assumed it was the same stuff I gave her last Christmas. It didn't compare with the fragrance of gardenias, but I couldn't deny Dabney did smell mighty nice when the wind blew in the right direction. The quarter moon peaked over my shoulder like a one-eyed bandit, threatening to rob me of my scruples. Fat chance, Mr. Moon. Dabney Foxworthy wasn't my type. There was only one girl in this world for me, and her name was Zann Pruitt. There'd never be another.

She was being too quiet. Made me want to turn around and head back in the other direction as fast as I could go. She'd done gone and got herself pregnant once, and if she had any ideas of pinning the blame on me, she could think again. The more I thought about it, the madder I became. Finally, I blurted out, "I don't know what your plans are, but I'll tell you in plain English, Dabney, I'm not interested in spooning, if that's what we're supposed to be doing out here."

She stopped abruptly and sank her hands on her hips. "Forget it, Kiah. I wanted to tell you everything, and I've been trying to get up the nerve, but you're so full of yourself, I don't think you care to hear the truth."

I sucked in a deep breath. "I'm sorry, Dabney. I mean it. That was low. Seems I'm always saying the wrong thing to everyone. Forgive me?"

She nodded. "I guess we're both a little edgy. Do you mind if we sit on the log for a few minutes?"

We walked over, took a seat and Dabney poured out a story so incredible, I had trouble letting it soak in.

She began by saying, "Kiah, I think you should know the Pruitts named the baby Alexandra Pruitt, after her mother."

I had to be civil if I hoped to get the whole story. "That's nice."

"That's all you have to say? That's *nice*?"

I couldn't decide if I was losing it, or if she was, but one of us was having trouble keeping our oar in the water. So the Pruitts named the baby after Dabney. What did she expect me to say? Frankly, at the moment I didn't care if Dabney's name was Little

Bo Peep, but it appeared she wanted me to care, so I tried to oblige. I grappled for words, and came up with, "So is your name Dabney Alexandra or Alexandra Dabney?"

She shook her head. "Neither," she whispered and buried her face in her hands. Her body shook with sobs. "My name is Dabney Sue."

Now, what had I done? "Look, Dabney, I don't know what I said to make you cry. Whatever it was, I'm sorry. I misunderstood, okay? I thought you said the baby was named after you." I stood. "Come on, let's walk."

"Kiah, you don't understand."

I felt like a firecracker with a short fuse, and I was afraid if this conversation lasted much longer, I was going to make a loud noise. Though it was becoming increasingly difficult, I made a concerted effort to keep my voice at a normal level. "You're right, Dabney. I don't understand. So try helping me. Please?" I contributed Dabney's erratic behavior to after childbirth blues. I'd read it was a common phenomenon and if any mother had a right to be blue, poor Dabney would be a prime candidate. No husband. And now, no baby. Poor girl. I decided to wait until she was ready to proceed. But I hoped we could soon dispense with talk about her baby and get to the real issue. Zann's death.

She wiped her eyes. "Kiah, Zann is a nickname for Alexandra."

So that was it. Well, why didn't she say so in the first place?

Perhaps Dabney feared I'd resent her illegitimate child having the same name as my precious Zann. I tried to set her mind at ease. "Dabney, when you said Mrs. Pruitt named the baby after her mother, I didn't know you meant after Mrs. Pruitt's mother. I suppose Zann was named after her grandmother, also."

Dabney cocked her head. Her voice was barely above a whisper. "No, Kiah. You aren't hearing me."

I sighed. It was difficult being patient with her. "I do hear you, Dabney. I've heard every word. You said Mrs. Pruitt named the kid after her mother. I'll admit I was confused at first, thinking you meant after the baby's mother, so I assumed she named the kid after you . . . until I figured out you meant the baby was named after Mrs. Pruitt's mother."

Dabney put both hands on my shoulders, and shook me gently. A look of panic stretched across her face. "No, Kiah. You aren't listening. Little Alexandra wasn't named after her grandmother— and not after her great grandmother—but after her *mother,* Kiah. Her mother."

My fuse grew shorter. I snapped. "All that's interesting, but if you don't mind, I have a lot of questions I need answers to, and at the present, I don't give a hoot about the origin of the baby's name." I cringed as the careless words flung from my lips. I sighed. I had to get a grip.

Dabney stared at me with giant tears streaming down her cheeks.

Then like a mighty ocean wave, the truth rushed toward me, sucked me under and left me gasping for air. I bit my lip. "Impossible," I mumbled.

She laid a restraining hand on my shoulder, her fingernails cutting into the flesh. "It's true, Kiah."

"Then what you're saying, is—" I locked my knees to steady myself, and suddenly felt myself wavering. The world around me was spinning at an incredibly fast rate of speed. When I came to, Dabney was kneeling beside me, her hand resting on my forehead.

"Welcome back to earth."

I reached up to touch the back of my aching head and felt warm blood oozing from a gash on the back of my crown. I looked at my fingers before wiping them against my overalls.

"You hit your head on the tree root when you went down," she explained. "I think you'd better lie here for a while. You may have a concussion."

"No. I'm fine." I stood, and tried to gather my thoughts. Then I remembered. My voice quavered. "Are you trying to make me believe the baby—" I couldn't finish the sentence. I glared at Dabney.

She nodded. "Yes. The baby is Zann's."

A sudden rush of anger came over me. It wasn't true. It couldn't be. If Dabney hadn't been a female, I think I might have hit her I was so infuriated. "Why would you say such a thing? Zann was your friend."

Dabney bit her lip. "Yes, and the best friend I've ever had."

I couldn't believe it. Wasn't losing Zann traumatic enough? Why rub my wounds with salt by trying to convince me Zann was no different than . . . than *her*? What was Dabney trying to prove? I swallowed. It wasn't true. It couldn't be.

Dabney placed her hand on my shoulder. "Are you sure you're okay?"

I jerked away. "Don't touch me. I don't know what your game is, but you're a liar. Zann would never have—" I couldn't seem to finish my sentences.

"She was raped, Kiah."

I felt sick. This couldn't be. But why would Dabney make up such an outlandish lie?

We must have walked five miles or more, most of them in silence, when she said, "Let's sit down on the grass. I'm getting tired."

I stopped. My legs felt weak. I looked at Dabney. "Raped?"

She nodded.

I repeated the horrid word. "Raped? But when? Where? Why didn't Zann tell me?"

"She couldn't, Kiah. She wanted to, but she couldn't."

The image of sweet, innocent Zann being compromised in such a horrid way by some low-down rascal like the foul-mouthed Arnold Evers was suffocating. I thrust my hands to my throat.

Dabney began to cry.

The hot rage that caused me to lash out at her, slowly cooled into an indescribable heartache as I faced the ghastly truth. I handed her a handkerchief. "I'm sorry, Dabney. Forgive me for being so cruel."

She snubbed and pressed the handkerchief to her nose. "Then you do believe me?"

I nodded. As much as I didn't want to believe it, I had no doubts she was telling the truth. "Start at the beginning." I clinched my teeth together, not knowing if I'd be able to stomach the horrid details.

Dabney wouldn't look at me. She glanced from the stars to the ground. "Remember the day school let out for Christmas break, and I brought you a note from Zann?"

"Yes. Go on."

"Well, she waited for you at the bridge. You didn't show up. However, someone else did. Zann ran back to the house, hysterical. I was there when she rushed in. Her pretty blue gingham dress was ripped away at the shoulder. Her neck was black and blue and she had a bloody nose. When she wouldn't name her attacker, her father naturally assumed it was you, since she'd gone to meet you."

I suddenly felt sick. Bad sick. I jumped up and ran behind a tree and heaved until my sides ached. I blamed myself for not being there for her. Tormented, I believed the only way to free myself from such misery was to die. How could I go on living, knowing I could've prevented Zann's death? If only—

I walked back to where I'd left Dabney and lay flat of my back on the ground. I stared at the stars. "Why did she let her father think I was the one who raped her?" In a coarse whisper, I kept asking the same question. "Why?"

Dabney sat with her arms wrapped around her legs. "Oh, she tried to tell him differently, but he insisted she was trying to protect you."

"But that doesn't make sense. Why would she want to protect me if I was capable of doing such a horrid thing?"

"Zann made the same point, but I think Parson Pruitt was so distraught it became impossible for him to think straight. You know how much he loved her."

It was becoming clearer. "So that's why he felt the need to be her body guard. It also explains why he and Mrs. Pruitt suddenly turned on me."

"Yes. Until Zann was able to convince her mother it wasn't you. Mrs. Pruitt explained to her husband that Zann was terrified of her attacker, whoever he was. It stood to reason, she wouldn't have defended you, if you were the guilty party."

I was on an emotional roller-coaster. My feelings reeled back and forth from sadness to frustration. "But she never mentioned a word to me about a rapist. Not one word. If only she'd told me."

"Kiah, she wanted to get it out of her mind. She was afraid if she told you, you'd never be able to forget it, and you'd look at her differently. I guess she was afraid you might think she didn't fight hard enough."

My eyes clouded. I groaned, "Oh, Dabney. That would never have entered my mind. Never."

Dabney looked down at me. "Kiah, would you mind if I were to lie down with you?"

Beads of perspiration formed on my brow. The apprehension I experienced at the notion of her issuing me such an open invitation, made me quiver.

Our gaze locked. I licked my dry lips and tried to swallow. "Sorry, Dabney. Thanks, but no thanks. I know you're trying to make me feel better, but that dog won't hunt."

The quizzical expression forming on her face gave me a start. Had I misinterpreted her suggestion? No. She was clear. I blew out a lungful of air. Why should her proposition surprise me? I squirmed, feeling antsy. An awkward silence lingered in the air, like an unwelcome Fuller Brush salesman loitering on the front steps. I could blame no one but myself for the embarrassing situation. Like a nincompoop, I'd led her to this spot—at this hour—giving her just reason to suspect my motives. I wiped beads of perspiration from my upper lip. I hoped I had not offended her with my retort, but Dabney Foxworthy had opened a door, which I had no intention of walking through.

With glassy eyes, she nodded. "I understand." She clasped her hands around her knees and held her head back, gazing up into the heavens. She rocked back and forth. Neither of us spoke for several minutes. I wanted to hear the rest of the story. Dabney's abrupt question had sent my mind on a different track and it took several seconds before I could think straight.

She had a peculiar look on her face. I couldn't read her. I couldn't tell if she was angry or just hurt. Of all the people I'd never want to hurt, Dabney Foxworthy was at the top of the list.

The sadness in her eyes spoke loud and clear, though her lips remained clinched. I cowered under the silent accusations, which I found impossible to refute. Undeniably, I had stomped on a tender spot and left her vulnerable heart bruised and hurting. What had happened to me? Why had I grown so cold and callous, caring about no one's feelings but my own? Had I given Dabney the impression I disliked her? That would be far from the truth. It was me I loathed. Spite and bitterness gnawed at my insides the way a mouse nibbles cheese—slowly and deliberately, until nothing is left. I'd become a shell of a man. From the outside, I appeared whole, but on the inside, I was as hollow as the holes in Swiss cheese. So what if I was right and Dabney had propositioned me? Was it a reason to reply in such a crude manner? Couldn't I have been a little kinder? Who set me up to be her judge?

She glared at me with wide, distrustful eyes. "Kiah," she said, "I know you may find this hard to believe, but you misinterpreted my intentions when I asked to lay beside you. My back ached from sitting in the same position for so long, and I—" She paused. "But

I don't blame you for wondering, my reputation being what it is." The tears welling in her eyes made a slow path down her cheeks.

I wanted to bite my tongue for being such a clod. With my head thrown back, my eyes closed, all I could say was, "Jeepers, Dabney, I'm such a chump. You're really a swell gal, and I guess . . . well, I assumed you felt sorry for me, and wanted to . . . uh . . . help get my mind off the pain. Forgive me for being such an ignoramus?"

She wouldn't look me in the eyes, but staring toward the stars, she gave a little nod and her lips made a weak attempt at a smile.

I sat up and pulled a handkerchief from the back pocket of my dungarees. I took the tip and wiped a tear trailing down her cheek. I smiled and said, "The stars look much brighter from a reclining position. Why don't we lay back?"

"Are you sure?" She asked.

I smiled. "You have nothing to be afraid of," I said with a wink. "I promise to be a perfect gentleman." I pulled off my shirt, folded it up and slid it under her head. We glanced up in time to see a shooting star blazing across the sky. "Look," I gushed. "Someone once told me shooting stars are the dead making an appearance, to bring us comfort. Do you suppose?"

Dabney turned her head toward me and smiled. Her voice had a soothing, compassionate tone. "No, Kiah. That was a star. Nothing more. Zann's not shooting across the sky. She's at peace in heaven, walking among the saints on streets of gold. One day,

I'm gonna be walking up there with her."

I supposed one legend was as good as another, so I didn't dispute it, though I found it to be quite preposterous. Especially, the part about her strolling around heaven with Zann. Didn't she understand? Even if there was a heaven, the golden gate wouldn't swing open for the likes of Kiah Grave and Dabney Foxworthy. Ludicrous. But I didn't want to debate her. Not now, anyway. I wanted Dabney to tell me every minute detail from the day Zann was raped, to the day she died. As painful as it'd be to hear, I had to know.

"Dabney, when Zann came back to school, she seemed so normal. I would never have guessed. How did she manage to hide something so traumatic?"

"Well, she did put up a good front. And as the weeks passed, I thought she was really beginning to put it behind her. She seemed to be doing fairly well, until she discovered she was pregnant. For the first four months, she didn't want to believe it, but when her dresses got tight, she couldn't deny it any longer. She told me first. Bless her heart, I felt so sorry for her, Kiah. I kept wishing it had happened to me and not to her. She was terrified of telling her father she was pregnant. Afraid he'd force her to name her attacker and he'd kill the boy. Frankly, I thought the rascal needed killing, but Zann was concerned her daddy would go to prison and it'd be her fault. But this was not the kind of news she could keep secret for very long. I held her hand in the living room, when she broke the news to her mama and daddy. As you can imagine, they were shattered."

Dabney screeched when a frightened animal—likely a 'coon—darted through the underbrush within feet of us, then scampered up a nearby sycamore tree. I instinctively grabbed her in an unconscious gesture of protection. It was a stupid move. Her eyes widened, and her lips parted. I squirmed, when I sensed she didn't realize it was nothing more than a reflex action. There was an uncomfortable silence.

I tried to hide my nervousness. "Uh . . . I hope you didn't think—"

She appeared flustered and quickly rolled over and sat up. "Forget it," she mumbled. With her lips tightly compressed, she dropped her gaze.

I swallowed. I wanted to forget it. Oh, how I wanted to forget it, but I wanted even more for her to forget it.

I sat upright and locked my hands around my knees. "Look!" A bat darted through the darkened trees. "Did you see it?" There was nothing spectacular about seeing a bat, but I was scrambling for an opportunity to replace the tenseness, which hung heavily in the air.

It worked. She craned her neck in the direction I pointed. "What? What was it?"

"A bat." I winced at the artificial enthusiasm in my voice. I couldn't have managed to say it with more oomph if I'd been pointing out a dinosaur flying overhead.

"Where?"

"Too late. You can't blink or they're gone. First you see them, then you don't. Amazing little creatures. Funny how they flit around in the dark, blind as can be, yet they seem to know where they're going. I wish I had their sense of direction."

"But you don't need it. You have eyes."

"True, I have eyes, yet I keep running into obstacles, every way I turn. I can't seem to find my way in life, Dabney. Maybe I'm blinder than the bats."

Dabney's voice quaked. "Oh, Kiah, you don't have any idea what it's like to be blind. You have excellent foresight. You can see a future. I admire you. You know where you're going and you know how to get there. Not me. I try to see ahead, but my future is as dark as my past. I can only see the here and now, with no yesterdays to comfort me, and no bright tomorrows, to promise hope." She covered her face with her hands. "Jeepers, I don't know why I rambled on so. You must think me a dim-wit."

I bit my bottom lip and shook my head. I couldn't tell her what I really thought. Frankly, I was surprised at the eloquent way she had expressed her feelings. If I hadn't seen her lips moving, I wouldn't have believed the words came from her mouth. For the first time, I felt I had a glimpse of the real Dabney Foxworthy. She had bared her heart. I was touched. I wanted to reach over and hold her hand, but what if she mistook my gesture for something more meaningful than a simple act of kindness? Instead, I bungled through something inane, like "Rambling isn't a bad thing. What's lovelier than a rambling rose?" Good Granny, where did that line come from? I lowered my eyes and gasped. I wanted to pound myself on the head for being so stupid. Stupid, stupid, stupid. My mouth went dry. I didn't want to look at her. Had I really said 'Rambling isn't a bad thing—what's lovelier than a rambling rose?' It didn't even make sense to me, and I was sure it made no sense to her. What if she was laughing? She'd have every right. I was such a dumb ox.

I slowly lifted my head and glanced her way. She wasn't laughing. She wasn't laughing at all. Giant tears made a trail down her cheeks. When she turned her head, the moonlight seemed to capture the softness of her skin, causing it to glow as if she'd been bathed with the silvery morning dew. I wondered at what point she'd stopped wearing the war paint. I hadn't noticed until tonight, but her face was as fresh and clean as Monday's laundry. She appeared pure and innocent, and if I hadn't known better—

"You're crying. Did I say something wrong, Dabney?"

"Wrong?" She smiled. "No, in fact it was beautiful," she whispered. "Thank you."

Now, I was really confused, but we had more important things to talk about. "You were telling me about Zann?"

She exhaled a heavy breath. "Yes. Now, where was I? I pure forgot, after the lovely thing you said. You know. About the rose.

It sounded kinda poetic."

Her voice sounded different—soft and wooing like—scared me silly to think I may have unknowingly said something that could've been construed as romantic. Certainly, it was not my intent. Me? Poetic?

Nevertheless, intent or no intent, she embraced my idiotic brand of poetry and clung to it tightly like a proud child with an all-day sucker.

I coughed in my hand. "You said you were with Zann when she broke the news to her parents. How did they react to the news? Had they suspected she might be pregnant?"

"I don't think so, from the way they carried on. Her mother went to pieces and said the only logical thing to do would be to send her away to a home for unwed mothers, where they could place the baby for adoption. Mrs. Pruitt said it'd be best to keep it a secret for the parson's sake. Knowing how ugly rumors get started, she said Parson Pruitt might be asked to leave, if folks thought his daughter had—well, you know."

"I don't get it. How could she have been so far along without me noticing?"

Dabney smiled. "Kiah, you wouldn't have suspected Zann Pruitt to be pregnant if she looked like she'd swallowed a watermelon. No one would've. But the truth is, she didn't gain much weight. I think she just stopped eating out of fear. When the parson said they wouldn't be able to hide it forever, his wife told him she'd let out the waist on Zann's skirts. Mrs. Pruitt said before Zann had time to really blossom, school would be out. The baby wasn't due until September, so she could be back home to start school in the fall, and no one would be the wiser."

I had a queasy sensation in the pit of my stomach.

"But things didn't go according to her mother's plans. Mrs. Pruitt intended for Zann to leave the baby and come home, but, oh my goodness, Zann wouldn't hear of it. She said she'd never agree to give up her baby. She and her mama went rounds over that one. Emotions were high and tempers flared. So I came up with a solution I hoped would suit everybody. They probably thought it dumb at first, until I explained how we could pull it off."

"Slow down, you're losing me."

"Don't you get it? I offered to fake a pregnancy. Then when Zann delivered, I'd pretend to have given birth, and the Pruitts could let folks think they adopted my child. No one would ever suspect it was Zann's baby and not mine. That way, Zann could be with her baby, and the little one would carry the respectable last name of the noble folks who adopted her. She'd never be looked upon as—" She clasped her hand over her mouth. "I'm sorry, Kiah. I wasn't thinking. I shouldn't have said that."

I shrugged. "You didn't say it. But even if you had, it would've been the truth. That was admirable of you, Dabney, to suggest such an arrangement. Not many girls would've done something like that for a friend."

"Zann's Mama hugged me and agreed it was the answer, but the parson, well, he balked and said it wouldn't be right and we had to come up with another plan. He called it deceit, but I made up my mind to do it, and I wasn't gonna let him talk me out of it. Zann cried and said she loved me for wanting to help, but she couldn't let me ruin my good name, just to save hers." Dabney smiled. "She actually said that, Kiah, and I think she meant it. I assured her my name wouldn't suffer. I really wanted to do it for her, and I reckon you might say I put my foot down."

I swallowed. "You're swell, Dabney. A real friend."

"Well, don't pin any roses on me, Kiah. It's true my main reason for doing it was to help Zann, but maybe I was doing it partly for me, too. I'd felt like dirt all my life and I wanted to do something worthwhile for a change. This was my chance to make my life count for something. It made me feel good. Like I was needed, you know?"

I had so many questions, yet there was really no right place to begin. "So where did you go when her daddy picked you up in the middle of the night? Mama thought you were going to visit the midwife." I swallowed hard as I reflected on the vile accusations I'd made, accusing her and the parson.

She glanced down. "Parson Pruitt received a call, saying Zann had delivered and she wasn't doing well. He came to pick me up and took me to his house, so I'd be there when they got back with the baby. After all, if I was supposed to be giving birth, I needed to be where my baby was, as soon as they arrived back. So I removed the padding Mrs. Pruitt had made for me to wear, and I waited at the parsonage for them to return with Zann and little Alexandra."

"Was she—" The words stuck in my throat. I tried once more. "Was she still alive when they returned home?"

Dabney's voice lowered. "Yes, but she was a very sick little mama. Oh, but if you could've seen her with the baby. We wanted to take the baby into another room so Zann could rest, but she insisted on having her with her in the bed at all times."

I choked. "How long did she live?"

"Six-and-a-quarter hours after they arrived home with her. She kept calling for you, and I really wanted to let you know, but I'd made a promise to the Pruitts that it'd be our secret. I couldn't go back on my word. And yet, now . . . now I've broken my promise."

I tried to console her when she cried. "Dabney, you had no choice. I made you tell me. You needn't worry. I'll never tell a soul."

Her eyes opened wide. She panted and stared at me like a frightened animal. "Promise, Kiah, do you promise?"

"Honest and hope to die," I said crossing my hand over my heart. "You can trust me. I have two very good reasons for not wanting to tell. One, you asked me not to. And two, because Zann would not have wanted me to tell. I know she wouldn't." Speaking of Zann in the past tense caused a lump the size of a frog to swell in my throat. I didn't want to cry, but I didn't know how much longer I could contain the intense pain.

She fumbled with the cheap ring on her pinky. "Kiah, there's something else I haven't told you."

I must have looked puzzled. I couldn't imagine there could possibly be anything more to tell.

She reached for my hand. There was nothing romantic in the gesture, but I stiffened, feeling the need to brace myself. When she hesitated, I sensed whatever it was she was about to tell me was going to come as a shock.

"There's a letter," she said.

"A letter?"

Chapter 16

Why did Dabney wait until now to tell me there was a letter from Zann? "Where is it? I want it, Dabney."

"I don't have it with me. It's at the house. In a safe place."

My heart throbbed at the thought of reading words written by Zann for my eyes only. As we neared Rooster Run, my imagination ran wild. What if she blamed me for leaving her at the bridge, unprotected? She had every right to hate me. What if she revealed her attacker? What would I do? There was no question about what I'd want to do. I wanted to kill him. But would I? Could I?

Dabney was dragging by the time we reached #3, and I'll confess I wasn't in tip-top shape, myself. Though I had no way of knowing, I guessed the time to be somewhere between one and two o'clock a.m. Dabney opened the screen door to her cabin, then turned and looked at me with pleading eyes. "Kiah, do you mind terribly if we wait until tomorrow? I'll get it for you first thing in the morning. I feel a mite washed out, and I know you'll have questions."

"No. You can't ask me to wait, Dabney. Where's the letter?" Why did she think I'd have questions? Had she read the letter? *My* letter? Did she honestly think I'd say, "Sure, send it over whenever it's convenient for you?" I couldn't wait another second. How could she expect me to wait another day?

She appeared reluctant, but motioned for me to follow her into the house. I expected her to light the lamp, but she didn't bother. The full moon let light in through the window, and I watched as she reached under her bed and pulled out a metal chest the size of a shoe box. She took a small key from a chain she wore around her neck. She reached in, pulled out a business sized envelope and handed it to me.

She mumbled, "Want me to light the lamp so you can read it?"

I clasped the letter to my chest and shook my head. "No thanks. Go to bed. I'll read it after I get home." I needed to be alone to absorb every word in privacy.

Though our houses were only feet apart, I was panting as if I'd run ten miles, by the time I reached the front stoop. I heard Mama snoring when I opened the front door. I lit the oil lamp and Mama grunted, threw her hands over her eyes and flounced toward the wall.

"Sorry," I whispered. Before I had time to tear the envelope open, she was snoring again.

My hands shook as I unfolded six pages of gold-trimmed stationary with the initial *P* in the top right-hand corner. As I read, I tried to drink in the words, as if sucking each syllable slowly through a straw. I couldn't imagine the pain she must have endured, as her tears had smeared the ink in several places.

My dear, sweet Kiah,

If you're reading this letter, it means I've gone to be with the Lord.

Kiah, I've deceived the one person who means more to me than anyone else in this world—you. Not by choice, but I wasn't allowed to make my own decisions. Dabney wasn't pregnant. I was. The baby is the result of a rape, but she's still my flesh and blood and I fought Mama and Daddy for the right to keep her. Now, it looks as if I'll lose her, anyway.

People in Pivan Falls will believe the baby's birth mother is Dabney, and that Mother and Daddy adopted the maid's baby. The idea was Dabney's. She's a real friend.

Kiah, I believe had I lived, you would've accepted my little Alexandra with open arms and loved her as I do. It would be a lot to ask of most men, but you aren't just any man. You're very special. I have a couple of requests, and I have no doubt that you'll carry out my wishes if the time should come.

Kiah, when she's of age, will you tell Alexandra the truth? Mama insists my little Allie should grow up believing she's their adopted daughter and I'm her big sister. Maybe it's selfish of me, but to think she may never know I'm her mother, tears me apart. Tell her, Kiah. Tell her I said she's worth the price I paid for her. Tell her I loved her more than life. I've named my parents as Alexandra's guardians, but in the event of their death, I've requested that you be named legal guardian. I couldn't choose a better father for my little girl.

I hate to leave you and Alexandra, but I'm confident God will send someone your way who'll love you as I do. She won't look like me, talk like me or act like me, so don't try to compare the two of us. Your love will be different, but just as strong as the love we shared.

When I was a little girl, I collected seashells. One morning I sat on the beach building sand castles when the tide rushed in and deposited a starfish at my feet. It was the most beautiful shell I'd ever seen. I left it on the sand, thinking it would still be there after I finished my castle. Minutes later, I looked up and the starfish disappeared when the tide ebbed.

Brokenhearted, I cried, but Daddy said, "You waited too late to retrieve it. Be patient, Zann, for God has many shells beyond the breakers, which will wash ashore with the incoming tide. The next one may not look like the one you lost, but will be equally beautiful. When it comes ashore, grab it, or it too, will disappear with the ebb tide."

So I sat on the beach that evening, waiting and watching. I'd almost given up, when the tide rushed in, and there on the beach was the prettiest pink conch shell I'd ever seen. This time, I knew what to do. I snatched it up, put it in my bucket and carried it home.

The tide's beginning to ebb, my darling, and soon I'll be no more. Don't mourn for what you've lost. God has something else in store. Watch for the high tide.

Until we meet again, all my love,
Zann

P.S. Dabney has instructions to give you this letter, if I don't make it. Please thank her for being such a wonderful friend. Goodbye, my darling.

I tried to keep the tears from falling on the pages and smearing the ink. I held the stationary to my nose, hoping to get a whiff of gardenias. But there was no scent. Not even the subtle smell of lavender, which I detected the day I purchased it from the drug store. I carefully folded the letter and slid it back into the envelope. "Why, God? *Why?* I can understand why you'd choose the loveliest flower in the garden but it doesn't seem right to pick one while still in the bud. She didn't have time to fully blossom before you plucked her. It's not fair. It's not fair at all."

I fell across my bed without bothering to undress.

Tuesday morning, Mama shook me. "Get up, shug. It's time to

get ready for school."

I grumbled and turned over in the bed. "I'm not going."

Mama didn't often raise her voice, but when she did, she could raise the roof. "Kiah Grave, I'll not stand idly by and let you destroy your life. Get out of bed this instant. You're going whether you want to or not."

Another grunt. Then I felt a sage broom pounding down on top of my head. I threw my hands over my face, but she kept beating me with a broom. It didn't hurt, but I got a mouthful of sage—not a pleasant way to start the day. I yelled, "For crying out loud, Mama, what's got into you? Calm down. I'm going, I'm going."

I pumped enough water to draw a bath. "My overalls are too dirty to wear," I yelled. "Did you iron my other pair?"

Mama grumbled. "Wear the ones you wore yesterday. You've only worn them once. They should be good for another day or two at least."

"Well, they're not."

She picked up my clothes that I'd thrown across a ladder back chair, and shrieked. "Land sakes, how did you get these in such a mess? Looks like you rooted with the hogs."

I was in no mood to explain my midnight walk with Dabney, or relate how I woke up lying on wet clay, after a fainting spell.

Mama reached in the wicker laundry basket and pulled out my overalls, neatly ironed and folded. "Kiah Grave, if you stood over a hot washpot to scrub denim, you'd be a little more particular about taking care of them."

"Sorry, Mama. What's for breakfast?" I wasn't hungry, but I knew if I didn't fake it, Mama would ask more questions than I was willing to answer.

"Oh, my stars, the biscuits need to come out of the oven."

"I got 'em," I volunteered. Wrapping a dishrag around my hand, I reached in and pulled out the hot iron griddle and sat it on top of the stove. I reached for one of the tender, flaky biscuits when my arm touched the hot iron, burning a patch of flesh the size of a half-smoked cigar on the back of my wrist. I jerked back and sailed the biscuit across the room.

Mama grabbed the syrup and insisted she put it on the burn. I turned away. "It's no big deal, Mama. Forget it." I walked over and picked up the biscuit from off the floor.

"But Kiah, shug, the syrup will take away the sting."

"Mama, that's an old wives' tale. Syrup has no medicinal value." Mama's remedies usually worked, but I decided I'd rather burn than be doused with thick cane syrup.

"Suit yourself, shug, but I'm telling you, it'll help cure it."

I sneered. "Yes'm, and so does kerosene mixed with sugar." She caught the intended sarcasm.

"Go ahead and poke fun. Kerosene and sugar might not cure burns, but it'll get shed of the croup, and that's a fact. I almost lost you one night, when you was a little bitty fellow. Your breathing was heavy and had a frightening sound. The nearest I can describe the awful noise coming from your throat, was like a bobcat on the prowl. You was gasping for air, and I put a few drops of kerosene on a spoonful of sugar, and it cured you in less than an hour. Your breathing eased and the hacking stopped." Mama's eyes glistened. "I sat up and looked at you all night long, just thanking the good Lord for a thimble full of kerosene. You woulda died without it, and that's the Gospel truth."

I'd heard the story too many times to fake an interest. I carefully reached for another biscuit, and loaded it down with freshly churned butter. When Mama's head was turned, I gently smeared a dab of cane syrup over the smarting wound.

All the way to school I questioned if I was doing the right thing. Should I continue on my way, or head back to the house to stand up to Mama and tell her I was capable of making my own decisions, good or bad. If I chose to quit school, I had the right. I was of age, and it would take more than a sage broom beating to change my mind. That's exactly what I'd tell her. I turned around and headed toward the house.

As I walked back, I considered the scholarship and what an education would mean to me and Mama. *To me and Mama*? The thought stuck in my craw. I'd wanted the scholarship so I could become somebody. Someone Zann would be proud to marry. The dream died with her.

Nothing mattered anymore. Not even my goal to become a famous college professor. Neither fame nor fortune was an incentive to continue with my education. Mama would have a fit if I mentioned dropping out of school, but only because she wanted a better life for me. She didn't want it for herself. Maybe she was perfectly satisfied living in Rooster Run, being a washwoman. Crazy thoughts stole my logic, twisting it until the absurd sounded reasonable.

I turned back and ran all the way to the school house. I slid in my desk, as the bell rang. When Mr. Thatcher wasn't looking, I pulled Zann's letter from my pocket, and held it to my nose again. I sniffed. Maybe there was the slightest scent. Or maybe I imagined the scent because I wanted to believe I could smell gardenias. I mulled over her last request and wondered why—why would she want me to fall in love again? If she could only know the pain I'd suffered because I allowed myself to love once, she wouldn't ask me to do it again.

Zann told me to explain to Alexandra that she was worth the price paid. I asked myself if loving Zann was worth the price I had to pay. The answer was yes. Would I do it again, even if I knew the heartache that would follow? In a heartbeat.

But love someone else, the way I loved her? Impossible.

The following days were filled with emptiness. I went to sleep, woke up, ate, went to school, went to work, and went back to bed—carrying on with daily chores, yet feeling like a zombie as

I moved from one task to another.

My hardest times came when the bell would ring for lunch. Every day, I trudged toward the big oak where we shared lunch so many times. I felt as if someone had thrust a butcher knife through my heart. I didn't bother to take a lunch pail. No need. I couldn't swallow. I sat down and leaned against the tree and cried like a baby. I didn't think anyone was close enough to see me, but even if they could, there was nothing I could do to stop the flow of tears. Oh, how I missed her.

When I heard my name called, I looked up to see Dabney Foxworthy standing there. She was holding a white wicker basket. Zann's lunch basket. "What are you doing here?" I asked.

"Do you mind?"

"Of course not. I'm glad you came, but I don't understand."

She sat down, pulled a napkin from the basket and handed it to me. I took the cue and wiped the wetness from my cheeks.

"This is Zann's basket," I said, as if she might not know.

She nodded. "Mrs. Pruitt packed us a lunch."

Now, I was really confused. "Mrs. Pruitt? But why?"

Dabney pulled out fried chicken and baked sweet potatoes. She smiled." I asked her the same thing, and she said she was doing it for Zann. It seems Zann left us all a letter."

I felt my brow furrow. "You mean . . . you have a letter, also?"

"Yes. I didn't know until this morning. Her mother found it among Zann's things when she unpacked her bags."

"What did she say?"

Dabney shifted her eyes away from me. "Personal stuff, Kiah. Mainly girl talk."

I wanted to press further. I wanted to keep hearing Zann's voice, even if it was only through her written words to someone else. But I understood why Dabney chose not to reveal the contents. I felt the same way about my letter. The words were meant for me and me only.

But I was even more curious to know what was in Mrs. Pruitt's letter.

Had Zann sensed that lunch would be a bad time for me? That the loneliness would be almost unbearable, so she asked her mother to send the maid to comfort me during my time of distress? What other reason would Mrs. Pruitt have for such an act of kindness? Still, it was too bizarre for me to wrap my thoughts around.

I wasn't really hungry. I hadn't wanted much to eat, since learning of Zann's death, but I felt a sense of obligation to eat a drumstick.

Dabney said, "Mrs. Pruitt sent some cookies. Do you—"

Before she finished her statement, I interrupted. "Yes, I like raisins."

Her brow lifted. "What did you say?"

"I said I like raisins."

She shrugged. "Uh . . . yeah, I remember. Sorry, though, I

don't have any. But how about a peanut butter cookie?" Dabney and I talked about a lot of things, but mostly about Zann. I was glad she came and surprised at how fast the hour went. After school I went by the old covered bridge before going home. There was something stuck to a cypress knee near the water's edge. I reached down to retrieve it. A blue satin bow ribbon. The bow Zann wore the day I was supposed to meet her.

The day I let her down.

Chapter 17

For the next three weeks, Dabney waited under the big oak in front of the schoolhouse at lunch with a basket packed by her employer. No longer did I bring my syrup bucket to school, since Dabney brought more than enough for the two of us.

"I just don't get it, Dabney. Why is she doing this? Sending you here with enough food for an army seems weird. I don't need her charity."

"Kiah, it isn't charity."

"Then what?"

"A mother's promise." She lowered her voice. "Kiah, what . . . what did Zann say to you in your letter?"

I chewed my bottom lip. A part of me wanted to tell her, but another part wanted to hold back.

She shrugged. "Sorry. I shouldn't have asked."

"Hey, if I remember correctly, I asked what was in yours, so why shouldn't you be equally curious?"

She smiled. "I'll tell if you will."

Maybe we *should* tell. It'd be like having Zann sitting between us. Perhaps it could bring healing to both of us. Before I could respond, the bell rang. I sucked in a deep breath, feeling a sense of relief. I didn't need to make a quick decision on such an important issue. I was glad she didn't press me for an answer. But Dab was like that. Seemed to have an uncanny sense of discernment. Almost as if she could read my mind at times.

Dabney gathered up the left overs and put them back into the basket. "You coming over tonight?" she asked.

I nodded. I missed Zann terribly, but I knew Dabney missed her also. Being able to share our grief seemed to be as important for Dab as it had been for me. A tangled thread of loneliness had wrapped around us and knotted us together. We spent almost every evening consoling one another. We sat out under the stars and laughed a little but cried a lot. Lately, though, I saw a mood change in both of us. Instead of crying a lot and laughing a little, we laughed a lot and cried a little. Sometimes I felt guilty, as if I had no right to laugh again. But I don't know what I would've done, had it not been for Dabney's friendship during those days following Zann's death. Sometimes my ramblings didn't make sense, but somehow Dabney could always comprehend what I was trying to say.

"Dabney, have you ever had a dream that was so real, so rich and vibrant that you didn't want to wake up? And when you did, you tried to close your eyes tightly with hopes to recapture it once more? To pick up where you left off?"

She nodded.

"I dream of Zann every night. Sometimes we're sitting under the old oak tree, and sometimes we're down at the bridge, traipsing down the shallow stream, hand in hand. Laughing. We're always laughing. Always. I can see her so plainly. I hear her laughter, and then it abruptly stops. I awake, and she's gone. It startles me so. My heart races so rapidly I feel I can't breathe. I'm covered with sweat. It's like losing her all over again. Night after night, she returns, and then poof. She's gone again. Will the pain ever go away?"

"Kiah, dreams can be thieves. They can lie to you—make you think you're having a real experience and then rob you. But memories are different. Memories are forever. They don't lie, and they don't rob. You and Zann shared many beautiful memories and nothing or no one can take them away from you. She's in your heart, Kiah, so enjoy the memories. When you wake from a dream, think on the good times and thank God for the time you shared together. Some people will live a lifetime and never know the kind of love you and Zann were privileged to share. What I'd give to know of love like yours for even a day."

"But our time together was so short," I complained.

"Kiah, tell me, truthfully. Would ten years have been long

enough?"

I understood what she was saying. I shook my head. "No. Not ten, not twenty— I'm sure if we'd had fifty years together, I would've shed no less tears. But I miss her so, Dabney. Oh, how I miss her."

Dabney and I spent countless hours together in the coming months, yet whenever I stopped to consider how little I knew about her, it shocked me. I didn't know where she came from, if she had a father, how her mother died, if she had siblings, or how she wound up in Rooster Run. She never talked about herself, and I'd been so consumed with my own selfishness, I never bothered to ask.

All my information, I'd learned from filthy gossip, which circulated around the school yard. The fellows had a name for her. I swallowed hard, knowing first-hand what it felt like to be branded. I tried to shake the guilty feeling stirring in my gut. Why should I shoulder the blame? I didn't put the label on her. She'd brought it on herself, hadn't she? She made the choice to be loose, so why shouldn't she wear the brand? Sure, I understood the pain of having people whisper and snicker when I walked past, but there was a big difference in our situations. I didn't choose to be fatherless. It wasn't fair that I bore the shame for someone else's sin. But Dabney deserved what she got. Didn't she? Then why did I die a little inside, each time I heard the snickers? True, in the beginning, I centered on me, with little consideration for her feelings and the pain she endured when she walked past and heard the crude remarks.

But lately, a transfer of feelings had taken place in my heart, and I wasn't even sure when it happened. I found myself wanting to become her protector. Maybe it was because she seemed so defenseless. Many of the lurid stories were nothing more than young men's fantasies. So why didn't she refute the lies? I'll concede she wasn't as pure as the water flowing from an artesian well—but jeepers, couldn't she at least let it be known that the school yard stories were greatly exaggerated? I wanted her to stand up and call them liars to their faces. What would she want with some little fourteen-year old, pimple-faced, foul-mouthed creep, without a red cent in his pocket? What would be in it for her? Dabney might not be as bright as a copper penny, but she was smarter than that. Anger burned on my face like a hot fever, intensifying with every snicker—every wayward look from evil-minded ignoramuses who lied about their wild exploits.

I wanted to spend every spare minute with her. She needed me, and I suppose as much as I hated to admit it, I needed Dabney Foxworthy.

Fall came and went, and I hardly noticed. It was my senior year, and I was still working for Mr. Farris at the stockyard. Christmas was upon us, and I found myself sinking into a deep depression as I recalled the events of one year ago. If only I had gone to the covered bridge at four o'clock. Instead of having a history to haunt me, I'd have a future to hold to. Four days before Christmas, we were sitting on Dabney's steps, all wrapped up in a wool blanket and looking at the stars when Dabney asked, "Aren't you going to get your Mama a tree? You know how proud she was last year of the one you cut for her, and she has all those beautiful decorations."

I grunted.

"Was that a yes?"

I turned and scowled. "No, it wasn't a yes. We're not having a tree this year."

"But why, Kiah?"

"No reason."

She lowered her head. "I was hoping you would."

"Why would you care?" I snapped.

"Because last Christmas was the best Christmas of my whole life. I felt like I was a part of a family when your Mama invited me over for dinner, and we sat and looked at the pretty ornaments on the tree and—" She choked up.

"And what?" I prompted.

"I was going to say I'd never had anyone to buy me a Christmas present before. Kiah, I never properly thanked you for the perfume, since I felt you didn't want anyone to know you bought it for me, but I Suwannee, it was the nicest thing anyone has ever done for me. I loved you for it."

I shrugged. "It was no big deal."

"It was to me." She picked up a stick and doodled in the sand.

"Okay, okay, I'll get a tree." I expected her to smile, but she acted as if she hadn't heard. She had a faraway look in her eyes.

"Kiah?"

"Yeah?"

"Did you know Arnold Evers is back in town?"

I grunted. "What do I care? I never liked him. He's a bully and a braggart."

Dabney held her head back and gazed at the stars. Her voice sounded strange when she said, "I don't like him, either."

I popped my knuckles. "I wasn't surprised when he dropped out of school. He goofed off and wouldn't have passed, anyway. I didn't even know he'd left town. Where's he been?"

"Somewhere in Alabama. I think he has kinfolk living around Montgomery."

I hadn't set my mind on Arnold since the day I busted his nose on the bridge. After then, he didn't have much to do with me. But Dabney had aroused my curiosity. I asked, "How do you know so much about him?"

She sucked in a deep breath. "He came by to see me last night."

I felt my jaw drop. "He what? I didn't know you two were friends." Even in the moonlight, I could see the color rising to her face.

"We aren't friends."

"Then why'd he go see you?" The minute the words fell from my lips, I gasped. I glared at Dabney and jumped up. "Well, I guess I get the prize for coming up with the stupidest question of the decade." My pulse raced. "Last *night*?" I gasped. The more I thought about it, the hotter I became. I lashed out. "I was sitting here on the steps with you until after ten o'clock last night. But I suppose you keep late hours." I ran my fingers through my hair. Arnold Evers hiding behind the iron gate, waiting for me to go home, made my blood boil.

Tears trailed down her cheeks. "But, Kiah, it's not the way . . ."

"Save it, Dabney. You don't owe me an explanation."

"Kiah Grave, you wouldn't believe me if I gave you one."

"You're probably right. Goodnight, Dabney, I reckon I'd better go. You might have customers lined up, waiting for me to leave. I'd hate to hurt your business." I stomped over to #4, madder than a run over dog. I'd stupidly believed her when she told me she'd changed. What a dunce I was. It was plain to see the only thing about her that changed was the company she kept, and that apparently had been changing on a nightly basis.

Dabney ran after me and grabbed me by the arm before I could open the screen door. "Kiah, you are the most stubborn person I've ever met, but you're going to listen to what I have to say, even if I have to hog-tie you."

I glared contemptuously at her hand, as she tightened her grasp. "We have nothing more to say, Dabney. I think you've said it all, already."

"No, I haven't. Kiah, you aren't being fair."

I reached over and prized her fingers from my arm. I scowled, "Go home, Dabney and leave me alone."

She commenced to bawling. Not crying . . . not weeping . . . but plain out bawling.

"Stop the blubbering," I said, trying to sound as if the tears hadn't moved me. But they had.

Dabney Foxworthy had fought many tough battles in her life and she was tough as old shoe leather. So why was she acting so much like a . . . like a woman? I sucked in a deep breath. "Look Dabney, it's late and I think we're both tired. Go home and we'll talk later."

"You can't forget, can you, Kiah? You'll never be able to forget what I was."

I swallowed. Hard. She was right. I couldn't forget. As much as I wanted to, I couldn't blot it from my mind, any more than the holier-than-thou folks couldn't forget what I was. As Mama would say, my finger-pointing accusations were nothing less than 'the pot calling the kettle black.'

Mama's moans could be heard when I opened the door. Dabney's eyes grew wide. She shoved past me. Mama lay sprawling on the floor. Dabney knelt down, gently picked up Mama's head and laid it in her lap. "Fennie?" She whispered, tears trailing down her cheeks.

"Mama, can you hear me?" I picked up Mama's limp arm to feel her pulse.

Dabney's eyes glistened. "Is she . . . I mean, she's not . . . is she, Kiah?"

I shook my head. "Her pulse is very weak. Dabney, if you'll pull back her covers, I'll lay her in the bed."

I picked Mama up, laid her down and sat on the edge of the bed beside her. Dabney ran to the sink and pumped water onto a dish rag, folded it and laid it across Mama's brow.

"Dabney, you stay with her and I'll ride into town and see if I can get the doc to come check on her."

Mama's eyes opened slightly. Her voice sounded raspy. "No, Kiah. No doctor."

The words gushed from my lips. "Mama, you don't try to talk. I'll be back in less than an hour."

Her eyes squinted. "Kiah Grave, you hear me out. No doctor. You hear? No doctor."

I bit my trembling lip. "But Mama, you're very sick. You need help."

She sucked in a deep breath. For a frightening moment, I thought it was her last. Halting after each spoken word, she said, "Kiah, I've known for some time that I was dying."

My voice quavered. "No, Mama. You're wrong. Don't say such things."

She reached up and stroked my face. "Kiah, I'm not afraid to die. Please don't mourn for me, son. I'm going to a better place."

I'd never wanted to believe in a place called Heaven, more than I did at the moment. Mama deserved a better place, and no doubt about it, anywhere would be better than Rooster Run. But even if it were true, and there indeed was a place called Heaven, would God let my Mama walk through the gate? I rubbed my hand over my face and thought of the Samaritan woman.

Mama turned and faced Dabney. "Oh, sweet, sweet Dabney. You've been like a daughter to me. I'm so proud of you."

Dabney laid her head on Mama's chest and sobbed. "Oh, Fennie, no one has ever been proud of me. Please don't leave us."

Mama patted her head. She looked up at me and formed a weak smile. "Kiah, shug, I'll soon see Zann . . . won't that be somethin'—me walking up there on them streets of gold and living in a mansion? And one day, my sweet Kiah-Cooter, you'll join us there. I believe that with all my heart."

Her eyes moistened as she fixed her gaze on me. "Son, I know you're filled with bitterness toward the church, but I've prayed for God to soften your heart. One day, you'll understand just how much He loves you."

I swallowed. I wanted to turn the conversation around. I'd never been able to give Mama much, and perhaps this was my last opportunity to do something special for her. "Mama, if you could make a wish, what would it be?"

"You mean something other than seeing you give your heart to the Lord?"

I winced. We'd covered the topic enough times for her to know we weren't going to reach an agreement. I'd been dogmatic before, and though I never admitted it to Mama, I did have questions—more tonight than ever. If she did go to heaven, and if Zann was there—then I'd be crazy not to want to go too. But I had plenty of time to settle that later. Mama's mind was already settled on the subject. She had no doubts. How I wished I could have her assurance. But of all the things I was, there was one thing I wasn't. I wasn't a fake. As much as it'd please Mama for me to say, "Hallelujah, I believe," she knew I'd never say anything I didn't mean.

She didn't bat an eye, before she answered. "Well, if I made a wish, I'd wish to die in Oklahoma, since that's my home." I gathered from her prompt reply that this was something she'd been thinking on for some time.

I determined then and there my mama would have her wish. The lump in my throat seemed to shrink. There was something Mama wanted, and I could give it to her. "Mama, you hold on, you hear? Hold on, 'til morning, 'cause you and I are taking a trip."

"A trip? Not to Oklahoma. We can't."

"Who says we can't? Of course, we can."

Mama frowned. "You can't miss school. I won't hear of it." She slurred her words, as her eyes closed.

"Don't argue, Mama. We're going, so you close your eyes and rest. I'll ride Dolly into town tonight and look at the bus schedule. We'll take the earliest bus available in the morning."

I wasn't sure how much she heard, since she fell asleep before I finished talking.

Dabney had already begun packing Mama's things. She fastened the clasp on the brown checkered suitcase, and said, "I think I've packed everything. I've made a pot of coffee, if you'd like a cup before you leave, Kiah."

"Thanks," I mumbled. "And Dabney, I'm sorry for firing off at you tonight. You've been a swell friend, and I have no right to tell you how to live your life."

She pulled two cups from the cupboard and poured the steaming black coffee. She sat down and took a sip. "Kiah, I want to go with you to Oklahoma."

I gave a short chuckle. "That's sweet of you, Dabney, but it's out of the question."

She raised her brow. "Why? Why can't I go, Kiah?"

I shrugged. "Why should you? I know you think a lot of Mama and she loves you too, but this is my responsibility. Not yours."

"Kiah, you asked me why? I'll tell you why, though I think it should be obvious. I love you, Kiah. I've loved you for a long time."

She caught me off guard. "Dabney, you don't know what you're saying."

"Yes, I do. I never expected you to love me. Zann was your type. She was sweet and innocent. You hated me for what I was, but I changed Kiah, and I did it for you."

I took a swallow of coffee and choked. "Yeah? Since last night when you and Arnold got together?" I wanted to cut my tongue out. Why did I keep hounding her as if it were any of my business how she chose to live her life?

Her face lit up like a neon light. Her voice trembled. "Kiah Grave, I can't stand Arnold Evers. How could I, after what he did to . . ." She stopped short. The color drained from her face.

My pulse raced. "Finish, Dabney. What were you about to say? After he did what to whom?"

"Forget it." She whispered. "I don't know what I was saying."

My heart pounded. "Sure you do. You were saying you hate Arnold because he raped Zann. That's it, isn't it?" The blood boiled in my veins.

Dabney sobbed. "Kiah, I didn't mean to tell you. Zann didn't want you to know."

I glanced at Mama to make sure she was still sleeping, when my voice rose. "And you—you entertained the creep last night, knowing he was the one who—?" Tears rushed to my eyes. How could she? Arnold Evers? I'd kill the jerk. First, I'd get Mama to

Oklahoma, but after that, I'd hunt him down like a blood hound and rip his eyeballs out of the sockets. He'd never look at another pretty girl, the way he looked at Zann.

Dabney reached over and placed her hand on top of mine. I jerked away. "Kiah, I tried to tell you I didn't entertain him. I didn't. Arnold showed up at my door, but I didn't let him in. He told me he'd been staying with relatives in Alabama, but would be hopping a train to Memphis after the holidays. Then he left. And that's the truth."

It no longer mattered to me why he was at Dabney's door, or whether he went in the house or stayed all night, for that matter. All I could think of was Zann and the horrid image in my mind of her helplessly trying to fight him off, while waiting for me to show up to defend her.

Dabney lifted her head. "Kiah, do you believe me?"

I looked her squarely in the eyes and had no doubt she was telling the truth. "Sure, Dabney. I believe you," I mumbled. "I do." I walked toward the door. "I have a favor to ask. Would you mind staying with Mama 'til I get back from town?"

She nodded. "You know I will."

I rode Dolly to the Greyhound Bus Station. The bus would be leaving at 6:15 in the morning. Not much time to get back, pack my things and get to sleep before time to leave again. But I wasn't sure I'd be able to sleep, anyway. I stopped by the yard to tell Mr. Farris I'd be leaving town. He offered to buy Dolly and the wagon and said he'd pick them up from the bus station the next day.

When I arrived back at the house, I dreaded saying goodbye to Dabney. She honestly thought she was in love with me, and I was unable to convince her otherwise.

She cried and threw her arms around my neck, when I walked her to her door. "Please, Kiah. Please take me with you. I know you don't love me yet, but you will. I'll make you love me. I'll do anything you ask of me. I'll make you a good wife. I will."

For a moment, I almost relented. Not because I loved her. Sure, I liked her. I liked her a lot. But I didn't love her. I'd never love anyone again, not after knowing the real thing. So why not take her up on her offer? She knew the score. She'd make a good companion. Someone to come home to at night. Would that be so bad? I put my arms around her.

"Dabney, Dabney, please don't cry. I don't deserve you."

She reared her head from off my shoulder, and stared into my eyes. "*You*? Don't deserve *me*?"

"That's right. You're a sweet kid and I'm a real chump. You've done everything to try and erase your past, but I keep bringing it back up. I don't mean to, but I do. I'm no good for you."

"Oh, Kiah, you're the only good thing that's ever crossed my path. Please, I beg of you, take me with you? You won't be sorry, I promise."

"But don't you see, Dabney? You'd be the one sorry, because

I'd keep throwing it up in your face. I'd hate myself afterward, but I'm the one who can't seem to change. It wouldn't be fair to you. One day, you'll meet a fine fellow who'll love you so much that he'll not only forgive your past, but he'll also be able to forget."

She tightened her grip and squalled. "I'll make *you* forget. I promise. I will, Kiah. I will."

I hated to leave her behind. I sucked in a deep breath and wondered if we could make it work. I, of all people, had no right to judge anyone for past mistakes. I'd made plenty, myself. Dabney was a swell kid, and I couldn't deny I enjoyed her company. The idea sounded appealing. But I had no idea how long it'd take to hunt down Arnold Evers. If I completed my mission, I'd wind up in the hoosegow. Maybe the electric chair. No. I couldn't take on the responsibility of a wife.

I pulled Dabney's hands from around my neck and pecked her on the cheek. "Goodbye, Dabney. I'll write when I can."

She wiped her eyes. "You aren't coming back, are you?"

I shook my head. "Nope."

With trembling lips, she pleaded. "Kiah, in less than six months, you'll have your high school diploma, and a college scholarship waiting for you. Surely, you aren't going to throw it all away."

I didn't answer. I didn't have to. She knew.

Chapter 18

Dabney opened the door at five o'clock the next morning and stuck her head in. "I saw the light from your window. I came over to help Fennie get dressed."

"Thanks," I said, grateful she was there, but dreading having to say goodbye all over again.

Seeing her all fresh and bright-eyed at dawn, took my breath away. Never had she looked more beautiful as she did in the pink chenille robe with her long, blonde hair falling loosely around her shoulders. My eyes traced the flawless outline of her features from her forehead to her cute little chin. Her well-scrubbed face made a radiant backdrop for eyes that sparkled like blue sapphires.

I had to be strong and remind myself that although Dabney had made a dent in my heart, I was not in love with her. I wasn't. What I felt was sympathy for someone I cared deeply for—and if I hadn't experienced true love in my lifetime, possibly I could've mistaken my feelings for Dabney for the real thing. But it wasn't and I couldn't fake it.

I doubted seriously that Dabney was in love with me, but she had nothing to compare her feelings with. She'd never known love, and that grieved me. As painful as it was to lose Zann, it was better to have loved her and lost than never to have loved at all. If I knew how to pray, my prayer would be for God to bring someone into Dabney's life to love her the way she deserved to be loved.

I watched as she tenderly bathed Mama. She picked up Mama's Sunday dress and drew the curtain, before dressing her. I heard her gasp. "Oh, Kiah, she's covered with a horrible rash. It's even worse than the break-out on her arms. Is it—?"

"Pellagra? Yes. I think so, but she won't let me send for the doctor. She's practically stopped eating. Says food makes her sick on her stomach. Mama's been puny for a long time, so I didn't see this coming. At the first signs of a rash, I assumed she'd gotten into poison oak while out picking poke salat."

Dabney pulled back the curtain, and I could see the tears welling in her eyes, when she reached down and hugged Mama.

A lump formed in my throat, but I couldn't let her moistened eyes hinder my plans.

I motioned for her to walk over toward the sink, then cleared my throat and whispered, "Mama seems a mite stronger this morning, though she appears to be a bit confused. She's still very weak, but I have hopes that we'll make it to Oklahoma. I was doubtful last night that she'd see another sunrise."

Dabney handed me a bottle, which she held in her hand. "This is paregoric. I got it from the pharmacy when Alexandra had a bout of colic. I've kept it in my purse, but she no longer needs it. It's for pain. The directions are on the bottle. Give Fennie a dose before you board the bus and it should ease her pain but it will also help her to sleep on the trip."

I picked up Mama's suitcase, and bundled up a changing of clothes for me in a red flannel shirt.

Mama hugged Dabney and pushed something in her hands.

Dabney threw her hand over her mouth and shrieked. "Your brooch? I can't take this, Fennie."

Mama smiled. "But you must. You're my only daughter, and the brooch is a family heirloom. Will and I always wanted more children, but we're so proud of you and Kiah."

I looked at Dabney. Her eyes widened. My throat tightened when Mama followed with, "Did you know Will is coming home to Goat Hill tomorrow and he's bringing me a chocolate set from England? I can hardly wait to see my darling. I've missed him so. He's been gone a whole month."

Dabney combed Mama's hair and played along, but I couldn't stand to listen to such lunacy. Though Mama had no idea what she was saying, the anger inside me reached a boiling point. I wasn't mad at Mama, or at least I didn't think I was. I sometimes felt my body was programmed to fly into a rage at the mere mention of my father.

I wanted to throw up when Mama said, "Oh, my sweet little Dabney. You've always been a daddy's girl. You've missed your father, haven't you, sweetheart?"

Dabney's lips trembled. "More than you know, Mama. More than you know."

Mama had a faint smile on her face. "Poor Will. Bless his heart, he loves us so, and it breaks his heart to be away, but he has obligations, which demand his time. Surely, you and your brother realize how much we mean to him. He'd be with us, if he could." She reached up and touched Dabney's cheek. "You do know that, don't you, sugar?"

Dabney sniffed. "Sure, Mama. We know." She tried to slip the brooch into my hand. I shook my head. "No, she wants you to have it." The brooch had been very special to Mama, though I couldn't imagine why. I thought of all the lean years when we both went to bed hungry, yet the expensive, antique brooch stayed pinned to the inside of Mama's purse.

Mama patted Dabney's hand that clutched the small, bejeweled pin. "Dabney, the stones are rubies, you know. Real rubies. It belonged to my granny, who passed it down to her first born daughter. Ma gave it to me on my eighteenth birthday, the day I left home. And now you can pass it down to your daughter."

Dabney glanced at me and smiled, sort of pitiful like, as if Mama was still talking out of her head.

My anger faded. Dabney's patience with Mama touched my

heart. If only I could be so kind. I whispered in her ear. "It's true, The stones *are* real, and it is an heirloom."

Dabney's eyes widened. "Oh, Kiah, I can't . . ."

"Sure you can."

"Why do you suppose Fennie was carrying on so about a chocolate set?"

I lifted my shoulders. "Something she dreamed, I suppose."

Dabney said, "I wonder if all these years she's yearned for one. You think?"

I shrugged. "Could be, but it's the first time I've ever heard her mention it." With Mama's state of mind, it was impossible to separate sense from the senseless. She rambled incessantly during her waking hours. About the time I'd think her mind was clear, she'd start talking out of her gourd again.

I smiled, thinking of Dabney's reply when Mama asked if she missed her father. I whispered, "So, sis, you really miss Pop, huh?" I smirked. "Me too. Good ol' Pop."

Dabney didn't seem amused. She answered, "Kiah, my response wasn't as far-fetched as you might think. I understood Fennie's dream and I must confess for a moment I wanted to share in her wonderful fantasy—that we're one big, happy family from Goat Hill, Alabama."

After Dabney finished dressing Mama, I helped her on the wagon, while Dabney watched from the front stoop. Our eyes met. I hesitated, then walked over to where she stood and kissed her lightly on the cheek. I felt like a heel, leaving Dabney behind. But wouldn't it be worse to marry her, knowing I'd never love her the way a man should love a wife?

"Dabney, I really wish—"

She didn't allow me to finish. "I know," she said in a flattened voice. No doubt she did, but it didn't make leaving her any easier.

"Promise you'll write?" She asked.

"I promise."

The trip was long and hard. Mama's mind came and went. At times, she was perfectly coherent. At other times, she thought I was my father, and she was Mrs. Will Lancaster, and we were on a cruise ship on our way to England. Had this been her fantasy for eighteen years? I'd loathed the man all my life, but now I hated him more than ever.

Even with the paregoric, Mama's pain became unbearable. The writhing pain on her face tore my heart in two.

In her lucid moments, she continuously murmured two words, "Promise, me. Promise me."

I pretended not to understand. She wanted me to promise I'd look up the scumbag who deserted her before I was born. I didn't want to make such a promise, but to calm her, I finally nodded. "Okay, Mama. I promise. Now, stop worrying. All this fretting is zapping your strength."

Whenever she dozed I panicked and checked her pulse, hoping

she'd hold on long enough to put her feet on Oklahoma soil. We were about twenty miles from her hometown in Dry Plains, Oklahoma when I reached for her arm and there was no pulse. I ran my fingers up and down her wrist, hoping I was wrong. She had to be alive. Had to be. But in my heart, I knew she was gone. I couldn't let anyone see my panic, for fear I'd be put off the bus before we reached our destination. As we drove into town, a large sign in front of a two-story house caught my eye—"Dry Plains Funeral Home."

We pulled up to the bus stop and I tied the red bundle onto my belt loop, then picked Mama up in my arms. I saw no need to retrieve her suitcase. She wouldn't need it. As I stepped off the bus, the driver questioned me. "What's wrong with her?"

"She's resting." I mumbled. "Mama's been very ill, but she'll be okay." It was the truth. Mama *would* be okay. All her troubles were over. But mine had only begun. What do you do with a dead body in a strange town? With her in my arms, I walked two blocks to the funeral home and rung the doorbell. It was late.

A tall, slender fellow in a double-breasted suit opened the door. He looked as if he'd never seen a corpse before.

"Young man," he gasped. "What have we here?"

I was tired, worried and not in the mood for needless chatter. "*We* have a dead body. She's my Mama and *we* need to bury her."

He ushered me to a back room and told me to lay Mama on a long table. After he determined I was poor and there was no need to go through his normal sales pitch he agreed to let me have a plain pine box. He said he'd lay her out and deliver her body to Potter's Field for ten bucks.

I waited on the steps of the funeral home for three hours, before the hearse pulled up and the mortician motioned for me to get in. We drove to the edge of town, and rode down a long dirt road to a large field, where graves were marked only with wooden crosses. Many had no markers at all. The moon was full and I had an eerie feeling as I listened to the sound of a hoot owl in the distance. We lifted the pine box from the back of the hearse. "Pick your spot," he said, showing little compassion.

What difference did it make? We sat the box on the ground. The mortician went back to the hearse and picked up a shovel and handed to me. "You can leave it here, when you finish," he said. "I'll pick it up later." I had naively expected him to help dig her grave, but he turned and drove away.

After digging in the hard soil for hours, I laid down on the cold ground beside Mama's grave, exhausted. I awoke at dawn, tied two sticks together with my leather boot strap to form a cross, and hammered it into the ground with the back of the shovel. The pain in my chest was almost unbearable. Mama deserved much better than what I could give her. I wondered if I'd done the right thing by leaving Dabney behind. Surely, Mama would've wanted her here for the burying.

I truly wished that I could've fallen in love with Dabney. I hated this lonely feeling, but it seemed to be my lot in life. I wanted to throw wild flowers on the grave and sing something appropriate, but all I could think of was "Yes, We Have No Bananas." The stupid lyrics to the song kept popping up in my head and I couldn't seem to erase them. Mama lay dead, and all I could think of was some silly song. "Oh, Mama, I wish I could go with you, where you're going. I really do—but I'm a mess. I'll never be good like you." I knelt down on the cold ground and began to hum a familiar tune. But what was it? I kept humming until the words came to me. "Just as I am, without one plea . . ." A sharp pain shot through my chest.

I stopped singing, lifted my head toward heaven and screamed, "Lord, you think I don't want to come? You think I wouldn't want to be up there walking on those golden streets with Mama and Zann? Of course, I do. But I can't. Not just as I am. I'm not good like Mama and Zann. I'm rotten to the core."

I tried to compose myself. Mama wouldn't have wanted me to yell at God. I recalled another song, although I wasn't sure it was a religious song. I started belting out the words to "You are my sunshine, my only sunshine." That one made me smile, for I could almost hear Mama singing it with me. I supposed it was one of her favorites, since she sang it often as she worked around the house.

I longed for a Parson to say kind words over her grave. It only seemed proper, though I didn't know why. Surely, Mama would've wanted Bible words spouted at a time like this, and though she'd read to me from the Good Book plenty of times, regretfully, I hadn't absorbed much. There was this one prayer that I'd heard her pray countless times. I tried to say it the way I remembered Mama saying it, even though I couldn't make sense out of it.

"Our Father, how be your name? Your kingdom come, your will be done—" There was much more, and it had something to do with daily bread, and forgiveness but I couldn't put it all together. I stood there for a good five minutes with my eyes closed, hoping the words would come. I drew a blank. Why didn't I pay more attention to my sweet Mama? I suppose I turned her off when she got to the forgiveness part. Will Lancaster didn't deserve her forgiveness.

After giving up on the prayer, I struggled to recall the words to one of her favorite Bible passages. I'd heard her repeat it so many times, I was sure I could say it if I put my mind to it. "The Lord is my—" A frog caught in my throat and I realized I had to improvise. "Lord, you were Mama's Shepherd and she was not one to want for more. She laid down in green pastures and— something, something, and—" I sucked in a breath and tried to think. Then it came to me. "Though she walked through the valley of the shadow of death, she feared no evil, for you walked with her." My pulse raced. All these years, I resented God and now all of a sudden I was grateful that He was always there to comfort Mama and give her peace, even in the worst of circumstances. With sobs billowing up from my diaphragm, I lifted my eyes toward the sky, because if Mama was right and there really was a Heaven, I reckoned that's where she'd be. I finished with the words, "And her cup ran over. Slap over the top. It ran over with love and poured out on me."

I was gonna miss her something terrible, but Mama would've been proud of me. I'd said the scripture verses for *her*, and even though I hadn't quoted verbatim, I found a strange comfort in the words that surpassed my understanding. Comfort in knowing Mama didn't fear death, because she had an unshakeable faith—a faith that let her believe she was going to dwell in a place called The House of the Lord. Forever. It was a lot for me to take in. Would she have experienced that same level of comfort if she hadn't believed in her heart that I'd one day join her there? I swallowed hard. She not only believed she was going, but she was convinced I'd follow her there.

I flinched. Mama didn't know what I knew. I couldn't join her, because I had to kill a fellow. Maybe God could forgive the Samaritan woman and my mama for their sins, but even with my limited knowledge of the Bible, I was confident if heaven was real, there'd be no murderers there.

I said farewell to Mama. I cried and made a promise to be back one day with a marble tombstone to replace the crude little cross.

I found a long stick and tied my clothes onto the end, slung it over my shoulder and headed for the railroad track. I had a mission to accomplish. I'd find Arnold Evers if it was the last thing I ever did. I worked odd jobs along the way, knocking on the back door of houses, exchanging labor for food. But I never accepted charity. I swept yards, chopped wood, mended fences. If there was nothing for me to do, I refused to eat their food. Since Dabney had said Arnold had relatives in Montgomery, Alabama, my goal was to get there and if my search proved unsuccessful, I'd work my way back upward.

The next seven months are a blur. I hardly remember leaving Oklahoma and arriving in Alabama. Dabney and I kept in touch. It was while working a short stint on a farm in Montgomery, that I received the following letter:

Dear Kiah,

Please excuse my hen-scratching but I ain't had much practice at writing. I miss you and Fennie so much. I wish you could see the baby. She's the spitting image of Zann. I'm still living with the Pruitt's. Poor Mrs. Pruitt ain't been herself since the funeral. She's just about slam crazy. Sometimes I think she blames sweet little Alexandra for Zann's death. The parson takes up time with the baby but Mrs. Pruitt can't stand to look at her, so I keep the crib in my room.

Life ain't easy for the parson with his wife half out of her wits. People in church are beginning to talk. Well, I don't mean it to sound like everybody, because it ain't. Most of the folks are real understanding, but a few women are stirring up a hornet's nest, wanting to believe there's hanky-panky going on with me living under the same roof with the parson. I've offered to move out, but he's begged me to stay and take care of Alexandra. I don't know what he'd do if I left. To be honest, it'd break my heart to have to leave my baby. Well, she ain't my baby, I know, but I've become so attached to her and she's attached to me.

I'm really in a pickle, Kiah. I wish you was here. I'm sending you little Alexandra's picture. Ain't she a doll? Well, I didn't mean to unload on you like this, but I'm feeling a little weepy.

Write soon.

Love,

Dabney

Chapter 19

I folded Dabney's letter and stuck it in my shirt pocket. Mixed emotions stirred within me. One minute I was angry with Mrs. Pruitt for blaming an innocent baby for being born and the next minute I found myself guilty of the same offense.

It wasn't fair to blame the kid, but neither did it seem fair for Arnold Evers' child to take the place of the girl I loved. Why did Zann have to die? My pulse raced as I pulled the picture out of the envelope. I looked into the face of a miniature Zann and trembled. Suddenly, the baby was no longer Arnold's child. She was Zann's and she stole my heart, just the way her Mommy had done.

I sat down on an old stump and let seven months of bottled up tears flow from my eyes. I wanted to go back to Pivan Falls. Back to see Dabney and the baby. But I couldn't. Not yet. I had to find Arnold Evers. For Zann's sake. At least, I wanted to believe it was for her sake.

I didn't mind farming, and would've stayed longer in Montgomery but I had a mission to accomplish, which wouldn't allow me to rest. I received a month's wages, hitched a ride with a trucker and rode to Huntsville, Alabama. There, I jumped the blinds, determined to search every town along the Southern Railway route until I found him. I'm not sure if I was driven by grief or hatred. All I know is that I searched every dive at each stop, and talked to anybody I could engage in a conversation, giving them Arnold's description. It seemed as if he'd disappeared off the edge of the planet.

Little did I know when I hopped on the Southern Railway in March, 1931 in Chattanooga, Tennessee, that I was about to become a part of Alabama History because of an alleged crime that supposedly took place on the train. Nine colored boys, accused of raping a white girl later went to trial in Scottsboro, Alabama, and it was in all the papers. The trial was billed as *The Scottsboro Boys' Case.* I never believed they were guilty, though I couldn't testify to the facts then, nor can I now. I believe the boys were in an adjoining boxcar when I hopped the train, but I could be wrong. Maybe they boarded later in Chattanooga. I gave little attention to the black dudes, since the object of my search was white.

I'm not sure what part of the state we were in at the time, but I do remember they were in the car when an old man boarded at Sheffield, Alabama. As the train pulled away, the elderly man with a long white beard, struggled to climb aboard. I reached down and gave him a hand. I couldn't help feeling sorry for the old gent. He looked to be at least eighty years old. Of course, I suspected he was younger, and that a hard life had aged him beyond his years. His silver hair reached his shoulders but it was clean and neatly combed. He was small of stature—not more than five-feet five and I guessed his weight to be between 115 and 120 pounds. He wore a clean white shirt, though it was ragged and worn. His black slacks were a couple sizes too large. A thin rope ran through his belt loops, causing the oversized pants to gather around his waist. His wrinkled, leathery skin looked weather-beaten. But there was something weird about the old gentleman. Nothing I could point to specifically, yet he was different from the other hoboes I'd met on my trip. Did he have a family? Had he once led an affluent life, and after losing everything in the crash, now resorted to hopping trains in search of work? I imagined all sorts of scenarios.

"Where you headed?" I asked.

"Heb'n." He said with a straight face. I tried hard not to chuckle. Perhaps like Mama, the old fellow had done gone loco.

"Did you say 'Heaven?'" I smiled.

"Yep."

Poor creature. He was obviously crazy as a bedbug. Not sure how to carry on a conversation with a loony, I mused, "Heaven, you say. And you think you're on the right track?" I bit the inside of my cheek to keep from laughing at the pun.

"Yep." He plundered through his bindle, as he spoke. "Sonny, I'm on the right track, all right. There's only one way to get there, and I've found the way." He pulled a dog-eared Bible from the small bundle tied to the end of a stick. "Jesus says in the Good Book that He's gone to prepare a place for me, and since He's gone to prepare a place, He'll come again for *me*, that where He is, I can be also."

I smiled. "Says all that, does it?"

"Yep. That and much more. You can join us there, if you're a mind to, ya know."

My pulse raced. What did he mean by join "us?" Then I let out a deep breath, when it occurred to me that he was referring to him and Jesus. Of course. There was no way for him to know I had loved ones up there waiting for me.

I had a mental picture of Mama meeting him at the pearly gate, saying, "Sir, do you know my boy, Kiah? I s'pose he'll be coming d'rectly." I smiled. In spite of my ranting and raving to the contrary, Mama had been convinced that one day I'd see the light, as she put it. I blinked back a tear. I was lonely. The possibility of seeing Zann and Mama again made me want answers to questions I'd never before asked. Did I dare ask the old man? If Heaven was real, I didn't want to be left behind.

The box car was crowded on the side toward the forward motion. The old man and I sat on the opposite end. I'd never met female hoboes before, but two girls whom I assumed were sisters were carrying on a bunch of foolishness with a herd of ruffians over in the corner. The raucous laughter soon turned into swearing. A fight broke out among a few white thugs and several black dudes.

With more energy than sense, I jumped up to join in. I got in one punch, when someone hit me over the back of the head with what I assumed was brass knuckles. I don't know how long I was out, but when I came to, the fight was in full swing. I jumped up to finish what I started, but the old man grabbed me by the arm. He was stronger than he looked.

"Sonny, what breed o' dog you got in that hunt?"

I looked at him and frowned. "No dog, I don't reckon." I rocked on my feet, dizzy from the blow to the head.

"Then let 'em be, Hezekiah. Ain't no sense in gettin' yourself thrown off the train for something what ain't no concern of yore'n." He led me back to our little corner.

He was right. Becoming involved didn't seem like such a smart idea, especially since I didn't even know why they were fighting.

The old man pulled out a small sack of cracklin's, which he shared with me. I liked the ol' fellow. There was something about him, which demanded respect. As I listened, I discovered he wasn't crazy, after all. His poor English belied his wisdom.

The train slowed, and four or five white guys were thrown from the train in Stevenson, Alabama. I got a glimpse of one of them. Arnold Evers? Could it be I'd been in the same box car with the grand rascal and didn't even know it? I couldn't be positive the fellow I saw was Arnold, but the notion haunted me. Was he one of the hoboes who boarded at Sheffield? Was it possible he was in the same car, only yards away and I'd been so amused by the old fellow that I failed to recognize him? Perhaps Arnold was the one who hit me from behind.

When the train came to a stop in Paint Rock, Alabama, the Bull walked up to the door, and demanded the nine colored boys step off the train. The old man fell asleep and I stayed hunched over in the corner next to him. If the Bull saw us, he pretended not to, for he didn't throw us off.

I didn't move, but I could see all the commotion from where I sat. Both of the white girls who'd been hoofing it up earlier with all the thugs, were now standing near a cop and putting on a show. I heard one of them say, "It was them colored boys who had their way with us, and we tried to fight 'em off, but they wuz too many of 'em."

The cop grabbed the youngest boy by the collar. "That true boy?"

"Nahsuh, it ain't so. We never touched them girls."

The tall girl yelled, "Liar, liar."

The nine frightened black boys all maintained an immoral act took place on the train, but insisted it was with one of the white guys, who was thrown off earlier. Said it wasn't rape, but consensual.

No one wanted to believe them. But I did, even though I didn't see what happened. There'd been something going on and now I believed more than ever that Arnold Evers was in the middle of it.

The cops were putting handcuffs on the boys, and questioning the Bull, when three hoboes slipped past and jumped in the boxcar. Two appeared to be seasoned vagabonds. The other, I could tell was new at jumping the blinds. We introduced ourselves. Hank and Coley maintained they were big-time gamblers. Judging from their shabby appearance and the fact they were riding in the boxcar, I presumed they were either liars or not very good at their profession. Posie, on the other hand was neat and clean. He was soft spoken and easy to talk to. Said he recently lost his job and was seeking employment.

That night I couldn't sleep. For months, hatred drove me to hunt Arnold the way a wolf hunts its prey. He didn't deserve to live and I'd be the one to see that he didn't. So when I saw him rolling on the ground, why didn't I jump from the train when it slowed—go back and do what I set out to do? I'd had the perfect chance.

I knew the answer. It was the old man. All his jabbering got to me. Killing Arnold no longer seemed to make sense. If the old fellow was right about a real place called Heaven—and he certainly seemed convinced—then did I really want to burn the bridges, which might help me find my way to Zann and Mama? I wasn't ready to cross that bridge, yet, but I saw no need in destroying even a remote possibility that I might see them again one day.

After all, Mama, Zann, Dabney and now the old man all seemed positive such a place existed. Were they all crazy? Or was I? Then I remembered the strange closing in Zann's farewell letter—"Until we meet again." I hadn't thought much about it until this moment. She was aware how adamantly I opposed anything having to do with Christianity. Yet, she didn't say "if we meet," but she used the word "until," as if it were only a matter of time. Was it nothing more than a cliché? Wishful thinking, or evidence of her strong faith? Though she never preached to me, I didn't doubt for a moment that she prayed for me.

The other three fellows didn't seem to have a problem catching Z's. Coley's loud snoring could drown out a train whistle. I hurt too bad to sleep. My head throbbed as I stretched out on the floor of the box car. Sticky blood stuck to my fingers, when I ran them through my matted hair. I must have awakened the old man, for he raised up, folded a moth-eaten wool army blanket and gently placed it beneath my head.

"Thank you," I whispered.

He nodded.

I was half-asleep when I heard him muttering something, which sounded rather peculiar. It was too dark in the boxcar for him to see how to read. Was he reciting poetry?

He was crouched over with his head resting on his knees, and his voice sounded soft and mellow. "For I was ahungered, and ye gave me meat; I was thirsty, and ye gave me drink: I was a stranger, and ye took me in. Naked, and ye clothed me: I was sick and ye visited me; I was in prison, and ye came unto me."

I lifted my head slightly. I could only see his silhouette. "Say, what were you quoting? Something from Shakespeare?"

He didn't move, neither did he answer my question. Instead, he continued to spout off strange sounding words in a low, monotone voice. I didn't doubt the old fellow was harmless, but there was something about the way he acted that gave me the heebie-jeebies. "Say, mister, you okay? Can I get you something?" The moment the words slipped past, I realized how utterly ridiculous I must have sounded. I was on a moving train, for crying out loud. What could I get him?

He was a strange bird, but I was drawn to him from the moment I helped pull him onto the train. Maybe he'd had a stroke and couldn't move. It was cold in the boxcar. I took the rolled up blanket, which he'd given me and spread it over his shoulders. He didn't flinch. My heart raced.

"Are you sick?"

No answer.

I expected to get a rise out of him when I said, "I suppose you saw no reason to answer a stupid question when I asked if I could get you something, but I wasn't thinking straight. You had me worried."

Without lifting his head, he said, "Verily I say unto you, Inasmuch as ye have done it unto one of the least of these my brethren, ye have done it unto me."

I couldn't tell if his eyes were opened or closed. Maybe he was dreaming. I shrugged, laid my head down on the cold, hard floor and drifted off to sleep.

Hours later when I awoke, the old man was gone but his blanket was under my head and the remainder of the cracklin's beside my bindle. What a kind ol' soul he was. Every hobo has a story. What was his? I picked up the bag of cracklin's and smiled at his generosity. This was all the food he had and he left it for me. But I sensed he'd given me much more than food for my body. He'd left me with food for my thoughts. I wasn't ready to swallow all of it yet, but I'd been given something to chew on.

I raised up and stretched. "Where are we, Posie?"

"Next stop is Goat Hill, Alabama."

Chapter 20

I jumped up, grabbed my bindle and the sack of cracklin's. "Goat Hill, you say? This is where I get off." The strange words, which I'd heard the old man utter, suddenly came to mind. "I was hungry, and ye gave me meat." I held out the sack. "You hungry, Posie?"

"You kidding? Man, I'm starving."

I tossed the sack his way. "This is all I've got, and it's not much, but they're pretty good. You fellows can share what's left."

"Thanks." He sat up, ran his hand into the bag and crammed cracklin's into his mouth before passing the sack to Hank. "Say, these are pretty good. Yo' mama make 'em?"

I shook my head. "The old man gave them to me."

"Old man?" His brow furrowed.

"Yeah, the one who was riding with us. I reckon he jumped off at the last stop. I was asleep."

"Ain't no old man been on this train. Last stop was at Paint Rock, and nobody got off there, except the hooligans arrested for the fight that broke out."

I shook my head. "No, the old man was here after we left Paint Rock. He was here when I went to sleep. You saw him. I know you heard him talking to me."

Posie lifted his brow. "Don't know what you been drinking but if you have any left, I'd be obliged if you'd give me a swig. I'm telling you kid, ain't no old man been on this train." He gestured toward Hank and Coley playing cards in the corner. "Just been the four of us, since the three of us jumped aboard at Paint Rock."

I pounded my palm on the floor. "He was beside me. Right here in this same boxcar with us. There's no way you could've missed him." The other two stopped playing, and were staring in our direction.

"You sick?" Hank asked, his brow furrowed.

"You talking to me?"

"Yeah, you. What's all the talk about an old man?"

I chuckled. "Posie seems to be having a memory lapse. Pretends not to know about the old man who rode with us."

"But there ain't been nobody, except—"

I yelled, "I know . . . nobody but the four of us. Are y'all crazy?"

I didn't know what was going on, but the furor stirring inside me continued to build. I fought to stay calm, though I felt I was losing the battle. Why were they lying? What reason would they have? Posie was in his mid-fifties—a family man, who proudly passed around pictures of his wife and children. He seemed honest enough. I even sensed compassion in his voice, when he said, "Kiah, don't let it upset you. I 'spect you've been under a lot of stress, and your mind is just a little mixed up. I'm sure you'll be all right."

I felt as if I'd fallen in a black hole. I yelled, "But he was here, I tell you. I didn't make him up."

"Okay, kid. Maybe we just didn't see him."

I sucked in a deep breath. It would've been impossible for them not to see him. He was lying right beside me. "Didn't you hear us talking?"

Hank looked sheepish. "We heard *you* talking, all right. You kept waking me up, mumbling in your sleep, something about visiting prisoners and naked people. That was some kinda weird dream you were having."

"No, no. That wasn't me. It was him. I think he was quoting something from the Bible, but he never did say."

Posie's voice sounded patronizing. "Okay, so maybe he was here and we didn't see him. Let's leave it at that. Where did he say he was going?"

I remembered the old man's words, when I asked him the same question. Did I dare tell the fellows he said he was on his way to heaven? They really would think I was ready for the loony bin if I tried to explain. I shook my head. "Dunno."

Coley stopped playing cards. "What was his name?"

I could tell he didn't believe me either. I suddenly realized the old man and I failed to introduce ourselves. "Dunno," I mumbled. Then I thought of something weird. Though I hadn't told the old man my name, I distinctly remembered him calling me Hezekiah before the other dudes boarded. How could he have known my name?

Was I losing my mind? No. He was real. He was as real as I was. And I had a sack of cracklin's and a wool army blanket to prove he was on this train. But how could it be that I was the only one who saw him? Were these guys pulling my leg?

In a condescending tone of voice, Coley said, "I hope your friend sprouted wings if he jumped from this train. We ain't slowed for even a crossing since leaving Paint Rock." Hank snickered.

"I don't care if you don't believe me," I mumbled. I thought about where the ol' codger said he was headed. And I thought about his invitation for me to join him there. Well, maybe I would. But I couldn't go yet. I had something to do first, and it had nothing to do with Arnold Evers. Bumping him off was a foolish idea. It wouldn't bring Zann back. But I'd made Mama a promise and I intended to keep it.

I grinned, at the mental picture of me going to Heaven and

knocking on the door of Mama's mansion. I imagined her shaking her finger in my face and saying, "Did you do it, Kiah? Did you do what I asked? Did you go meet your daddy?" I wouldn't be able to lie to her—not with God looking over my shoulder.

The train slowed for a stop, and I grabbed my bindle.

Posie said, "What's in Goat Hill?"

I smiled. "Just a promise."

"A promise of a job?"

I shook my head. "No. It's personal."

"Well, if you need a job and you're a mind to pick cotton, you might wanna go to the Gladstone Plantation and ask for a man they call 'Mr. Will.' He owns it. I don't recollect his last name, but I hear tell he's a right nice fellow to work for. I'm going on to Mobile, myself. I'm gonna try to get on at the paper mill."

"Lancaster," I shouted, standing in the doorway with my bindle over my shoulder, ready to jump.

"Huh?" Then his eyes widened. "Yeah, that's it. Will Lancaster. You know him?"

"No, but he'll know me before I leave Goat Hill."

I jumped from the train and caught sight of a brand-spanking new Model A Ford, driven by the prettiest girl I'd seen since Zann Pruitt died.

She and her girlfriend soared past the depot, full throttle. When she spotted me, she slammed on the brakes but didn't bring the car to a full stop. She turned, smiled at me and threw up her hand. Though the car was still in motion, I ran toward the vehicle, thinking she'd slowed down to offer me a ride. I stopped in my tracks, when she kept inching forward while eyeing me in her rearview mirror. I could hear her laughing, as if she'd pulled a prank. She drove down the road a piece. I felt a little put-out at first, thinking she'd played me for a sap, making me think she was gonna give me a lift. But suddenly, the brightly colored scarf tied around her neck flew off and hit me slap-dab in the face.

I chuckled when she looked back and winked. That's when I caught on that she meant to let go of the scarf. The little flirt. But why would a gorgeous rich dame flirt with a scrubby-looking hobo? Was I fantasizing? Maybe she hadn't winked. Perhaps there was something in her eye.

I kept walking toward her, and she kept easing forward, as if to tease me. She drove several yards, and the car stopped. She backed up, then cut the wheels and lunged forward, heading straight for the ditch. It was almost as if she aimed for it.

I stiffened when it looked as if she might hit the fence. I ran toward them. "Miss, can I help?"

She tucked a strand of platinum blonde hair behind her ear and flashed a quick smile. "Why, thank you. I certainly hope so." She tried to feign a look of desperation, but I'd seen better actresses in Grammar School plays. She raised her brow as I stepped back and eyed the imbedded tires.

I tried to keep a straight face. "Don't worry, Miss. It's not as bad as it looks. I'll run up the road and see if I can find something to put under the wheels."

She smiled, kind of coy, like. "You're very kind. You can throw your . . ." She looked at my bindle and fumbled over her words. "Put that . . . I mean your—"

I raised my brow. "Rags? Is that the word you're choking on?" She shot her chin in the air. "I wasn't choking. I simply didn't know what to call it."

"Allow me to educate you, to keep you from appearing ignorant in the future." I held my bindle in the air. "This elegant red bundle dear lady holds my winter wardrobe. The only difference between a vagabond and a banker is that we men of distinction pack our morning coats in red flannel when we travel, to keep from lugging around a smelly old cowhide suitcase."

She hid her mouth with her hand. "Sorry." Flipping her hair back with a toss of her head, she said, "You don't have to be so snippy. I was merely telling you to toss it on the rumble seat."

Then she giggled. I didn't know whether to laugh with her, or give her the what-for.

My jaw jutted forward and I snapped, "I suppose you're accustomed to telling folks what to do, but I don't happen to be in the habit of taking orders."

She seemed amused. I took a step backward and tried to appear agitated, although I must admit I enjoyed the banter. The girl had spirit. Her quick wit made me laugh and feel alive again.

She was lively and sharp-witted. She took my sarcasm, rolled it up with her own, and socked it back in my face with a punch as powerful as a mule's hind legs. Never had I come in contact with such a gutsy female. Nothing shocked her, but I can't say the same for me. I was unprepared for her smart-mouth. But I suppose that was part of her appeal. She was different. There was nothing about her that made me stop to compare her with my darling Zann.

Instead of stirring up feelings of melancholy, she stirred something else inside me, though I couldn't define it. I figured if I ever did fall in love again, no doubt I'd wind up with someone like this exasperating little poker. That's exactly what she was—a fire poker. She managed to stoke away at love's left-over ashes, and without my consent rekindled a tiny, live ember in the depths of my heart. When Zann died, I was certain the fire she lit under me left and that I'd never see the light of love again. Now, I wasn't so sure.

The blonde smiled when I laid my bindle against the fence post. "Don't forget to come back," she said with a giggle.

I raised the corner of my lip in what I hoped resembled a snarl. "And you don't forget to stay put."

She need not worry her pretty little head. I'd be back. And I hoped she'd still be waiting. I wasn't convinced the car was really stuck, and I had a feeling that neither was she. I grinned, thinking there was barely enough clay to cover the tread on the tires. A slight tap on the accelerator would send the car in either direction.

Nevertheless, I'd return with the boards, and we'd both pretend I saved the day.

As I turned to walk away, she yelled, "Where you going?"

Had she not been listening? "To get the boards," I said, rather sharply.

"No, silly, I mean what are you doing in Goat Hill? Where are you headed?"

I chuckled. "To see a man named Will Lancaster. Know him?"

"Everyone knows 'Mr. Will.' She looked at her friend and giggled. If you help get us out of this mess, I'll drive you there."

After rounding the bend in the road, I saw a deserted barn in the distance where I might be able to salvage a couple of old boards. My heart beat double time. Conflicting emotions gnawed at my insides. What was wrong with me, allowing a snobby, smart-alecky girl to steal a corner of my heart, when it belonged to another? I didn't even know her name, or why I was instantly attracted to her. A sassy little thing, she had a come-back for everything I said. So why did I enjoy scrapping with her?

I jammed my hands in the pocket of my overalls and stepped up my stride. Confusion wracked through my body like an electric current.

She was nothing like sweet, agreeable Zann, who was as lovely on the inside as she was on the outside. The mere thought of the treasure that ebbed from my life without allowing me to say goodbye, made me ache all over. I felt like a knife had been thrust through my heart. I'd become proficient at conjuring up her image in my mind, which I sometimes viewed as a strength. Other times, it became my weakness. There seemed to be an almost intoxicating effect, whenever I'd reach into the confines of my memory bank and pull her near me. The mind can do strange things when employing a wild imagination.

I'd never needed Zann to come to me as I needed her now. With a heavy heart, I sucked in a breath and there she was, as plainly as if I were gazing at her through a looking glass. The proficiency with which I'd learned to pull her into my thoughts with such clarity, had come through hours of practice. Having a mental picture of her steadied me, as it always had. Though I could see her image, I'd never again be able to feel the softness of her skin, any more than one can feel the warmth of flesh by laying a hand on a mirror. Yet, there she was, in the corner of my mind, smiling back at me. Her long, black curls blowing in the wind— her lips like plump, luscious pomegranates and those big brown eyes twinkling as she smiled. I could hear her giggling as she twirled around and around in an elegant gown—a gown, I'd only seen in my thoughts, yet she'd described it so perfectly, I could see every detail. After all these months, I still missed her terribly. Such a lovely creature, yet she never grasped how stunningly beautiful she really was. Humility was only one of her many virtues.

Sure, the other girl was a fine-looking dish, but my first impression led me to believe she didn't underestimate her gorgeous looks. An aura of unmistakable confidence oozed from every pore in her body. How strange that I'd be attracted to such opposites.

Her neatly styled hair was the color of corn silks. Her eyes the color of emeralds. Her sun-kissed skin glowed, reflecting a healthy diet. Her cheeks were soft like rose petals. But it was her laugh that drew me in. Her lips parted wide, then her eyes twinkled and giggles erupted into soft, fluttering sounds like a huge covey of sea gulls flapping their wings over the ocean. Even when she goaded me with her wise-cracks, she made me laugh. Ah, how good it was to laugh again.

Yet I felt ashamed that I could laugh so freely. Guilt overwhelmed me. Was it wrong for me to have feelings for a stranger? I'd love Zann Pruitt 'til I drew my last breath. But there was something special about this girl. Something that made me want to live again.

When I reached the old barn, I walked inside. A setting hen fluttered from the rafters, causing me to jump and stumble over a broken cow-stall gate, lying on the ground.

A frightening scenario caused my mouth to dry. I swallowed hard. What if I returned to discover there was no car. No girl. Perhaps she was a mere figment of my imagination. Had the bump on the head caused me to hallucinate? Or had I conjured her up in the same way I brought Zann to my remembrance when I needed her? But if I'd dreamed up this beautiful creature, I did a bang-up good job. I couldn't have imagined a more perfect apparition—one with the power to bring life back into my body. Not only did I want to live again, but I wanted to love again. I'd been led to believe that for every man and woman there was only one love. Now, I wasn't so sure. Was it possible for true love to come twice? Zann seemed to believe it. She'd prayed for it to happen. If God answers prayers, then surely Zann's wishes would get top priority. My pulse raced. What if—?

I reached into the pocket of my overalls and pulled out a yellowed envelope. Carefully unfolding the thin pages, I read the words, which I'd read so many times I could quote them from memory:

"God has many shells beyond the breakers, which will wash ashore with the tide. The next one may not look like the one you lost, but it will be equally beautiful . . .

The tide is beginning to ebb, my darling, and soon I'll be no more. Don't mourn for what you've lost. God has something wonderful in store. Watch for the high tide. This is my prayer.
May God keep you, 'til we meet again,
Zann"

I sat down inside the barn on an old milk stool and bawled like a colicky baby. With an uncontrollable compulsion to speak to a precious memory for what I sensed would be the last time, garbled words flowed from my lips. If I failed to say them quickly, I might never say them at all. I needed closure.

"Zann, Zann. My sweet Zann," I cried. "The day I learned of your death, I felt as if I'd been sucked in by an undertow and pulled beneath the dark, murky waters. With no will to live, I drowned in my loneliness and self-pity. I died with you, my darling. I believed it impossible to ever love again. But moments ago, something strange happened. I saw a girl. I can't explain it, but when our eyes met, my body short-wired—the way it did the first time I laid eyes on you."

The memory of Zann sitting across from me in the little school house brought a smile to my lips. I turned to the last page of her letter and read it a final time before wadding it up and tossing it into a rusty barrel nearby. It was time to say goodbye.

"Oh, my precious Zann. I loved you to the—" I stopped, recalling the funny little words, which Mama and I had quoted so often to one another. The peculiar phrase brought a slight smile to my lips. "Yes . . . Zann, I loved you to the ocean and back." I swallowed hard, picturing my beautiful, sweet shell pulled away from me by an ebb tide. She wouldn't be coming back. She was gone. Swept away. I reached in the back pocket of my overalls and pulled out a handkerchief to dry the tears washing my face. If I wanted to see her again, I'd have to go to her, and there was no question in my mind where she'd gone.

I looked toward Heaven and shot my hand upward in a wave.

A sudden cool breeze caused my hair to blow. I wanted to believe it was Zann waving back. I tried it once more, but the wind stood still. I could no longer visualize her. I knew she had raven curls and big brown eyes. I knew her smile could melt a glacier. I had the memories, but I couldn't see her. Could no longer hear her voice. She was gone.

"Rest in peace, my love. God willing, we'll meet again." My heart pounded. Why did I say, 'God willing?' Surely, He was willing. It was I who'd been unwilling. I'd been wrong about so many things, but I was alive again with a chance to start over.

"Until," I whispered. "Until we meet again." Suddenly, something came to my remembrance that I hadn't thought about in a very long time. Parson Pruitt once told me that God answers our tears. Today, I felt He'd heard my cry and answered my tears. I had so many questions. If only I'd asked the old man . . . I was sure he could've answered them. That is, if there really was an old man. I was so confused. After all, I'd suffered a blow to the head. But if I dreamed him up, then where did the cracklings come from? And the blanket? Whether or not he existed, I couldn't say. Yet, the experience, whether real or imagined had given me a new perspective. I felt different inside. The heaviness in my heart had lifted.

I couldn't understand why someone like Zann Pruitt had set her sights on me, any more than I could understand why the lovely creature in the Model A would pretend to be stranded in order to get my attention. But she did. She liked me. Even with her sharp wit, I could tell she was as enamored with me as I was with her. The chemistry between us was electrifying. I hadn't imagined it. We both knew it. I could hardly wait to grab a few boards and get back.

I picked up the broken gate, ripped off a couple of cross boards to put under the wheels and scurried down the road.

Though I can't explain it, a change had taken place within me. For the first time since Zann died, I had a strange urge to reach out and take hold of my life. But was it too late? How could I possibly recapture the dream of becoming a professor, since I'd lost the scholarships?

Then, as clear as the ocean's emerald waters, a verse mama often quoted popped in my head: "Nothing is impossible with God." It was as if my sweet mother was walking beside me, encouraging me to live again. I could hear her saying, "You're still young, Kiah. You can do anything you set your mind to, my precious lamb." I began to laugh and cry at the same time. Mama was right. She was always right. I could do it and I would.

My pulse raced as I rounded the curve and saw a shock of yellow hair glistening in the sunlight. I stepped up my pace and sucked in a deep breath of clean, fresh air. Pecan trees were beginning to bud, red clover blanketed the ditch along the edge of the road and the sweet scent of honeysuckles filled my nostrils. Spring had come, signaling new life. What a wonderful season—a magnificent time to be alive.

I squinted my eyes, when the morning sun blinded me. I blinked and blinked again. For a moment, it looked as if the trees and grass had vanished and the whole world had become a blank canvas. Color seemed to disappear. I ran with a board under each arm. I broke out in a sweat. Maybe the heat was getting to me.

Weird, but I felt as if I were running on the beach, the feel of sand squishing between my toes. I could hear the roaring of tidal waves and the distinct call of sea gulls. I rubbed my eyes and the girl in the Model A came into clear view.

Had my mind played a trick on me? Or had God given me a glimpse of what to expect beyond the breakers? I couldn't say, though I chose to believe the latter.

With the wind to my back, thrusting me onward, I ran, excited to discover what lay ahead.

It was a brand new day, and the tide was coming in.

FROM THE AUTHOR

(Please turn the page for short synopses and sample chapters from the sequel, WHEN THE TIDE RUSHES IN, and other books by this author)

WHEN THE TIDE RUSHES IN

Book 2, Grave Encounters

Confident that her mother is responsible for Kiah Grave's mysterious disappearance, Eliza Lancaster tearfully writes her own obituary and leaves home.

Seven years later, filled with bitterness and regrets, Lizzie, as she is affectionately called, returns to Goat Hill to attend her estranged mother's funeral, determined to unearth the Grave secrets buried long ago.

PROLOGUE

Goat Hill, Alabama - 1931

Lizzie Lancaster announced her death with the following obituary and had it printed in the morning paper on October 15, 1931. She thought it fitting. Her mama was not at all amused.

HEIR TO THE GLADSTONE PLANTATION SUCCUMBS

Eliza Virginia Lancaster's spirit departed this earth at the setting of the sun October 14, 1931. She was a mere eighteen years of age with cherished dreams for a long and wonderful future, but alas, the romantic dreams led to her untimely demise. Lizzie, as she was affectionately called, was a Lancaster and Lancasters are forbidden to dream. If you choose to mourn, don't mourn her death. Mourn her life.

Robert Loch was fired from The Tribune for printing it. Lizzie's daddy owned the paper, and her mama said Robert should have known better. Eliza cried for days when she found out she caused Mr. Loch to lose his job. An older man, he lived alone—the newspaper was his love. She understood too well, the pain that comes from losing something or someone you love.

CHAPTER 1

Seven Years Later

Eliza Lancaster parked her shiny new Packard behind the hearse. "Congratulations, Mama. You had to go and die to get your way, but you finally got us together."

Throngs had gathered in the Gladstone Cemetery, but the first face Eliza recognized was Oliver Weinberger's. She slumped in her seat and groaned when Oliver waved and sprinted toward her. With his long, skinny legs and big, brown doe eyes, he looked like a panic-stricken whitetail deer on the first day of hunting season.

She glanced at the hordes of people staring in her direction and wondered how many had come out of sheer curiosity to gawk at a marked woman. Or at least one presumed to be marked. Privy to the nasty gossip that had continued to circulate through the small town, her pulse raced. Eliza didn't need to hear the whispers to know what they said about her. *Surely, Oliver knows. He lives here. Jeepers, has he no pride?*

He hunched over with his head slightly leaning toward the open window and panted. "Ah, my sweet. I trust you received my telegram."

She feigned a smile and nodded. Eliza hadn't responded to the wire. Now, sensing a flicker of hope in his high-pitched voice, she wished that she had. He seemed to interpret her failure to reply as an affirmative answer to his request.

Eliza had no desire to create the illusion they were a couple and give rise to his fantasies, but neither could she humiliate him by spurning him publicly before a mob of curious spectators. She'd accept his offer to escort her to the memorial service and deal with the consequences later. At the moment, it appeared she was holding up a funeral.

Oliver jerked open the door. "I was beginning to worry, Eliza. We mustn't tarry. The preacher's waiting." He lifted his felt hat and blotted his damp forehead with a handkerchief. "I'm sorry about your mother—she was a grand lady. We were quite close, you know."

Eliza nodded. "Yes. Mama reminded me often."

His face lit up. "She told you we were close?"

"No. She reminded me often that she was a grand lady."

His brow furrowed.

"I'm teasing, Oliver. Yes, she was quite fond of you." Eliza had known since grade school that Oliver was everything her mama had ever wanted for her. But she wanted much more—or according to one's viewpoint, perhaps she wanted much less. In either case, Eliza knew what she wanted and Oliver Weinberger was not his name.

Excerpts from Chapter 2

. . . Eliza didn't dispute the fact that according to the latest census, her birth took place on May 2, 1914. Yet, she didn't begin to live until eighteen years later—May 4, 1931—the day she and Bonnie went joy-riding in Lizzie's new Model A and met Kiah Grave on a narrow dirt road near the railroad tracks. Had it really been only seven years? It seemed like such a long, long time ago. But she remembered it well—

"Did he get it? Did he?"

"He did, Lizzie. The scarf flew in his face." Bonnie squealed. "Isn't he a dreamboat? You think he jumped off the morning run, or do you reckon he's waiting to hop the next train?"

"Why don't I turn the car around and ask him." Lizzie snickered.

"Are you crazy? You can't turn around here. If you get out of the ruts, we're likely to slide in the ditch, and we'll be in big trouble—Uncle Will warned you not to cross the tracks."

"So he did." Lizzie crinkled her nose and grinned.

"Lizzie. I don't like the expression on your face. I hope you aren't planning something stupid."

"Stupid? Of course not." She clutched the steering wheel

tightly and stomped the brake to the floorboard, causing the car to come to a jarring halt.

Bonnie buried her face in her hands, slumped down in the seat and moaned. "Eliza Lancaster, you know your mama will have a conniption fit if she finds out you flirted with a hobo—and you know she'll find out. You can't spit in this town without someone reporting it. "

"All the more reason to do it, dear cuz—let's give them something to talk about."

"Lizzie, no. Don't. It's not proper. We don't even know him. He's a . . . a tramp, for crying out loud. Let's go. Suppose someone sees us? What if your daddy takes your car away?"

"I'll cry." Lizzie chuckled. "Daddy can't stand to see me cry." The gears made a loud grinding noise when she jerked the shift into reverse. "Besides, we can't possibly leave," she said as the car shot backward. "He has my favorite scarf."

Bonnie screamed. "Watch out!"

Lizzie's shiny new Model A Ford, which her daddy had given her for her eighteenth birthday, spun around on the wet clay road, and slammed into the ditch.

Bonnie clasped her hand over her heart. "I knew this would happen. Lizzie, we're going to be in—" Her eyes widened. "Oh no! He's running toward us. What are we gonna do?"

"Flirt, silly." Lizzie pinched her cheeks and fluffed her hair. "How do I look?" She glanced in the rearview mirror. "Oh,

Bonnie, catch me, I think I'm falling in love."

"And what's new?" Bonnie rolled her eyes. "I declare, you're so dramatic."

"I mean it this time. Isn't he dreamy? Take a gander at those arms."

"I see them. They're red . . . just like his neck. Lizzie, you can forget him. I can imagine what Aunt Ali would say if you brought *him* to the family picnic."

Lizzie smiled and batted her lashes when the handsome fellow approached the vehicle.

He propped his bare foot on the running board and bent forward, his head slightly leaning into the window. The hairs on the back of Lizzie's neck bristled, when she felt his warm breath on her face. Slung over his shoulder was a red bundle and a pair of worn brogans tied to the end of a pole.

"Can I help, ladies?"

Lizzie tucked a strand of hair behind her ear and flashed a quick grin. "Why, thank you. I certainly hope so."

He stepped back and eyed the embedded tires. "Don't worry, Miss. It's not as bad as it looks. I'll run up the road and see if I can find something to put under the wheels." After taking a few steps, he turned around and pulled a scarf from his pocket. His blue eyes twinkled. "I believe this thingamajig belongs to you. Maybe you should tie it next time."

"Thanks. You can throw your—" She eyed the pole and

fumbled over her words.

"Bindle? Is that the word m'lady's choking on?" His fingers raked through a mass of inky black curls.

Lizzie's face burned. Yet, in an odd sort of way, she found it quite charming that he wasn't afraid to speak his mind. "I wasn't choking. I simply didn't know what to call it."

"Try clothes." His square jaw jutted forward. "I gather you don't know the difference between a vagabond and a banker. We men of distinction pack our morning coats in red flannel when we travel, to keep from lugging around a smelly old cowhide suitcase."

"No need for such haughtiness. I merely wanted to tell you to toss it on the rumble seat."

He stiffened. "I suppose you're accustomed to telling folks what to do, but I'm not in the habit of taking orders." He shoved his bindle against the fence post and stalked down the road, looking madder than a run-over dog.

Bonnie crinkled her brow. "Lizzie, I can't figure him. He's almost rude."

"Don't be silly. He's playing hard to get."

"But isn't that what we're supposed to be doing?"

Lizzie gave a short laugh and took a second look at her reflection in the rearview mirror. "Well, I think he chose first, but I invented this game."

Within the half hour, the handsome hobo returned, carrying

two four-foot long boards on his shoulder. After making a track in the clay, he said, "If you ladies will kindly step out, I'll crank 'er up. I think I'll be able to get it out."

"You *think*?" Lizzie cocked her head to the side, attempting to look coy. "Do you know how to drive?" It seemed a logical question, since he obviously didn't own wheels.

His nostrils flared. "I wouldn't have volunteered if I didn't know how to operate an automobile Miss, but if you think you can get the car out of the ditch, I'll not trouble you further." He threw up his hand and with a smirk, muttered, "Toodle-do, ladies. Have a nice day."

Lizzie flung the door open and leaped out. "Please! Don't leave us stranded. I'm sorry."

He trudged back to the vehicle, slid in and sat on the soft, gray seat covers. The motor revved and the car rocked. Then with a jolt, the Model A made a quick lunge and settled into the well-traveled ruts. Sporting an arrogant grin, he stepped out and strutted like a proud banty rooster. His gaze traveled from the front bumper to the rumble seat as he strode around, admiring the car.

Lizzie whispered, "If only he'd look at me the way he's eyeballing this piece of metal."

He gasped. "What a beauty. A real sweet patootie."

"Why, thank you. I thought you'd never notice. Oh, silly me. You were referring to the car, weren't you?" Lizzie shrugged when he ignored her. "Where are you headed?"

"Miss, do you have a habit of making everyone's affairs your own?"

She feigned a pout. "Forgive me. I didn't mean to pry. I was offering you a ride."

His blushing face grimaced. He grabbed his bindle stick and mumbled an apology, albeit a weak one. "Thanks. A ride would be swell." With his head lowered, he added, "If it won't put you out." His next words caught her by surprise. "Would you happen to know the whereabouts of the Gladstone Plantation?"

When the handsome stranger jumped up on the running board and plopped down on the rumble seat, goose bumps raced across Lizzie's arms, causing her to shiver. Cleoda, the maid, called such shivers "a rabbit running over a grave," which didn't make a dab of sense. Lizzie knew exactly what caused her to tingle all over, and he looked nothing at all like a furry little creature with long ears.

LUNACY

Book I – Switched Series

Advised by a quack doctor in 1915 that her unborn child is at risk for lunacy, a wealthy woman pays a midwife to secretly switch her baby with the newborn daughter of a penniless couple. Twenty-one years later, the truth's revealed in a *Last Will and Testament* and Harper Harrington is forced to swap places with Veezie, the rightful heir. Harper leaves the palatial estate and moves to a rundown shanty in Goose Hollow, Alabama. But she soon discovers the unattached, young country doctor there has something far more valuable to her than the affluent lifestyle she left behind. Yet, to take it from him will break his heart. If he wasn't so stubborn, Harper could fall for a man like Flint.

When Dr. Flint McCall learns Harper is secretly attempting to sabotage his plans, he begins a quest of his own. How could he have fallen in love with such a pig-headed woman?

PROLOGUE

Flat Creek, Alabama

September 24, 1936

The executor's brow furrowed. "She left a letter, Paul. You'd better brace yourself."

"A letter?" The attorney gave a short chuckle. "Can't say I'm surprised." His swivel oak desk chair squeaked as he leaned over to spit a wad of Prince Albert Chewing Tobacco into a nearby cuspidor. "Confounded woman's determined to have the last word, even after death."

"But she claims . . ."

"Don't let it rattle you, ol' man. In a few minutes, it'll all be over."

"You think?" The executor jerked an envelope from his breast pocket. "Wait until you read this. There's gonna be trouble Paul.

We should've retired after Gordon died."

Paul Aycock, a portly man in his late seventies had served as the Harrington estate attorney for three generations, and now with the widow Harrington's recent demise, his semi-retired status would change. Numerous pictures of him posing with President Hoover, President Roosevelt, Governor Graves and other dignitaries lined the shellacked pine walls of his office.

Paul couldn't deny he'd had a great ride, but he was tired. In less than twenty-four hours, the doors to the conference room at Nine Gables would open and he'd read Ophelia Harrington's *Last Will and Testament*, ending his long career. He was eager to exit the legal jungle and take the South sea island cruise he promised his wife ten years ago.

The wiry executor shoved the envelope toward Paul. "Here, take a gander, then tell me you aren't rattled."

After adjusting his spectacles, Paul unfolded the pale blue stationary and read aloud:

"My name is Ophelia Harrington. For twenty-one years, I have denied my birth daughter, known as Veezie, her rightful place as a member of the Harrington family."

Paul stopped. His gaze locked with the executor's. "Veezie? Who is this Veezie?"

The executor made a slight motion of the wrist. "Keep going. You've only begun."

When a scandalous thought passed through his mind, Paul's

jaw dropped. "Good gravy, Ralph. Is Ophelia saying she gave birth to an illegitimate child?"

"Finish."

He shrugged and nodded.

"Though I erred in life, I hope to make amends at my death. It was not until after I became pregnant twenty-one years ago that I made the horrific discovery my husband's mother had given birth to two children suffering from lunacy. May the child of my womb and the child I reared forgive me for putting my trust in a foolish quack who led me to believe my husband carried a flawed gene and my baby would be born a lunatic."

With his fingertip, Paul traced his pencil-thin mustache. "Sounds like—"

Ralph cut him off. "She tells all in the letter, friend. Continue."

"I was sorely grieved that I had the means to provide a good life for a healthy child, and yet my baby would be doomed to live out his/her life in an attic. Knowing the dire financial straits of the O'Steen family and having been informed our babies were due approximately the same time, I reasoned I was doing right for all concerned when I paid a midwife to switch babies. My husband and I could provide a good life for a child. The poor O'Steens could not. For a paltry sum, a midwife came to understand my predicament and made the swap without the O'Steens' knowledge. I now see the error of my ways, but feel it understandable that in my frenzied state of mind my reasoning was skewed.

After making inquiries, I have recently learned my birth daughter is alive and well and in possession of all her faculties. The startling news has left me sorely distressed. Not the fact my child is sane, but that she's been deprived of the love and adoration of her natural parents. As hard as I tried, I formed no affection for the child I named Harper. I am convinced heredity is a much stronger influence than environment.

May God forgive me for denying my own flesh and blood. I feel no sympathy for the child I reared, for she's enjoyed a life of plenty, which her biological parents couldn't have provided. Now, it's time to provide for my own."

Paul drew a deep breath and deposited his spectacles in his coat pocket. His knees wobbled. "This is insane. What are we going to do, Ralph?"

"We have no choice, Paul. Poor Harper. She's a good kid. I knew Ophelia was a wicked woman but I never expected something like this."

Unwed

Book II – Switched Series

Veezie Harrington, a backwoodsy young woman with a seedy past, experiences difficulty fitting in to her new way of life after she inherits a wealthy estate in Alabama during the 1930's. When she falls in love with handsome Shep Jackson, the local pastor, she sets a goal to overcome her redneck ways and become a real lady, worthy of the love of such a fine Christian man. Is the bar too high?

Reverend Shepherd Jackson, a forty-year-old widower, causes an uproar in the church when he falls in love with the ill-bred Veezie, who is half his age. Will he risk his God-given call for the love of a fallen woman?

Chapter One
May 07, 1937

A shrill cry, sounding more like a bat screeching than a newborn baby, caused Veezie Harrington's arched back to fall flat onto the plump feather mattress. Sweat drenched the satin pillowcase beneath her head.

The doctor blew out a heavy breath, as if he'd been the one doing all the work.

She reached down and rubbed her belly. Every inch of her body ached from twelve long hours of pain, but it was over. *Over?* Was she loco? It'd never be over. The real pain had just begun.

Beulah, the Harrington maid, stood next to a dry sink beside the fancy-carved poster bed. Her calloused brown hands wrung a wet rag over a porcelain bowl. When she turned, her mouth flew open and an eerie-sounding groan tumbled out.

Veezie's throat tightened as she focused on Beulah's pinched face. She dared not ask questions for fear her curiosity might suggest the idiotic notion she was changing her mind about the fate of the child. A thousand times a thousand she wished to renege, but for the sake of her baby, she had to stick to the original plan. Boy? Or girl? Did it matter? She didn't want to know. Didn't want to see it. It'd be easier that way.

The soaked cloth in the maid's hands fell to the floor when she slapped her hand up to her head rag, allowing water to trail from her wrist to her elbow. Her lip quivered. "Oh my stars, doc, po' little creature ain't no bigger'n a wharf rat. I ain't never seen no baby what had—"

He cut her off. "I've delivered a lot of babies, Beulah, and without a doubt, she's the most beautiful newborn I've ever seen. You have a little girl, Veezie. Look at her."

She jerked her head in the opposite direction. "No. Take her away." She'd known Flint McCall since the first day he arrived to practice medicine in the Goose Hollow community, about twenty miles from Flat Creek. She supposed she knew him better than most folks and the raspy sound in his voice told her something peculiar was going on. Why didn't he let Beulah finish her sentence? *What's wrong with my baby?*

"Look at her, Veezie." His voice quaked. "She's perfect. Like a flawless diamond. Take her in your arms and hold her."

When Flint made an attempt to lower the tiny creature, Veezie clinched her eyes shut. Why was he taunting her this way? Didn't he know how she ached inside? How she longed to keep her baby?

Well, she wouldn't give in. She couldn't. "Leave me be, Flint."

"Veezie, I'm not asking. I'm telling you to turn around and hold out your arms. Now! Your baby needs you."

Her hands knotted into tight fists at the roughness in his voice. She opened her eyes and glaring into his troubled-looking face, she whimpered, "*My* baby? *Mine*? I ain't got no baby. Take her home to your wife, Flint. That was the plan. Remember?"

Beulah wiped Veezie's sweaty brow with a cold, damp cloth and pushed a wisp of hair back of her ear. 'There, there, sugar. You just got the blues settin' in. Why don't you do like the doc says?"

Veezie's throat couldn't have ached more if she'd swallowed a bullfrog. If Flint only knew how she longed to hold her baby in her arms and to count all the little fingers and toes. But how could he understand? He was a man. The tears she'd shed since that first kick inside her belly could fill a gallon drum. She dared not look for fear she'd never be able to go through with her plan.

Flint's brow furrowed. "Veezie, I'm sorry I couldn't administer the ether, but it would've been too risky for the baby. You went through a lengthy, painful delivery. You're hurting and you're tired. I get it. But this is not about you and your feelings at this point. The baby came early and there's a frightening chance she won't make it. You can have all the poor-pitiful-me parties you want after today, but at the moment you have a responsibility to this little girl you brought into the world." His voice trembled.

"She may not make it, even if you hold her . . . but I'm pretty sure she won't if you don't."

The tiny bundle cuddled against his broad chest could've fit in a cigar box. If she took one look at her baby's face, she'd never be able to let her go. *Don't you worry, baby girl. He ain't gonna let you die. He's a doctor. Besides, he wants you for his own.*

Flint said, "Beulah, you didn't get any milk at all when you pumped her?"

"Not nary a drop. It just ain't coming."

He leaned over the bed. "Veezie, you're going to hold this baby if I have to tie your arms around her, so you might as well reach for her now."

She glared at the way his throbbing temples pumped in and out when he gritted his teeth. The cold eyes and unfamiliar gruffness in Flint's voice reminded her of the scene from the picture show, *Dr. Jekyll and Mr. Hyde* when Jekyll claimed all human beings are made up of both good and evil. With Flint's sleeves rolled up to his elbows, his shirt tail hanging out and his trousers crumpled, there seemed to be two people living inside one body. There was nothing about the rumpled, hateful-talking doctor that hinted of the neat, gentle friend she knew as Flint McCall.

With a toss of his head, he slung a shank of brown hair away from his bloodshot eyes. "You idiotic, bull-headed woman," he bellowed. "I won't allow you to lie here and let this precious baby die, simply because you're feeling sorry for yourself. Get over it,

Veezie."

Beulah crossed her arms over her plump bosom. "Begging yo' pardon, doc, but that kinda talk ain't getting us nowhere. There's a heap o' truth in the ol' saying, 'honey draws more flies than vinegar.' Reckon we ought to send for the preacher? I 'spect Brother Shep Jackson can pray a body into doing most anything. Seems to have a knack for it. Understands troubles, he does." She shook her head gently. "God bless him, he's had his share. Want George to hitch up the wagon and go fetch him?"

Veezie burst into sobs. "A *preacher*? You crazy? Y'all might as well announce it in the newspaper that Veezie Harrington gave birth to a little—" She bit her lip. Couldn't say it. "No! I don't want nobody to know. Nobody, ya hear?" She pulled the covers over her face and rubbed the soft satin comforter between her fingers, comparing it to the moth-eaten woolen army blanket she'd slept under for twenty-one years. Yet, she'd gladly give up all the silks and satins and go back to the way it was, if only. . . But there was no going back.

ABOUT THE AUTHOR

Kay Chandler is a multi-award-winning author of Southern Fiction with a speaking ministry called LIFE ROCKS. An enthusiastic motivator, she shares personal experiences seasoned with humor, to illustrate that life rocks when God's in the center. If you're interested in having Kay speak at your church, civic group or book club, she can be reached by email at kay@liferocksministry.com. Her Facebook account is Kay McCall Chandler. Kay and her husband, Bill, have retired and have moved back to Geneva, their hometown in lower Alabama.

If you'd like to see more books by this author, please leave a review on Amazon.